Roddy

Ballycarson Blues

Ballycarson Blues

Roderick Paisley

Matador
9 Priory Business Park,
Wistow Road, Kibworth Beauchamp,
Leicestershire. LE8 0RX
Tel: 0116 279 2299
Email: books@troubador.co.uk
Web: www.troubador.co.uk/matador
Twitter: @matadorbooks

ISBN 978 1784624 835

British Library Cataloguing in Publication Data.
A catalogue record for this book is available from the British Library.

Printed and bound in the UK by TJ International, Padstow, Cornwall
Typeset in 11pt Garamond by Troubador Publishing Ltd, Leicester, UK

Matador is an imprint of Troubador Publishing Ltd

Gewidmet sei dieses Buch meiner Frau, meinen Kindern sowie meinen Eltern, die mir viel Gutes getan haben

ENDNOTE

The normal state of affairs is often reversed in Northern Ireland. In homage to this principle, the introduction is at the back of this book. Those seeking a brief guide to some of the persons and events mentioned in the story may find it there. So too this endnote is at the start and may encourage those who wish to read no further. Others may decide to plunge straight into the text and consult the tail-end repository of wisdom only when they encounter something they do not understand. Reflecting Ulster politics, those who seek answers will often be disappointed. Of course, the only real introduction to politics in that province is actually to have been there and, perhaps, to have remained confused by what occurred. Nevertheless, it is hoped this book will convey some of the flavour of events in the north of Ireland.

Although mired in the general history and political culture of the six northern counties of Ireland, nothing in this book should be taken as denoting any living person. This is a work of fiction. So far as the author is aware, there is no town with the name "Ballycarson" anywhere in Ireland or elsewhere. In one respect this book is also deliberately misleading and unrepresentative of real life. Noone is killed. Even in a novel the author would not wish to see that occur again.

A final warning: those who are colour blind should not bother to read on.

CHAPTER 1

THE WALL

Beside the public lavatories in the very centre of Ballycarson a new impressive granite memorial had just been unveiled. On its polished black surface it bore the golden inscription in freshly cut letters:

> Dedicated to the memory of the unknown Republican Heroes, this memorial is erected by public subscription organised and collected by Councillor Finvola O'Duffy and her fiancé, Councillor Eugene Gerald Fitzmaurice. Their names shall live for evermore.

Those in attendance at the unveiling (and there were many) had been reminded of why they should not forget. The long, stirring political speeches had stirred long-held emotions. The stirred-up crowds now headed home with a longing to stir their tea. As the serried rows of the organised political manifestation dispersed, the two Nationalist councillors named on the memorial had a great view from the temporary stage erected on the flat roof of the public conveniences. They could be more than content with their extended oratorical and political efforts. At the very centre of events, at public expense, they had been immortalised. The Unionists had been pushed to the fringes of town. The future had forgotten them.

With suitable municipal swagger the councillors moved off the temporary stage on the lavatorial roof by means of a ladder and descended to the level of the mob below. The politicians were immediately replaced on their pedestal. Senga Rae, a very plump local artiste, long past her best as a country and western singer, had been lifted onto the same roof by means of the bucket of a large, but somewhat rusty, mechanical digger. "Digging Done Daily by Doug the Diggerman" was the strapline painted on the arm of the digger by the machine's owner and operator, Doug himself. Not for Senga was the indecorous clambering up of a ladder leaning at an ungainly angle. Such a method of elevation showed a certain lack of class, she thought, and it also involved more effort than she could easily expend when her focussed efforts were needed for her imminently expected musical extravaganza.

Suitably elevated and with her false teeth adjusted, Senga began to tune up with her octogenarian lead guitarist. Just in case she, the lead singer, might be mistaken for her overly mature musical companion, she was wearing a white tee-shirt bearing her name "Senga" in black block capitals. Thus her fame and identity were simultaneously announced to the world. Her two roadies, of equally advanced age, wore similar white tee-shirts, but these bore in large black letters the title of the most recent song by which Senga was seeking belated local musical stardom. It was an old Elvis Presley number with a personal twist intended to publicise the crusty old *chantreuse*: "Return to Senga". Unfortunately, the manifestly ripe age of the roadies coupled with the emblazoned title of the golden oldie led to a somewhat odd impression. The visual combination suggested that the workers might be suffering from Alzheimer's dreaded affliction and the large print was intended to encourage the public to volunteer their assistance and to lead the wandering employees back to their boss. But noone at all was bothering to offer assistance even if it had been required. By the time the roadies had managed to set up the amplifiers and associated musical kit, the town square was empty. The fat lady started to sing, but the evening was already over.

Senga had done her real job before she had even started to

croon. She had been well worth her modest fee paid out of the public purse for crowd control services. Music indeed has charms and Senga's persuasive sound had won any argument long before hostile words and gestures had been exchanged. Indeed, this public success was a repeat performance for Senga. Whenever the Council needed a potentially restless crowd dispersed without altercation, they did not require water cannon or rubber bullets. Such overtly aggressive methods would be unthinkable in the age of the Peace Process. Instead, the new Nationalist administration merely employed the longest standing of the local artistes, Senga Rae. The Peace Process had given her singing career a new lease of whatever half-life it had ever had. Indeed, it was much better than that. The proper fulfilment of her municipal duties to assist in the avoidance of street violence and political agitation had led to the Council awarding her a personal title of some dignity. This came in the form not of a warlike medal or ribbon but, instead, was a title of honour, a designation of peace, which she was encouraged to use on her publicity material as a leading local artiste. She bore this peaceful municipal acclamation with pride. It was clearly visible underneath the reproduction of her smiling face on the two large temporary banners that had just been set up beside the entrances to the "gents" and the "ladies". It read: "Senga Rae, Peace Artiste".

So the entertainment drew the evening to a speedy and peaceful end like a noose drawing close on a neck. Senga, as anticipated, had emptied the town square. The "evening of peace" or, as the Council's public relations department, in what they considered was a tasteful emulation of French Revolutionary and Republican ideals, preferred to call it, the "Peace *Soirée*" was over.

But at eastern approaches of the town something was still going on. The bus approaching Ballycarson bore the number "000" and the destination "Not In Service". The driver, however, knew better than that. He liked to think of his personal number as "Double Oh Zero". He knew, or at least, since these matters were never officially confirmed, he strongly suspected, that he was a secret agent. So secret was he that he was not even officially listed amongst the known secret agents on the well-tended list of colleagues serving overseas who paid their slate at the Ballycarson transport cafeteria once a month after returning from long-distance missions. No, he was in a league of his own as an ex-directory, unlisted, off-register, off balance-sheet secret agent whose very existence afforded plausible deniability. His advertised destination, "Not In Service", was almost certainly deliberate misinformation rather than a mechanical fault with the bus equipment. All the evidence, when balanced and weighed carefully, indicated that he had to be in the Ballycarson secret service. His present mission was to transport, in secret, his passengers into Ballycarson two or three times a week and he made sure he never set off or arrived on time so noone could lie in ambush. He was reliably unreliable and predictably unpredictable. In fact, he was so irregular in his timings that an outsider looking on would have thought it was just a normal bus. Here he was hidden in open sight.

But, like everything else in rural Ulster, all the locals knew the truth of the secret. If a secret shared is a secret halved, this one was infinitely divisible in this divided society. Anybody asking for this particular bus was directed to the bus stop that didn't exist, although it did have a specific location – right in the centre of the enormous empty car park of the Ballycarson Yankees' Baseball Stadium just beside the bridge over the Union Canal. That landmark was where the passengers would disgorge to begin their new lives. There was plenty of space there. The large electronic sign beside the entrance to the totally empty car park advertised in big bright orange letters "Parking: 1690 Spaces Available".

The journey that didn't officially exist, at least in the mind of the deluded driver, was now coming to an end and the time had now come to inform the uninformed and officially non-existent passengers. Careful as always to abide by the Council's recently imposed requirements to convey information in at least three officially recognised languages, the bus driver called through the bus sound system: "Ballycarson, Ballycarson, Ballycarson." With an over-enlarged sense of undue responsibility, he pronounced each word identically to ensure equality of esteem for each of the represented linguistic traditions, whatever they were. His vehicle had just passed the Ballycarson town sign with another coach-load of immigrants and he had timed his announcement for maximum effect on the increasingly mystified passengers. The driver had made this journey so many times in recent years he did not have to ask any questions. He wasn't interested anyway. But, for others, and in particular, for anyone new to Ballycarson, a brief introduction was needed. Who were these people on the bus? Why had they made the journey here? The answers were surprising.

After the reunification of Germany, a deluge of former East Germans headed west for freedom and jobs. Many fondly imagined that they would find a happy haven by flying into New York. Some pictured themselves steaming into the American harbour past the Statue of Liberty. Unfortunately, dreams don't always work out in full. Of those happy band of eastern pilgrims, quite a few did make it west but not as far west as they had originally dreamed. Eventually, they found their sanctuary in Ulster; more precisely, they found it in Ballycarson.

The nervous refugees' first sight of the town itself came from their bus as it passed the huge painting of King Billy on the gable end of the salami factory beside the main road into the east side of town. The only sign of huddled masses here was the group of painters tarting up the detail of the weapons held by German mercenaries standing behind the Dutchman on the white horse crossing an Irish river. Disconcerting? Not at all. With such symbols of integrated European civilisation and culture clearly on show, it couldn't be such a bad place after all. And for those amongst the bus-loads of incomers with a less visionary outlook on the world, there was work at the salami factory.

After a few more minutes of routine vehicular manoeuvring, the final halt in the momentous journey was reached. The bus drew into the vastness of the Ballycarson Yankees car park and, as it passed the barrier, the advertised number of free parking spaces altered, by automatic electronic subtraction, to read "Parking: 1689 Spaces Available". In recent years, 1690 and 1689, by happy political coincidence, were the only two numbers used on the sign as, by unhappy commercial underperformance and lack of appeal to the masses, the imported sporting facility had ceased to be used for sporting events. The passengers disgorged somewhat bleary-eyed into the gigantic vacant tarmac space as the spotlights came on to light up the evening gloom. The luggage was unloaded but not before the hopeful immigrants read the advert on the boot of the bus, "Ballycarson Yankees Forever", to which had been added a side note "Now Disbanded".

This particular bus-load was nothing special in itself, but it formed part of something much larger and particularly remarkable. This bus-load was just one of many similar bus-loads comprising the third wave of substantial German immigration to Ballycarson in as many centuries. Together the three waves had given rise to the largest single German community in the British Isles outside London. Nervous and anxious though they were, these most recent incomers represented the future for a town stuck in the past.

A combination of good fortune and detailed planning ensured that accommodation in Ballycarson had not been a problem for the new German incomers. A specially produced Council brochure in English (with an interlined Ulster-Scots and Irish translation) welcomed them to the town and advertised the facilities. Nobody bothered to produce it in German. The German incomers were informed that the Ballycarson Council had policies "aimed" at the German immigrants and special schemes "targeted" for their welcome. The Council would "leave no stone unturned" to make them feel at home. In addition, it confirmed that they would have easy access to amenities in Ballycarson given that everywhere was "a stone's throw" from everywhere else. Initial problems in extempore translation led many of the Germans to fear that Ballycarson was a scene of continual riots. For the more poetic amongst them, the words of Friedrich Schiller came to mind. Here was a place where the pace of time was threefold. The future arrived nervously, the past stood still eternally and the present moved at the speed of a projectile.

However, advance planning by the Ballycarson Council had served to curtail the potential of projectile diplomacy. To dampen the enthusiasm of possible rioters, a fifteen-foot-high Peace Wall had been built separating housing estates in the east of the town from similar locations in the west.

Of course, compromises had to be made even in relation to such a strategic frontier structure. A small, awkward salient of Loyalist- and Unionist-occupied Council houses in a sea of Nationalists and Republicans was walled off just within the west. The Council indicated it would have been too expensive to extend the wall and bend its line of construction to incorporate these minority occupants into the east. The local authority was not going to organise an airlift to keep them fed if they remained where they were. A short-lived experiment with a reconstructed medieval trebuchet to lob food parcels over the wall had merely confirmed the worst fears about fast food. Intimidation in its various forms gradually convinced the small body of Loyalists and Unionists to move out and the entire enclave was slowly abandoned. The process was complete just as the first bus-loads of the most recent Germans arrived. They all entered the town in bright orange buses bearing on their side the large blue logo "Transports of Delight". This was a reflection of the political affiliations of the bus fleet's owner: "Big David" as he sometimes liked to be known. They would find out much more about this man during their stay. In addition, they would discover that the locals had endowed him with another, more accurate, name:

"Camp David". This latter appellation indicated that he had once lived in a refugee camp but also reflected his ostensibly effeminate manner. There were only very few indeed who were aware that Camp David was not gay at all. He had affected the mannerisms of effeminacy as he had realised that there were not a few in the local political establishment who had difficulties in handling the notion of a gay politician in rural Ulster. And if they had difficulties with the concept, reasoned Camp David, they would have difficulties in handling him. So much the better: it gave him an angle and left them without a handle. In due course of time this version of Camp David's name had inevitably been shortened to CD and his gang of associates, "David's Volunteer Defenders", was known as the DVDs. It would not be long before the Germans realised the people who called the tune in the east side of town were CD and the DVDs. However, David himself did not like the idea of being associated with anything compact or with technology that had already become out of date. For him, to match his ambitions, the only appropriate name was "Big David".

All this, however, was still to be the subject of a soft introduction for the Germans as they braced themselves for a soaking in the traditional Ulster steady drizzle and walked across the vast car park to a row of Council minibuses parked outside the barrier. This was indeed an accurate indicator of a disintegrated transport system full of petty hold-ups and minor obstacles. Why did they not park the minibuses just beside the big bus to make life easier for those arriving? Experience had taught the Council that the 100-yard walk dragging possessions in the cold and wet was just enough to make the incomers grateful for any seat, any transport, any shelter from the rain. Why should the Council stint on Nature's bounty and the outdoor experience especially when they were free? The Council minibuses were hardly luxurious. Getting into their new means of transport, the Germans were welcomed by the comforting sounds of piped potted speeches of welcome from local politicians. This was the last leg of their epic journey from the centre to the fringe of Europe. It would last only a few minutes, but the tired speeches were intended to make the last lap feel like hours so the exhausted European incomers would gain the impression that the elevated fee for the minibus trip was worth it.

The minibuses set off to their final destination where vacant houses awaited the passengers. On their seats the passengers had found literature to assist them. The Germans were informed by the Council brochure that some of the locals had given up their houses just for them. You cannot get much more self-sacrificing than that. However, the truth was that these houses were the abandoned properties located in the former Unionist and Loyalist enclave. Some of the more insensitive of the political hacks in Ballycarson had regarded the potential availability of such newly vacated houses as a dividend of the great divide. A few of the Nationalist councillors considered that this was an ideal opportunity for democracy to flourish. They could select new electors more to their liking after the old ones had moved out. That would be democracy in action at its very best. Nevertheless, it became politically inexpedient for the Ballycarson Council to re-let the vacant houses in this area to local Nationalists and Republicans as that would be seen to have condoned the dubious but effective methods of persuasion that had led to the exodus. But no other Loyalists or Unionists wanted to move in. They had been entirely persuaded to stay out. The councillors hit on the solution of resettling the East German incomers in this abandoned area right beside the Peace Wall, complete with a new watchtower and large, powerful searchlights. For the former East Germans it was the perfect physical surroundings to bring forth a warm glow of remembrance about the place of their origin. True to their German tendency to analyse and define, they even had a German word to describe their collective feeling: "*Ostalgie*". Nostalgia about the east.

"You'll feel at home here," was the uplifting comment of the chairperson of the Council to the first of the families to move in. "And you can paint the big wall any colour you like – as long as it is not white, red and blue – we have already given it a good coat of green primer."

Of course there were several among the more conservative elements in Ballycarson society who took the view that all change was just an illusion. Even if it did exist, it was a reality that was best ignored. "When it's not necessary to change, it's necessary not to change" was a long-standing principle that had become a cliché and then a stale political dogma that they had committed to memory and practice. These conservative elements of society attempted to continue the traditional pigeonholing of everyone in Ballycarson regardless of their extrinsic origin. Some of this was relatively light-hearted banter, although liberal academics denounced it as "sound-bite sectarianism" or "sectarianism with a smile". As almost all of the newly arrived Germans found work in the salami factory located well within the Protestant east of the town, a few Loyalists labelled them "the part-time Proddies". A select few were named after the electrically charged implements by which they persuaded the doomed cows to enter the salami factory: "the Cattle Prods". Still, this was always better than the name applied by the extreme Republicans to the native Loyalist workers at the factory: "the Protestant Pigs".

However, most of the attempts to continue the parochial political pigeonholing were claptrap pumped out by a single extreme Republican newspaper printed in the building it shared with the cheese factory. Both occupants of the stone-built structure dominating Irish Street produced a diet unaltered for centuries. In a land with too much history, the newspaper represented a constituency with a memory supremely well matched with its inability to learn. It had forgotten nothing and learned nothing – or even less, if that were possible. The leaders of that constituency could never admit to having made a mistake at any time in the past as their followers might just begin to wonder if their leaders were making a mistake in the present. In a special Christmas issue, this narrow-minded broadsheet dredged up what it described as "disgusting pictures" of British and German soldiers fraternising on the western front on Christmas Day 1914 and warned its readers "Saxon and Anglo Saxon are natural allies."

Fortunately, even in Ballycarson, this was not the universal approach and the vested political ideologies had not wholly rooted out and destroyed the last vestiges of humanity. What the extremists of the political classes feared most was something, or more importantly someone, they could not classify within the frame of fossilised philosophies and platitudes of the Peace Process. Many ordinary people in Ballycarson, on both sides of the sectarian divide, recognised that the Germans had brought something new: the possibility of change and hope for the future. In particular there was the prospect that one of the Germans would open a decent cake shop in the town to supplement the already slightly cosmopolitan diet of Viennese biscuits, Danish pastries, Paris buns and Swiss rolls.

CHAPTER 2

UNDERCURRENTS OF ANGST

The East German incomers, now living in the tiny enclave in the west, had to pass through a manned gate in the wall every day to reach their place of work in the salami factory on the other side. There was a border control system and a set of traffic lights to manage the flow of people. Only when the little green sandman appeared on the lights could the procession of workers move from one side to the other. As might have been expected, this gateway between east and west quickly became known by the populace as "Checkpoint Charlie", leading to energetic denunciations from Councillor Eugene Gerald Fitzmaurice to the effect that this was a tasteless throwback to a rejected political system. It would cause extensive local offence, he asserted, as the name "Charles" was too closely associated with the British royal family. Still, the name stuck, causing Councillor Fitzmaurice to up the tempo of his campaign.

"All street names, signs, symbols and banners of British rule should be removed forthwith," thundered Councillor Fitzmaurice through a large green megaphone in his weekly tirade from the back of a green pickup parked on the fringe of the town green. The fringe of the green was, in fact, the only part of the green where grass grew and all that this amounted to was a narrow margin of untended weeds. A few months previously, in a money-saving exercise to cut uncontrollable mowing costs, the Council

12

had covered virtually the entire area with concrete paving stones coloured green. It had all been a direct result of the notorious supergrass trials. These bold experiments under the prior Unionist administration had failed utterly, despite the promises of ultimate reward for society as a whole. Some Unionist boffin had come up with the idea of a new strain of supergrass that would be stunted by genetic design. It would grow only to a certain minimal height and thereafter it would never need mowing. The parsimonious prospect of cutting the costs of cutting grass appealed to the accountants and those with hay fever in the Unionist administration. The smell of new-mown hay and perfumed paper handkerchiefs would never again blight the town of Ballycarson. In a massive community effort to spend the Council budget before the end of the financial year, every patch of traditional, genetically un-modified grass within the town boundary was dug up and the new improved seeds sown.

The seeds of hope produced a harvest of despair. The experiment went badly wrong. Almost immediately after its planting, the carefully blended and selected grass seemed to mutate and, proving remarkably invasive, it grew wildly and beyond control. The green belt rapidly expanded into a green blanket covering every open surface in what seemed to be an omnipresent bed of weeds. Ballycarson was turning into an urban jungle. There were protests on the streets of Ballycarson and at least one outraged letter in block capitals and green ink sent to the local newspaper (gardening section). But little could be done as the Unionists had also sold off the Council mowers to reap a double dividend of cost savings. In despair, but inexorably attracted by the name of the product, the Unionist Council decided on the use of the horticultural weapon of last resort. They applied to the American consulate to purchase an undisclosed number of barrels of the notorious defoliant known as "Agent Orange", which they had come to understand had been left over from the Vietnam War. The containers were lying rusting in what was suspected to be a CIA warehouse in Belfast. There were even several Huey helicopters in the same warehouse that could assist in the spraying. The whole batch of the evil herbicide in liquid form and the small fleet of vintage helicopters were acquired as part of a deal negotiated in a shady spot beside a service station near the motorway to Belfast. However, the hand of political fate intervened before the project could be implemented. The Unionists lost the Council elections and a new political broom swept in.

It fell to the new Nationalist administration to deal with the aftermath of the supergrass crisis. Agent Orange was off the agenda for obvious reasons. But the Nationalist-led Council found a suitable dumping ground for the offensive material by emptying the now unwanted barrels into what had been the Union Canal. The Huey helicopters, in contrast, might prove useful for crowd control or even as a municipal fleet for fast transport of the new councillors to essential Council events. In any event, their existing green colour reflected the loyalties of those holding power in the new political dispensation. So, the superannuated helicopters were spruced up and stored away for a rainy day.

Attention was then turned to the supergrass infestation. A green, foul-smelling weedkiller derived from a distillation of the extract of Donegal seaweed was sourced from a reputable dealer somewhere on the internet. It was applied by the tanker-load and fire engines were employed to spray it lavishly on the spreading plague. There was almost instant die back.

But it is not all easy in local politics. Some sentimentalists in the new administration longed for some link, however tenuous, to their romanticised, rural origins. A political compromise was reached. All of the areas in the centre of town where the over-energetic, genetically modified grass had been exterminated by liquid poison were ploughed, harrowed and then slabbed over with green-painted concrete. Continuity with the past was retained by the maintenance of signs at strategic points around the perimeter of the area in the centre of Ballycarson indicating that visitors should "Keep off the Grass". Admittedly, this was more a fond memory or lovingly retained myth than a statement of fact or recognition of reality – but what did that matter? In that regard the spurious message of the signs was utterly consistent with many other of the new Council's policies. The mowers were not repurchased and the money notionally saved in the whole exercise was reinvested in recruiting a number of new Council employees to translate the new signs into various minority languages. The Council appreciated that for the people speaking such equally esteemed but easily overlooked languages life could be a struggle at the fringe and it was determined to make life in Ballycarson equally attractive for all. So the permanently green plaza in the centre of town became a barren space where everyone stayed at the fringe.

The very centre of the green plaza contained a large empty green plinth. It was a vacant memorial set up by the new Nationalist administration to the "As Yet Unborn Future Republicans" who would, in the words of the dedication plaque in the new civic interpretive centre, "Take the lead in the Republican struggle in the decades and centuries to come". In their enthusiasm for the brilliance of their own imagination, the members of the Nationalist administration had failed to see that the public inscription suggested that the Nationalist campaign was not going to succeed for a long time yet. The fact of the matter was that the Nationalist administration had actually run out of existing heroes to honour as they had already set up a multiplicity of statues to the past achievers in the Republican and Nationalist causes at the end of every street, lane and alley in the west of Ballycarson. There were plenty of streets and plenty of heroes, but some of these commemorations were less successful than others. It was perhaps surprising that the statues of various hunger strikers had proved the greatest embarrassment. The Nationalist administration now needed to divert public attention away from the inscription below each hunger striker's statue, which set out their individual names and dates of death, and then proceeded to hail each of them as "A Living Legend". "So where is he living now?" was the unanswered question of a small child in the minute's silence at one of the many Republican services of dedication. To silence the critique of the representative of the next generation, the interrupted minute's silence was immediately followed by another minute's silence. However, what was written in stone was not chiselled off just in case it might amount to the admission even of a small mistake. A stroke of self-certified political brilliance served to move on public attention and to save the day. "Let us look forward and not back" became the Republican slogan and the plinth for the "As Yet Unborn Future Republicans" then materialised like a work of avant-garde art in the centre of the town plaza.

This vacant if not vacuous structure was not the only manifestation of a political wish for cultural emptiness at the centre of civic life. At the edge of the permanently sterile green plaza Councillor Fitzmaurice proceeded to invite the new German arrivals to join his new movement to pull down and replace all public reminders of British rule – "the Street Traffic and Signs Initiative", or "STASI" for short.

Indeed in its implementation of the Peace Process the Council had been most energetic in taking down what were now regarded as reactionary and offensive signs. Apart from areas in the eastern enclaves where Loyalism still held sway, the public areas of Ballycarson had been stripped of any hint of links with the British royal family and the United Kingdom. The policy was zealously enforced. Even the Jehovah's Witnesses had received an official letter from the Council inviting them to consider altering the name "Kingdom Hall". It was further rumoured that the poker club at O'Neill's bar had been requested to examine their decks of cards and substitute president and first lady cards for the four kings and queens. There was no issue about the knave as every political system, Royalist or Republican, possessed such a character. The proposal, so the rumour went, had not been implemented, only because the newly elected feminists on the Council had vetoed the priority given to men in the highest value card. The Unionists stirred the pot further by objecting to the identification of the remainder of the playing cards by Roman numerals. The local newspaper, the *Provincial Enquirer*, picked up on this political game of poker and reported the debate about the decks of cards under the inquisitive heading: 'Royals to be Flushed Away?'

Despite all the hot air and controversy, one coincidence of political strategies proved a happy one. In honour of the recent German incomers and, more importantly, to further the Peace Process, the councillors passed a resolution urging the local bakeries to re-name "Empire biscuits" with their original name "German biscuits". Sweeteners were offered for compliance. If the bakers co-operated, the councillors would instruct their canteen to place a special order for Battenburg cake.

"If you want to see symbols of British rule, then you should go over the border" became the official Ballycarson Council policy immediately after the Nationalist and Republican coalition took power.

This policy was based on the strange irony that in border market towns in the Irish Republic the most impressive pre-1922 buildings were still adorned with the British Royal Crest and Arms. Indeed considerable sums of European Union money were being spent to retain and restore this heritage in the South whilst twenty miles away in the North the same money was being spent in removing it. A business, known as "the arms trade", grew up of selling the heraldic items removed in the North to eager purchasers in the South. The policy of removal of symbols was accelerated in the North by the increasing demands from the south. In his oft-repeated speech of welcome to each newly arrived group of German refugees, the Ballycarson Council vice-chairperson, Councillor Seoras O'Duffy, made extensive reference to this policy of "reconstructive anonymisation". The truculent tirade culminated with the words of triumph: "We want refugees to come here and feel stateless!"

For the first few years all appeared to be going well in the tiny German enclave within Ballycarson. However, there must have been some unperceived undercurrents of angst. Whatever it was, it was not picked up by the health board social workers as they gathered at their frequent case conferences. These meetings were styled as a modern form of collective quasi-religious confession to reveal, explore and discuss human failings and frailties. Of course these flaws of character were not the participants' own failings and frailties but those of other people. Each with a six-month part-time study diploma in social work from the local university (thank goodness, it was no longer just the technical college), the participating social workers were the only people in a position to carry out this important work. All those who lacked such undoubted success in certificated formal education, in their collective view, were stupid. Thus the health board social workers were able to raise themselves above the common herd.

That said, only so much dirty linen can be washed in public at any one time and the ladies in question had no desire to make themselves feel like common washerwomen. It simply would not fit their desired image, as most of them were doctors' wives with a certain standing in the community. The remainder comprised wives of Council-employed environmental health officials who wished they had been doctors' wives. A few of this remainder still struggled to alter their status should opportunity arise, but, with only three medical practices in the town, there was a limited supply of the objects of desire. So, rather than insult their collective intelligence by considering the lives of stupid people for the entire length of the meeting, the tawdry business of social work proper was confined to the first five or ten minutes of every gathering. As for the remainder of the meeting the following two hours were turned over to more select activities.

The principal task at these case conferences was to exchange notes on the various types of Blackforest gateaux in the newly established Schwarzwald Konditorei located in what had been the Ballycarson market square. So the case conferences, by fortunate typing mistake, became known as the "cake conferences". For the owner of the cake shop establishment the business of salacious gossip brought with it the prospect of filthy lucre. By attracting such luminaries of the social science world, the baking establishment had got off to a flying start. It probably had a lot to do with the notice in the window of the establishment: "Genuine Ersatz Coffee". If an enquiring scientific mind can uncover all sorts of shady practices, then a suitably vague answer can produce a satisfied customer. And so it was when a social worker enquired where was the origin of the coffee, the German host was able to respond that Ersatz was a major coffee and timber-producing province in Bolivia. The social workers then began to dream of holidays in Ersatz, sitting under an Ersatz sun, acquiring an Ersatz tan, participating in an Ersatz conference to obtain an Ersatz diploma. Yes, there was a genuine need for all things Ersatz.

With all this daydreaming the world can slip by. The social workers found it difficult to realise there was a real world outside their wooded glade of pseudo academic discussion and genuine cake consumption. Their motto could easily have been: "Ours not to do or die; ours is just to eat the pie." Clearly there was a complete absence of reasoning why. Reality, however, eventually did knock on the door even of the Schwarzwald Konditorei. Whatever the cause, one morning the neighbourhood awoke to find that two German neighbours living side by side in semi-detached houses had fallen out over something. Whatever the differences were they were irreconcilable. The social workers made a suitable report to the Council. Under the heading "Needle in Close Knit Community", it was full of analysis and tentative conclusions but wholly lacking in suggestions, recommendations or advice. The Council were left in a moral and political vacuum to decide what to do. Perhaps the report was not so bad as first seemed. Arguably, it comprised advice tailored to the character of the client. However, a practical solution substituted for an absence of any principle. For the elected members of the Council, separation of the ways was deemed a suitable solution. But the Ballycarson Council did not wish to be seen to force out any of the welcome newcomers who had already been collectively deeply offended by the window advert of a local travel agents reading "Do Us a Favour and Go Away". The pictures of the smiling Germans at the Munich beer festival and on Rhine cruises in the immediately adjacent window posters had not assisted the overall impression.

The local authority's quandry in the face of this general sensitivity and the particular passions of the two German neighbours was solved in a special general meeting of the councillors. Both German protagonists were invited to remain in their present houses but were given planning permission to separate their backyards more completely by building a fifteen-foot wall, complete with a barbed wire flourish at the top. To avoid offending the two German belligerents, it was declared at a Council meeting that the new construction was never to be referred to as a "wall". Such a word could only inflame an already difficult situation. Instead the construction was to be known by the more acceptable euphemism as a "Separation Structure" – or "S.S." for short. Each of the Germans would be given a grant to pursue their separate but equal development. There was much backslapping at the drinks party after the Council meeting. A tricky situation had been solved. The Council had given a certain and decisive lead. Maybe there was more room for such decisive acts in the future? Maybe the separate but equal doctrine could be introduced on a wider scale with even greater benefits reaped as a result?

The enthusiasm was not shared by all. For many in Ballycarson the acts of the Council were divisive and not decisive. The *Provincial Enquirer* summed up their mood when it ran a headline:

Division Decision Deserves Derision.

"Uncertain Street" was the main shopping street leading to the area previously known as the market square in Ballycarson. Completely rebuilt and renamed after repeated bombing in the 1980s, Uncertain Street had received its new name immediately prior to one local Council election. At that time noone could predict exactly which political party would win. The Council official dealing with the street renaming did not wish to blot his copybook with anyone who was about to become his new political master, so he had completed the form for the new name of the street with the word "Uncertain". The name stuck. Nobody could ever agree on a replacement. The "market square", however was renamed as soon as the Republicans gained power. The traditional name was seen as having direct links to capitalism and overtones of Masonic ritual. It was hastily renamed "the Communal Rectangle". Fortunately, the new name did not stick. Even in official Council correspondence, the centre of town was still referred to as "the area previously known as the market square". If anything, the episode seemed symbolic of a political regime adept at getting rid of things but utterly incapable of putting anything useful in its place.

Despite the constant revision of names, when anyone wanted to know which way the political wind was blowing in Ballycarson, they went to Uncertain Street and not just to stick their finger in the air. More exactly, they went to Cecil Pitman's newsagent at the top end of Uncertain Street to read the headlines. Rumours of sales of top shelf material by Cecil Pitman had led to suspicion amongst the more proper elements of Ballycarson society. The suspected salacious sales had earned for Cecil Pitman's establishment the nickname "the Cess Pit". Due to repeated tip-offs prior to police raids, the rumours were never substantiated and the Cess Pit continued to deliver what some regarded as an essential, if sordid, semi-secret service.

The shop, like Cecil himself, appeared to have a split personality. As well as diverting the attention of the locals into the gutter of life, the shop contents genuinely did assist in broadening the horizons of the locals to some extent. Maybe it was just a very broad gutter. The tiny shop was hardly an internet café, but it provided a link with the outside world even though most of the news was local. Outside the Cess Pit, the advertising boards of the *Provincial Enquirer* heralded the latest developments in the locality. The principles of the Peace Process had required that there always would be two headlines (even if there was no news) so that the paper had something to offer each community. This was based on the principle that politics in Northern Ireland was always a zero sum game. According to this theory any event that conferred an advantage on one community would naturally and inexorably confer an equal disadvantage on the other. Those interested in realpolitik found pseudo-justification in Newton's Law: "To every reaction there is an equal and opposite reaction." This was the Eternal Truth for political commentators in Ulster. Consequently, for the politically correct class in Ulster, things could never get worse and things could never get better. The province was preordained to a perpetual plateau of petrified political platitudes. However, looking on the bright side, in broad overview, all news was neutral in its effect. The two posters outside the newsagent were intended to implement this policy of political stagnation, or "golden stagnation" as its proponents named it.

The orange paper poster on one board on the right foot of the main door of the newsagent – known as the "right footer board" – followed the latest neighbourhood developments from the point of view of the Loyalist and Unionist community. The other, a green poster, set on the left foot of the door – the "left footer board" – contained matters of interest to the Nationalist and Republican community. Often, the two headlines bore different, indeed starkly different, if not wholly opposing and irreconcilable, "takes" on a particular incident. They were a true reflection of society in Ballycarson as viewed by the traditional political pundits. This was typified on one particular day when the newspaper headlines addressed the incident of Councillor Eugene Gerald Fitzmaurice writing to the *Provincial Enquirer* to complain that the Ballycarson Bluegrass Festival Committee were disclosing unsuitable political bias in their very name.

"Every idiot should know that grass is emerald green, particularly, traditional Irish grass. Just look at our new town plaza to see the truth," ran his polished published pontification.

The headline on the right footer board ran: "Councillor Sounds Foolish Note". The left footer board commented: "Councillor Does Not Sound Foolish Note". Equilibrium was maintained by the dissonance.

But stories relative to the German community had broken the mould and noone had yet got round to producing a third noticeboard. The small space above the door of the Cess Pit was already taken by a hastily hand-painted sign reading "Licensed for the sale of alcohol and racy literature". With the middle ground already occupied by these more important matters, the result was that the most trivial of partisan aspects for each local community was sought out in any story affecting the Germans. If none could be found, the story was ignored.

On this particular day the story of the wall-building German neighbours was regarded as of marginal interest to the Loyalists and Unionists because the local Loyalist big man, Big David, had got the contract to paint both sides of the newly erected Separation Structure keeping the feuding Germans apart. That had been a relief to him as he had lost out in painting the new town plaza green. With the German aspect dominating the new painting story, no positive angle could be found for the Nationalist community. The result was that their noticeboard simply contained the usual blandishment used by the newspaper to advertise itself when there was no news of interest. However, even on this day one could not avoid reading one community headline like a comment on the other. The first of the adjacent noticeboards shouted in block capitals:

```
┌─────────────────────────┐
│                         │
│      PROVINCIAL         │
│      ENQUIRER           │
│                         │
│    LOCAL GERMANS        │
│      FALL OUT           │
│                         │
└─────────────────────────┘
```

The second gleefully observed:

```
┌─────────────────────────┐
│                         │
│      PROVINCIAL         │
│      ENQUIRER           │
│                         │
│       THE BEST          │
│       NEWS YET          │
│                         │
└─────────────────────────┘
```

And what was so great about this news? Well, perhaps the Germans had started to assimilate. Maybe, they would soon fit the local mould and engage in unfathomable and irreconcilable disputes. However, there was still hope.

CHAPTER 3

NO-MAN'S-LAND

Not all messages are as short lived or as easily removed as those on the publicity boards of local newspapers. In a country such as Northern Ireland where the past had been ongoing for a long time, something more permanent had to be sought. Usually, the solution was several layers of exterior gloss paint. And this was all the more so as it was now the second half of June and the time was fast approaching the traditional July marching season.

That particular day William Henry's paint job at the Queen Anne Boleyn Bridge was complete, at least for that particular morning. Another Ulster landmark had been renovated for the benefit of locals and any more German incomers who might be bussed into the town. William Henry set down his paint pot and brush and surveyed his work.

William Henry always did what he was told. As a conscripted member of Big David's Volunteer Defenders, he was a loyal "No Man". He alone was responsible for the "NOs". This gave him status – and *political* status at that. Here was no artist struggling in obscurity without recognition. He was a man of influence and his work was world famous, if only locally. So influential, indeed, was he that the very name of the site of his recent artistic efforts was linked to him. The site of the disused railway bridge over the main road into the east side of Ballycarson was known locally as "No-Man's-Land".

It was not the case that this title of No-Man's-Land indicated a shell-marked strip of land beyond the control by any one side in the Ulster divide. The six tattered Ulster flags (one for each county in Northern Ireland) and the various slogans painted on the bridge all shouted to the contrary. This indeed was the last redoubt of Loyalism.

Right in the middle of the archway over the roadway, in big, white, block letters, was the traditional rallying call:

NO SURRENDER

And that was not all. Clearly there was continued loyalist resistance in this place, despite the onslaught of the Peace Process. Immediately underneath the big "NO" in a vertical column of unmistakable loyalist assertiveness were three other recently completed NOs. These were the still wet product of William Henry's very recently accomplished painting mission. It was "NO SURRENDER" and three times "NO".

But this was not evidence of a community hard-boiled in bigotry or fossilised in prejudice. No way. Not at all. Not a bit. The entire space under the word "SURRENDER" and beside the added NOs was blank. The three recently painted NOs were the unaccompanied and unadulterated denials of something yet to be determined. The local loyalist big man, Camp David (although William Henry would never use that version of the name, as he might be asked to decamp), had told William Henry to paint on three more NOs and nothing more just yet.

Whatever Big David did not like in the future could easily be added from time to time into the spaces immediately to the right of each NO.

This was no predetermined route of intransigence defined only by past events. It was no political vacuum. It was a blank space for tomorrow's adept political comment. Here indeed was preparation for the future and a willingness to adapt. This blank space was the symbol of a willingness to look ahead and reject the future whatever it was. It was a case of "Ulster Says No" to something yet to be thought up. Indeed it could assist Big David in making a fast response to the volatile political situation that was expected to arise later this month with the arrival in the province of the United States president. And he might have to act quicker than that because security concerns might mean the exact timing was not publicised. The rumour was that the president might even appear unannounced in the next few days just ahead of the marching season. The *Provincial Enquirer* had picked up on the possibility and thundered its news with a dramatic headline: "President Avoids March by June Arrival". Staff in the American consulate in Belfast were bemused. They were aware that time stood still in Northern Ireland, but noone had previously told them that the powers that be could delete several months just to suit present political circumstances. It was a wonder there weren't rioting crowds in the streets demanding the return of their lost months.

These complex calendar calculations were the last thing on William Henry's mind. He paid heed only to a much briefer timescale. His thoughts were always for the short term and his foresight invariably short-sighted. Speed was everything and consequences, well, they were for someone else.

It was a good job Big David had ordered that quick-drying paint, thought William Henry as he surveyed the bridge of many colours. Actually, it was a bridge of only three colours: red, white and blue. For William Henry, three was a large number.

This bridge-painting mission had always been and always would be a team effort. William Henry had just done his bit. Other specialists from the chosen few contributed their skills to complete particular additions from time to time. William Henry had a special and refined talent for painting big white NOs, or, at least, so he had been told. Every year during the months of June and July that was almost all he did for the Big David organisation. Someone else would decide which political developments had to be denounced. Someone else would order other words to be added in paint. Someone else would decide the colour of the paint. Someone else would ordain the completion of the blanks beside William Henry's NOs. That someone else was Big David.

"Just do what you are good at," was William Henry's motto.

So he stuck to painting his NOs and did very little else during the months of June and July. How would posterity sum up his literary skills? If posterity noticed them at all, perhaps this might suffice for a line in an overstated oration at his funeral. "Other political commentators wrote a column in the newspaper – William Henry painted a column on the railway bridge."

But one should not underplay ability. William Henry's extraordinary talent for such street art had been spotted at an early stage. The local Council had employed him at the age of sixteen as an apprentice road painter. On his first day he had been given the stencils to paint big traffic directions on the pristine tar.

"This word will suit you down to the ground," the foreman had said, with a smirk, as he handed William Henry the four big wooden stencils for the word "SLOW". "Just use each letter only once for each job and you can't go wrong," he continued. "The stencils are numbered. So you use this one first and then this one and then this one…"

So William Henry went off to paint parts of the town white. He stuck to his job, aligned the stencils on the ground in the order he had been told and poured the white street paint into the gaps. It was only the next day that he knew his efforts had led to eternal fame – or at least such fame as lasted until the street paint could be removed. The reporter from the local *Provincial Enquirer* wanted to interview him as the man who had decorated the main road into the east side of Ballycarson with the word "SLOM".

Panic gripped the publicity department of Ballycarson Council. Of course they had well-laid contingency plans for various possibilities arising from spelling screw-ups. It was not that something similar had never happened before. But noone had ever conceived of a catastrophe on the scale of that which had just occurred. If only William Henry had painted "LSOW", it could have been explained away as shorthand for "Loyal Sons of William". Or if he had decorated the road with "LSWO", it could have been glossed as a rather Teutonic instruction to the recent German incomers and appealing to the democratic sentiments of the elected representatives on the Council: "Leaders Speak, We Obey." However, from the slim lexicon of the publicity department of Ballycarson Council, all that could be conjured up to explain "SLOM" was "Sacred Legion of Mary". The appearance of such an obvious reference to a competing religious tradition at the main entrance to the east end of Ballycarson was incomprehensible, impossible to ignore and inconsistent with long-established local tradition.

There was no up-side to the upside-down story for the Ballycarson town councillors. Local political wrath from both sides of the community demanded heads should roll.

But, because of the "Peace Process", William Henry could not easily be sacked.

The union officials and the human rights lawyers dictated the terms. The new politically correct dogma of "Equality of Esteem" of all traditions (which in practice could be translated as *both* traditions) meant that the sacking of a Protestant should also require the sacking of a Roman Catholic. It was known locally as "The two heads are better than one" rule.

William Henry was fortunate that there was noone from the other side of town who was precisely his equal. Malachi O'Leary had been briefly considered. During the recent Council election campaign, he had been sent out to paint the "Sinn Fein" name all over the west side of town. But the basic rules of spelling beat him. He had painted an endless row of luminous green six-foot-high "SINE FINE" slogans on the old railway embankment wall running along the main entrance to the west side of town. Even Protestants from the eastern side of town had driven past to wonder at the meaning of this interminable political comment. How could Malachi O'Leary have misspelled the party name that was supposed to be written on his heart and engraved on his very soul? Party prestige was dented because of the potential public disgrace. But Malachi's skin was saved by the euphoria of Nationalist electoral victory coupled with the distinguished classical scholarship of Bishop Eugene Miguel O'Hagan. He was sure that the words meant something in Latin, although, having lost his dictionary on an excursion to the races, he could not remember exactly what. However, his learned input was sufficient to allow the relevant party committees to trade tautologies and eventually report: "The reality of the situation is that these words mean something and therefore they must be meaningful." Such an indisputable conclusion could not be contested – indeed that was the whole idea – and led the Nationalist majority to mount an upbeat and robust defence of an attempt to terminate Malachi's job at the Council cleansing department. Malachi was obviously fluent in an ancient European language, albeit he did not realise this himself. Such a man of previously hidden talent and latent scholarship the Council could not afford to lose. Furthermore, as part of the newly elected ruling coalition, the Sinn Fein councillors rejected his dismissal on the basis Malachi had been engaged exclusively on party business and he had not acted on the instructions of anyone engaged in local government. Those constitutional niceties were important, especially as they were now in power. There was no point in setting a precedent for having anyone resign.

In any event O'Leary's subconscious lapse into the mellifluous Latin language was partially disguised amongst the multiplicity of "Viva Argentina" slogans on the same embankment wall still surviving from the time of the Falklands War. The quality of the exterior gloss paint in the early 1980s was clearly excellent.

So by finding a parallel on the other side of the local political universe, William Henry escaped the chop and a new role had to be found for him. It was determined that he was to be assigned to another post to be agreed with the main shop stewards "Union"

Jack Presley and Seumas "Iceberg" Quinn. The political loyalties that gave rise to Jack Presley's nickname were obvious enough. The origins of Seumas Quinn's sobriquet were more obscure. His habit of thumping the table during negotiations so hard that it usually broke indicated the origins had nothing to with any cool temperament on his part. It seemed likely that the source of the nickname was to be found in his complete obstinacy in the face of any argument no matter how reasonable or overwhelming. Seumas "Iceberg" Quinn would not move even if he knew the *Titanic* was steering straight towards him. He personally had wrecked and sunk virtually all attempts to update and streamline the work practices at the Ballycarson Council for over two decades. Now these two employees of major stature but limited talent decided the fate of William Henry and sent him on to the management for implementation of their decision.

William Henry angled himself towards the human resources department to find out the next development in his career. There he sat for a day and a half whilst the staff searched in vain for his personnel file. The new computer system simply could not cope. It was only after the staff checked the name on the collar of William Henry's anorak that it dawned on them that they were dealing with an aristocrat with a double-barrelled name. Yes, William Henry was one of those honoured few with a double Christian name and a surname he rarely used. His recorded personnel details were eventually found under "Anstreicher, Wilhelm Heinrich", a name that betrayed his ancestors as having been among the German-speaking Moravian refugees who had fled from the fringes of the Austrian Empire in the eighteenth century and had headed west for religious sanctuary in the New World. Clearly several dozen of them had got as far as Ballycarson and had thought that was far enough. And it was there that their talented descendants had remained to this day as the remnants of the first wave of substantial German immigration to Ulster.

"Mr. Anstreicher, we have been instructed that multitasking is probably more your speciality," said Miss Sweetly in the Council's human resources office. "First of all, we need to sort out your footwear." She handed William Henry a large black Wellington boot to try for size. He proceeded to put it on his right foot. It was a snug fit. Well pleased with his new footwear, William Henry picked up all his bits and pieces and headed to the door. "Wait a minute," shouted Miss Sweetly, "you'll need a second one." And so, a second boot of similar size being proffered to him, William Henry was kitted out in full.

Miss Sweetly's co-worker Immaculata Concepta Fitzgerald, known as "Immac" for short, pointed William Henry towards the back of the Council yard where a row of three identical small wooden sheds stood against the fence. This line of buildings comprised the modest property portfolio of Donald Oskar Gormley, the lost property officer and dog warden. It was a combined role to supervise the waifs and strays and, in their earnest desire to further the Peace Process, the big-wigs amongst the councillors regarded it as ideal for William Henry.

To symbolise his new role Miss Sweetly had handed William Henry a pre-typed, orange-coloured, laminated badge containing a photo, a bar code, a job description and a cartoon of a dog on a bicycle to pin to his anorak. "You are to be Donald Oskar Gormley's assistant," indicated Miss Sweetly, "the new Deputy D.O.G."

CHAPTER 4

HOUNDED OUT?

So William Henry reported for duty at Donald's row of chalets. After completion of the usual paperwork, he was given responsibility, subject to Donald's supervision, for lost property. This mainly comprised washing machines, bicycles and dogs.

It seemed that nothing much else was ever handed in for Donald's tender care. Too much was otherwise recycled by the families of tinkers who lived beside the local municipal tip. One of them ran a second-hand shop in Irish Street entitled "What Everyone Doesn't Want". Despite the name, it was always mobbed out, especially during the happy hours on sale days when boots and shoes were sold at the discount of three for the price of two.

But the relative dearth of donations to lost property probably had more to do with the immediate topography than with local retailing patterns. Most of the centre of Ballycarson was built on a hill. When they went shopping the local population went "up town" and not "down town". So the daily uphill struggle meant that bicycles were never much in demand except for the occasional few that were dumped in the canal at the foot of the hill beside one of the railway bridges. Perhaps some reformed feminist in the town really did consider that fish did need this form of two-wheeled transport. Perhaps it was a side effect of wealth cascading down in the consumerist and mobile society that comprised uptown Ballycarson. Whatever it was, the former Union Canal united Ballycarson with nowhere anymore. The erstwhile commercial artery had become a manifestation of stagnation, silt and corrosion.

In fact, there were only two bicycles and three tricycles in Donald's lost property shed. There they had rested, unclaimed, for several years. The cycles had not been recycled. But there were several small boxes of books with the word "Classics" written on the side and a large crate full of bicycle pumps.

The "classic" contents comprised mainly dog-eared doctor and nurse romances previously enjoyed by Miss Sweetly. She felt a real affinity with such medical matters given that she looked after the office first aid kit and had once assisted at the removal of a large splinter from a bin man's hand. The books may have been discarded by Miss Sweetly just as romance had consistently discarded her, but the crate of bicycle pumps was a real mystery. Rumour had it that it had been mistakenly ordered by a temporary employee in the Council's cleansing department when he had ordered "black pumps" as lightweight industrial footwear for the office cleaners. That was the problem with ordering anything from an English supplier. The English had always misunderstood the English language. Or maybe it was just as the Nationalist politicians continually asserted: the English knew perfectly well what Ireland didn't want and yet they sent it to Ireland anyway. Yes, a serious issue like this had the potential to cause a major constitutional crisis unless the councillors engaged in some neat political footwork. So, at the time of the black pumps scandal, a special meeting of all the councillors had been convened to discuss what to do with the unsatisfied order for footwear.

There followed a lengthy debate in the Council chamber. It was eventually decided, with a cross-party consensus, that in future the local Ulster Scots word "gutties" and a suitable Irish translation (to be researched and approved at the next meeting of the full Council) would be used in all orders of black pumps, sand-shoes or similar footwear. If the English did not understand this terminology, they could just look it up in a dictionary or phone the Council help line in the new department of "Communication, Reports and Publicity". Such a mouthful of a title had inevitably been shortened and henceforth, but only outwith the hearing of the councillors, was referred to as "UAD" standing for the "Unfortunate Acronym Department". The UAD had previously been established with the generous assistance of a grant from the European Union to foster the study and use of Irish and the Ulster Scots language in local government affairs. It was incumbent on the Council to make sure the European Union got its money's worth by examining every aspect of this multi-faceted affair of the "black pumps" and the "gutties".

The debate on the gutties dragged on into the small hours with pedestrian points being made in grandiose style. The climax came when councillors Eugene O'Driscoll and Montgomery Cherry wished it to be minuted that, contrary to the Council's policy of access to information, neither of the Ulster Scots or Irish languages had been included in the nineteen European languages used in the suppliers' booklet of instructions that accompanied the bicycle pumps. In an inspiring show of cross-party unity, the councillors resolved unanimously to note the linguistic failure with restrained reproach and dignified disappointment. The chief executive was instructed to write a letter of formal protest to the English suppliers and, in addition, to the manufacturers in North Korea. The future use of the word "gutties" was to be demanded. Hardly had there been a more satisfying political outcome to such a potentially serious situation.

"GUTTIES GET GREEN LIGHT" ran the headline in the *Provincial Enquirer* that week.

This caused a row amongst the Unionists as they asserted that this put a colour on the story that it would not bear. They wished it to be known that the Nationalists should not get all of the credit for the cross-community initiative. The carefully constructed political consensus collapsed. The footwear had become a potential election embarrassment for all concerned. The politically charged box of bicycle pumps was then shoved into the lost property shed to get it out of the way.

The lost property shed in the Council yard was only the first of the three identical wooden sheds set up against the back wall. It was Donald Oskar Gormley's private H.Q. and over the door in black paint it bore his initials "D.O.G.". The other two sheds were used as kennels on regular short-term lets – usually to canine inhabitants, although overnight stays by inebriated councillors, or those hardworking local public servants who had been ejected by their spouses or cohabitants, were not unknown. Both residential functions helped the statistical returns of the Council confirming official time spent at the workplace. All the sheds were now part of William Henry's new property portfolio that he was to manage under Donald's supervision. The more sophisticated part of the new job was to feed the unclaimed stray dogs living immediately next door and awaiting destruction in the stainless steel contraption known as "the Zapper". Someone else was paid to look after the Zapper and William Henry was only to attend to the dog feeding. For this he was given the specialist equipment of a can opener, a spoon, several cans of the locally produced dog food, "Happy Mutt", and two stainless steel bowls, both bearing the word "DOG".

"Those are not my initials," indicated Donald Oskar Gormley as he handed over the specialist equipment to William Henry with the further comment that William Henry's priority was to make the lost property shed habitable for them both.

So the various piles of beer bottles in the shed would have to be thrown out.

"People keep handing them in because there is no deposit to be paid on them," he explained.

And that cleaning operation William Henry could do whilst Donald was off attending to his other jobs as part-time greyhound walker, retail consultant and literary importer.

"Make sure you wear these ear plugs, but don't turn the music off," was Donald's last comment as he headed off towards the town centre.

So William Henry, wearing an oversized pair of industrial ear defenders, was left on his own to run the recycling business. He had the shadow of power without a shadow of responsibility. Nobody was going to bother him as he made half an hour stretch into an entire day. As William Henry was about to find out, Donald Oskar Gormley had discovered the best way to keep people out of his shed was not to display a "No Entry" sign but to keep an ancient but still functioning music centre playing the most appalling music he could tolerate. With his own particularly effective set of ear plugs, Donald's pain threshold was especially high. The assault upon the ears presently blasting from this source was a rendition by a local artiste Charlie Rae of the classic "Take These Chains". The sentiment had a wide appeal extending even beyond a human audience. The two dogs chained up outside were howling along in chorus. It was entertainment in the very widest sense of the word.

After throwing most of the contents of the lost property shed outside only to see it urinated on by the two guard dogs, William Henry discovered three small cans of paint at the very back of the shed. In addition, he found a selection box of brushes, a tin of white spirit and a bottle of gin. The diverse elements of the assortment had something in common – all were tools for refreshment of various types. The contents of all had been sampled but not exhausted. Donald had painted the bicycles and tricycles every year to stop them rusting. It had seemed to him a sensible precaution to prevent the wastage of such important assets, but it hadn't been a big job.

His familiarity with the various bottled substances made William Henry feel immediately at home. After checking them out, however, his aspirations grew to be more extensive than the mere preservation of a modest transport fleet from the depredations of rust. Instead, he intended to renovate the property empire of his new boss. Levering off the paint tin lids with the dog food mixing spoon, William Henry discovered that there was just enough in each tin to paint each of the three sheds a different colour.

William Henry's internal exile as a property conservator and developer lasted a bare two days during which time Donald Oskar Gormley never returned from his dog walking, retailing or importing. Then Big David arrived in the Council yard. After the usual check of the site security provided by him, Big David with his well-known and ostentatiously effected mincing gait headed straight for the canine death row. As ever, he had a quick look over the doomed animals to see if any were suitable for site security at the salami factory. That day the elderly three-legged poodle and half-starved mongrel were not up to scratch for such active service. However, they might fit the bill for other enterprises and he would come back with the van and trailer later. Orders for such dogs were flooding in on an hourly basis on Big David's Dalmatian-spotted black and white mobile phone, which had a ringtone of dogs barking out the introductory bars of Beethoven's fifth symphony. With business as brisk as it was, a dog dealer such as Big David could not afford to be kept on a leash and tied to a desk with its inefficient landline communication. Indeed, fast and fluid communication and fast and fluid action were the order of the day. Big David would have to get a move on because the political temperature had been raised considerably since the Unionist defeat in the local elections.

One of the big campaign issues in those elections had been who controlled the Zapper. The sociologists at the local new university were agreed that this focus of attention showed the Ulster political parties had matured and were now concentrating on major life and death issues. With the Nationalist victory it was widely expected that the Zapper would be privatised soon. That remained the case even though some of the Nationalist political rivals to Council Chairperson Finvola O'Duffy were lukewarm to this policy. "How could Nationalists undo nationalisation?" they queried as they gnashed their teeth. The fact that words could have a number of meanings had escaped them. The political heat was rising. Whatever was the state of affairs amongst the Nationalist politicians, there was a real possibility that Big David's interests would be left out in the cold.

With such a black future staring him in the face, Big David cast his eyes towards William Henry and the colourful product of his labours. He was immediately impressed to see that the three kennels had been newly painted. One in red, one in white and another in blue.

"I could use your talents, kid," he said to William Henry.

This was not just the offer of a job. It was a transfer.

CHAPTER 5

ROOTS

It was no coincidence that Big David had spotted the newly painted kennels. He had been tipped off by his all-seeing spies in the shelter at the Spion Kop bus stop. From their vantage point on one of the seven hills of Ballycarson, the spies had observed the painting efforts of William Henry almost immediately he had started to renovate the sheds. These spies really did like watching paint dry – especially when it was red, white and blue.

The glass structure comprising the bus shelter at the Spion Kop bus stop provided an unrivalled view around the east side of Ballycarson and, in addition, enabled a glimpse into the mysterious west. The shelter was constantly occupied by a rota of pensioners in the pay of Big David with at least three residents in the bus shelter at any one time. They acted as lookouts, talent scouts and general gatherers of information. Because of the location of the vantage point and the age of the occupants, the bus shelter was known generally as "the old crows' nest". The vintage of the spies also enabled Big David to claim legitimately that he did not practise age discrimination. The only precondition for the employment was that they were not short-sighted, or at least they had a decent pair of glasses to share amongst the members of the trio. Despite the constant watch kept on the town, Big David rejected the claims of his political rivals that it was a case of "Big Brother Is Watching You". In reality it was more sinister even than that. It was a case of "Great Granny Is Watching You".

Whatever one's view of the miniature crystal structure on the hill, it has to be admitted that it was an unusual and comfortable establishment. Equipped with internal luxuries such as lace curtains, three recliner seats and electric power, it was linked to the outside world with a satellite dish, email and a large orange-painted aerial. A public convenience had been constructed immediately beside the structure for the benefit of those with weak bladders. The words "Public Convenience" on the sign above the door had been struck out and replaced with a claim of ownership so that the notice now read "Occupied". Even though a certain degree of privacy was thus ensured, the whole complex at the top of the hill was so obvious it could be no secret. For the benefit of all and sundry, the Council had erected a large arrow-shaped sign at the bottom of the hill pointing upwards to facilities described on the sign in large black letters as "Public Convenience", "Public Viewing Area" and "Restricted Area". Although the confused messages ensured that there were not many uninvited visitors, the hub of social activity and intelligence-gathering at the top of the hill was occupied twenty-four hours a day by shifts of appropriately talented pensioners and those suffering from bladder weakness. To make absolutely certain that there would be no overcrowding and overuse of the public water supply and sewers, the Council initiated a scheme whereby anyone entering had to show a special pass to a man in a small orange-coloured hut at the foot of the hill. This security measure sounded impressive, but the requisite document of travel really was an orange-coloured pensioner's bus pass adapted only slightly from similar documents issued by the local bus company, "Transports of Delight". Not much of a security measure really even if coupled with a barrier that was lifted only after suitable presentation of documents. However, it was the very location of the hilltop structure that made entry off-putting. The shelter at the Spion Kop bus stop was accessible only by a long set of concrete steps or by the funicular railway recently installed by German-speaking Swiss engineers at a massive cost funded by Europe. This transport acted as a chairlift for the pensioners accessing the bus shelter and was an unqualified success until hijacked by a drunk demanding to be taken to Belfast in exchange for releasing one of the pensioners he had taken as a hostage. Matters looked serious when the police realised the drunken man was armed with a chainsaw and he was threatening to use it on the hostage he disliked the most. However, police negotiators relaxed considerably when they discovered the chainsaw was an electric one stolen off a building site. As part of his demands the inebriated man issuing the threats of human dismemberment had asked for an extension cord so that he might plug it in. The siege eventually ended when the man sobered up and realised that the hostage suffering from his particular disfavour was his wife.

Whatever one's view of the bus shelter, it was really the view from the establishment that impressed Big David. With their binoculars and telescopes the pensioners provided him with an unrivalled source of information. Only one part of the Loyalist side of town could not be seen from the vantage point. This was the valley that ran down to the Union Canal. This freedom from supervision, however, was bought at a price. Because of their depressed situation, none of the inhabitants in that particular area could receive television signals. So the whole area was known as "the valley of the unobserved and uninformed", or, more loosely stated, "the valley of the hidden idiots".

Ever since he had left the employ of the Council, William Henry found that the crystal shelter at the Spion Kop bus stop formed a major part of his life. It was to this structure that he reported every day to pick up his instructions. He had made the journey so often now that even he could not get lost more than once a week. The routine had helped the time to pass quickly. By now William Henry had been in the employ of Big David for almost four years. Despite the depression of the wider political situation and the local reverses suffered by the Loyalist cause, those were years of personal glory for William Henry.

And this particular day was a continuation of the trail of

42

glory. Upon completion of his painting mission at the Queen Anne Boleyn Bridge, William Henry was due to head back up the hill to deliver his report at the Spion Kop bus stop. Thereafter he was to take urgent dispatches to the L.H.O. hall where Big David had his H.Q. on the first floor.

The L.H.O. hall belonged to the Local History Organisation and from that fact of ownership the initials were derived. On the ground floor a legion of local genealogists were busy putting together chart after chart of family trees. The whole enterprise was aimed at the surviving overseas relations of those who had left Ireland for promised lands such as North America in the 1700s and the early nineteenth century just as German-speaking refugees were moving into Ballycarson.

The pictures on the wall of the various celebrities that the Local History Organisation had been able to link to ancestors in Ireland included an array of statesmen from much earlier times and many modern personalities such as Elvis Presley, Dwight D. Eisenhower, Ronald Reagan, Richard Nixon, Barack Obama, Bill Clinton and Jessie Jackson's third cousin. However, there did remain some controversy about Jessie Jackson's third cousin as they could not prove whether his antecedents were the Jacksons of Tyrone or the Jacksons of Tipperary. Therein lay the potential for a serious cross-border political row, so, to avoid serious embarrassment, noone wanted to finish off the research and get to the true facts. However, face was saved when the newly elected Nationalist Council in Ballycarson voted to create a new brand of honorary title that they could award to all their American friends who had not yet come to live in Ireland. And so was created the Council award for "Overseas American Friends". Jessie Jackson's third cousin was reported in the *Provincial Observer* as delighted to be nominated as an OAF. Even the Unionists had to swallow their misgivings. For the Nationalists the solution to this potential embarrassment for Ballycarson represented a unique combination of historical accuracy and political sensitivity. What a masterstroke! Two weeks later the Council officials buried the news that Jessie Jackson's third cousin's personal staff had returned the ostentatiously proffered medal in outrage. The American reaction was all perfectly understandable – but nonetheless deeply regrettable – given that whoever had engraved the medal for the Council had mistakenly omitted the word "Overseas" and replaced it with "Oversized".

The L.H.O. hall had originally opened early in 1964 in the same week as the John Fitzgerald Kennedy memorial hall had been dedicated on the far side of town. Unfortunately for the Local History Organisation, it was noticed at an early date that the initials L.H.O. could also stand for "Lee Harvey Oswald". An unintentional coincidence no doubt, but names, phrases and even spelling mistakes make history in Ireland. The whiff of complete tastelessness had never completely left the place since then, despite the strenuous efforts of the genealogists to attach to their completed charts as many Irish harps and angels as Americans were willing to pay for. Yes, even in this Unionist enclave, this was real proof of an outward-looking and tolerant spirit. The colour of money did not matter and Big David was prepared to accept as many green-backed dollars from the great republic over the water as the home-sick third- and fourth-generation Irish-Americans would send to him. For them it was true that "nothing knocks nostalgia" and Big David was prepared to sign up to the philosophy of that motto as long as the cash rolled in. He did indeed have principles, but he preferred that they be fluid principles, well oiled by the universal solvent.

And who had conferred this genealogical opportunity on the Loyalist citizens of Ballycarson? In another of those ironies of life commonly encountered in Ulster, the boom time had resulted from an earlier boom time, albeit one of a different nature. The original event was what Big David characterised in his typically pompous manner as the "hostile actions of a foreign foe in a foreign land". In 1922 the IRA had blown up the Public Record

Office in Dublin, the capital of the newly emerged Irish Free State. Following upon the consequent fire, shredded official papers and burned birth certificates had rained down on the city for days, together with the soot and ashes. Consequently, since the 1922 partition, every church in Ireland, north and south of the border and regardless of denomination, did a nice sideline in providing birth, death and marriage entries and information to genealogists. Particularly well off in this regard were the older churches that had records going back before the foundation of the United States of America.

The Fourth Independent United Reformed Dissenting Congregational Church of Ballycarson had refined the exploitation of this stream of income by publishing a particularly profitable series of picture postcards of tombstones located in their graveyard. Visiting Americans were encouraged to send home a picture of great-great-granny's sister's or brother's final resting place. If an actual tombstone could not be found, the grieving American relatives could purchase a newly painted inscription on the large tombstone comprising the rear gable of the church. This would confer on their long-lost (and still unfound) deceased relative the status of occupier of a temporary honorary place of interment in the churchyard. Again, a photo of the inscription on the tombstone would be supplied for a modest additional outlay. Only once had the Church cause for minor concern about the message these tombstone cards were sending out. This was when the Church elders received a complaint from the FBI via the American Consulate about a death threat written on one such picture postcard. The card had featured a photo of a particularly impressive mausoleum and was sent by a tourist from Brooklyn to his mother-in-law. On the back had been written the message: "Wish you were here". Still, it hadn't been any worse than the slight scandal that had threatened to erupt in the previous year when the minister had posted out his New Year gift of a church calendar to each member of the congregation. In a nice personal touch, but as part of a misplaced attempt to show he had a sense of humour, the minister had added on the back of each envelope the hand-written message "Your days are numbered". It was fortunate that only two of the elders had called the bomb squad who proceeded to destroy each envelope in controlled explosions.

There was an executive board meeting at the L.H.O. hall this very afternoon and, as a director of the Local History Organisation, William Henry needed to be there. Yes, he really was a director, although he gave no directions to anyone and had no real idea which direction he himself should follow. As a non-directing directionless director, William Henry had been asked by Big David to sign all the forms, the tax returns, accounts and to appear on all notepaper as a director of the Local History Organisation and so many other related companies and organisations, he had no idea what they were or what they did. What a decent and modest man Big David was – he didn't appear anywhere!

"You can take the glory, son. I'll take the decisions," was how David explained the paperwork and division of labour.

It sounded more like dictation than discussion. But in a neighbourhood where you could have any colour you liked as long as it was orange or green, as the case may be (depending entirely on which side of town you lived), it was nothing unusual. It was merely a perfectly normal manifestation of the local variety of democratic centralism practised for decades by local politicians. They had no intention of letting these fine traditions die.

Whatever the possible criticisms of the manner in which business decisions were to be made, it remained the case that at this afternoon's high-level meeting of the executive board on the first floor of the L.H.O. hall there would be real and substantial issues on the agenda. The main item was the final planning for the big event to demonstrate the Renaissance of Loyalist culture following upon dual disasters of the Nationalist election victory and the great flood. Since those combined calamities the pensioned-off political pundits in the shelter at the Spion Kop bus stop were of one mind – there had been nothing except two dry, barren years for the Loyalists of Ballycarson. Indeed, for many of that particular political persuasion it did appear that the centre of the town was now no mere political wilderness – it was a real complete desert with the symbols of their tradition being sandblasted from all public buildings.

But the very fact that there was an executive board meeting clearly showed all was not lost. Without a doubt there were exciting plans for a re-plantation of Ulster culture. And how was this hoped-for re-flowering of Ulster traditions to be manifested in this oasis of Loyalism? The planned event in question was the grand re-opening of the flute band practice room on the first floor of the L.H.O. hall and the dedication of the new band uniforms. And this time no expense had been spared. It was no longer to be music on a shoe string. In addition to a generous insurance pay-out following the destructive deluge, Big David had managed to lay his hands on European Union money that had been ring-fenced for the fostering of freedom of expression and cold weather payments. Clearly it seemed that the providers of European funding did not want even hard-bitten Loyalists to become frostbitten.

CHAPTER 6

WASHED OUT

The reason for the big splash of cash may just have been that the lesson of recent local history had been learned at the "Watery Wednesday Enquiry" ordered by the L.H.O. hall's insurers after the much debated midweek inundation at the L.H.O. hall.

Whatever the reasons were for the present liberality, it was largely the skinflint approach of the previous band leader, Larry Niven, that had caused the financial problems in the first place. Five years previously the last redecoration of the flute band practice room had clearly been done on the cheap. No expense had been spent. There was no heating whatsoever in the practice room. It had always been uninviting and cold. So frosty indeed was the atmosphere that each flute band member had kept his coat on whilst practising as the volunteer musicians collectively marched up and down the practice room. These were the cold warm-ups for the annual big day, 12th July.

At that time of undoubted and unchallenged Loyalist ascendancy there were greater priorities than heating or decorating the L.H.O. hall. These greater priorities included the retouching of various gable wall murals, the painting of strategically located kerbstones and bus shelters, and the erection of the loyal archways at the entrances to the town. The L.H.O. hall redecoration had not even been contemplated at all until vociferous complaints were received from the genealogists on the ground floor about the marching noise from the practice sessions of the flute band on the floor immediately above. Important transatlantic telephone and email orders for great-granny's sister's second cousin's birth certificate simply could not be processed as the melodies of party songs from the first floor and the accompanying drumming and marching not only raised the roof but also penetrated the ceiling below.

Larry Niven assured the genealogists that the problem would be solved by laying three thick carpets on the floor above. Unfortunately, this deep pile led to deep trouble or, more precisely, deep water.

Despite the fact that these three layers deliberately comprised a sandwich effect of white, red and blue, there was a major scandal when it was discovered that the carpets were seconds from Councillor Finvola O'Duffy's carpet and linoleum factory on the far side of town, the west side of town – the Nationalist side of town. Someone had to be carpeted. Someone needed to be decked. But the resulting row over the "Republican Reject Rugs" could not be swept under any floor covering. At one stage it threatened to be almost as serious as the "Pat's Pan" incident a decade previously when it was discovered that the bread for the sandwiches supplied to the flute band on the twelfth of July had come from south of the international border. However, even the most aggressive and implacable Loyalist critic in the row about the carpets was eventually silenced when it was suggested in an anonymous letter to the *Provincial Observer* that by walking all over Councillor O'Duffy's products, the Loyalists could practise symbolically walking over all of her constituents. Those traditional walking patterns required to be preserved at all costs even if it required some temporary political sacrifices and some fancy footwork. And if the members of the flute band were encouraged to walk up and down the room whilst practising, it would generate so much heat that Larry would not have to spend any cash on heating the room. Yes, this was a case of savings all round. A political saving of face and a financial saving of cash.

Compared to the flooring arrangements, the sound dampening

of the walls in the flute band room was a greater technological challenge. No available wallpaper was thick enough to deaden the sound. Plasterboard was too expensive even if rescued from bombed-out buildings. However, the problem was solved by a newspaper collection. Volunteers were encouraged to turn up with boxes full of newspapers, preferably the thick Sunday editions. Those with a Sabbatarian conscience were content after it was made clear that they were all printed on Saturday and not a word had ever been read on the following day. These pristine works of literature would be placed into bundles six inches deep and then nailed onto the walls and the doors with rivet guns. Care was taken to ensure that the newspapers were placed with their backs to the wall and that the inside faces comprised news reports of previous Loyalist triumphs trumpeted by headlines such as "Not an Inch", "No Concessions" and "Ulster Says No". Clearly the lining of the walls with such dense and detailed historical records and positive propaganda resulted in the flute band practice room becoming slightly smaller. Nevertheless, with the memories of their former illustrious exploits and victories adorning the walls, the Loyalists were unworried about the marginal shrinkage of the borders of their empire.

Newspapers could not be nailed to the windows for obvious reasons. It wasn't that the occupants of the L.H.O. hall wanted to see what was going on in the outside world – that was usually irrelevant anyway. Rather it was that light was needed for them to read the surrounding headlines as well as the music scores of the flute band. Larry Niven originally intended to install second-hand Venetian blinds, but someone objected to the proximity of their city of inspiration, if not origin, to the city of Rome. With such a provenance they would certainly not suit traditional sash windows. The plan was scrapped and the Venetian blinds returned to the "What Everyone Doesn't Want" shop via the town dump. So it was a case of curtains for the blinds and, as it happens, curtains instead of the blinds. Purple and orange velvet curtains would have burst the available budget, so, instead, white net curtains were painted onto the inside face of the glass of the windows.

"They will never need to be washed or dry cleaned," was the great advantage indicated by Larry Niven.

And there was more than enough painting talent close at hand to complete the job of the ever-clean net curtains. William Henry and his colleagues were on call twenty-four hours a day seven days a week for that urgent Loyalist painting job.

The real snag in this complex sound-dampening arrangement was that noone had thought of the ceiling in the flute band practice room. One Tuesday night a few weeks after the sound-dampening was complete there was a sharp frost. The water pipes in the attic burst leading to a deluge into the flute band practice room. The walls in the room were duly washed down with cascading water. It left a foot deep of paper and literary sludge on the newly carpeted floor and a remnant of nails in the walls that resembled the work of an insane circus knife thrower.

"It wasn't much of an improvement when that stuff was readable," observed one of the L.H.O. hall cleaners the next day as she peered round the door on what became known as "Watery Wednesday".

Special squads of flute band volunteers were instructed in the use of buckets and shovels to remove the filth on the floor that had become almost as hard as concrete after it dried out. Unfortunately, imbedded in the mass on the floor were not only the various works of Loyalist literature, which had previously adorned the walls, but also the debris of all the band uniforms, the flags, the banners, the drums and, worse still, many of the black wooden flutes. The band had been stripped and silenced. Even the Republican terrorists had never achieved that in decades of violence and destruction. So whilst the flute band members wielded their shovels and buckets, Larry Niven carried the can. The flute band management committee awarded Larry Niven for his services to music the D.C.B., meaning "Don't come back".

The grim-faced Mr. Niven was pictured in the *Provincial Observer* with the caption underneath: "Happy as Larry."

The eagle-eyed economists in the shelter at the Spion Kop bus stop noted that all this happiness did have a modest trickle-down effect, at least within the L.H.O. hall building. On the floor below, the dripping water had soaked all the paperwork of the genealogists. However, the oil of foreign currency was poured on their troubles with an overall settling effect. When they dried out, their records and charts looked more original, ancient and authentic than ever before and commanded five times the price from those seeking records of past personalities and long-forgotten unknowns. Now the Americans were supplied not only with ersatz ancient histories but also with genuine ante-deluvian records.

Key to the documentary dry-out was the tanning salon next door to the L.H.O. hall. Business had been slow for the "Golden Pigments" tanning shop after their landlords – the Fifth Ballycarson Free Non-subscribing Associated Independent Congregationalist Church – had taken umbrage at newspaper reports of the riotous living of some young Ballycarson holidaymakers when they visited certain destinations in the Aegean. The elderly elders of the churlish Church did not subscribe to the philosophy that their premises should be used to pre-prepare such tourists for sun, sea, sangria and sex – particularly, sex. So the leasehold terms were altered to require the tenants, the operators of the tanning salon, to make sure that their make-believe sunbeams should not shine equally on the righteous and the unrighteous. Anyone taking a tanning session had to sign a form confirming they would not be visiting certain listed Mediterranean destinations. The *Provincial Observer* ran the headline "Blacklist Frowns on Sun-kissed Towns" and followed it up with the story "Tourist Hotspots Become Blackspots". If that wasn't enough to strangle trade, most of the painted letters on the "GOLDEN PIGMENTS" shop sign above the frontage had flaked off like old desiccated skin. It left the shop sign consisting only of the letters "...OLD... ...MEN...". There could hardly have been a more demonstrative advertisement of the adverse consequences of premature skin ageing. The absence of a daily queue of budding Adonises left the tanning salon ready to accept the task of drying the paperwork of the genealogists under the tanning lamps. Fortunately, overly rapid ageing and discolouration were exactly what the genealogists were after.

On the upper floor of the L.H.O. hall there had to be some radical rethinking. Leadership of the flute band was entrusted to an enthusiastic German immigrant Eva Pfeiffer who had come to Ballycarson the previous June in response to an internet advert headed "Flute-players Urgently Required". Despite her slightly dictatorial approach, leading to her nickname "Eva Brunette", it was clear she was the right woman for the job. She clearly had musical talent and was the only woman in the town who could whistle party songs such as "The Sash" whilst smoking a cigar. It seemed that the several large gaps between her front teeth facilitated the feat. In addition, if any additional qualification was at all necessary, someone in the flute band community had heard that prior to arriving in Ulster Eva Pfeiffer had played in someone's conservatory in Leipzig.

"If she was good enough for that glass house, she could serenade us here in the bus shelter. She'll do rightly for the big marquee in the demonstration field on the twelfth of July," observed one of the music critics in the shelter at the Spion Kop bus stop.

That remark was truer to the mark than could ever have been expected. When an outsider looked at the Ballycarson 1690 Young Defenders Flute Band what they often saw was a bunch of gullible fools playing in a "Kick the Pope" flute band. With her upbringing in the former D.D.R., Eva knew the pressures to toe the party line. She also knew that some compromises had to be made to have any life at all. When she looked at the band what she saw was a group of real musicians with real talent and real potential. She had the wit, however, not to tell anyone that. In England and elsewhere one might be damned with faint praise. In Ulster, as in the former D.D.R., one could be damned by any praise at all. It was best to keep your head down and get on with it. So much the better if the local politicians thought of her as no more than an eccentric who would never amount to much and be of little use to them.

But it was the financial, organisational and administrative skills of Eva Pfeiffer that were equally, if not more, important than her low public profile. After the Watery Wednesday washout, she would have to attend to the total restructuring of the flute band, the obtaining of new instruments and uniforms, and the rebuilding of morale in a difficult political climate. For that her credentials were impeccable if slightly unusual. How could anyone better the individual who, in the space of a few months, had successfully implemented the long-delayed conversion of the main production line in the Ballycarson salami factory from black pudding to salami? So ruthless had she been in pushing through the sausage reforms at the factory she was promoted to financial and sales director. In that position she promptly earned the loving title "The Hun at the Till".

Over the next few months it became more than clear that the appointment had paid off. Eva arranged a temporary practice room for the flute band in a renovated nissen hut in the old WW2 prisoner of war camp. And emanating from that hut every Tuesday evening passers-by could hear the flute band's rendition of her own arrangement of classics such as Elvis Presley's "Suspicious Minds". Here indeed was an acceptable mix of novelty and continuity. New tunes, new melodies, new arrangements, a new sense of direction but with a sufficient hint of the same old political message. Eva had clearly hit the right note.

Loyalty cannot be bought except when it is sold. But when it comes to genuine, rock-solid loyalty, it pays to make sure by compulsory purchase. Despite her attempts at public invisibility, Eva became publically audible and unavoidable as a result of her innovations with the flute band. So Eva was put on the Big David payroll, whether she liked it or not. An investigation on her background was launched and accompanied by some obvious surveillance. But even after the recommendation from the character analysts in the shelter at the Spion Kop bus stop, her political reliability remained a little uncertain. Big David sent someone else on his payroll to keep an eye, or rather an ear, on Eva and the flute band.

For this musical nursery, I need a plant, thought Big David and smiled as he thought he'd come up with a new joke.

William Henry was the man in question. He was deputised as a reluctant political commissar to beat the drum of political correctness at the band practices. Fortunately for Eva, both William Henry and Big David were tone deaf and had no idea of musical timing, rhythm or pitch. For William Henry a sheet of music was like a roll of Chinese script. Given Big David's reputed oriental origins, it was clearly something else for him, but whatever it was, it remained unintelligible. So William Henry's musical reports to Big David were a case of the deaf speaking to the deaf. What was the upshot of this misinformation? Big David may have paid the piper, but Eva called the tune.

Fortunately for her and for musical progress, Eva spotted the plant immediately and had just the job for what she informed William Henry were his very special talents. He could paint the sides of the new base drum. Originally Big David had insisted that his face be featured on both sides of the drum. But then, information having been received, he had backed down. Eva had told him she was delighted to have his face on the drum. It was an image of inspiration to all musicians. But she didn't think it would do his image any good to have someone beating the lining out of it in public even if accompanied by music. Faced with his image receiving such a hammering, Big David agreed that the sides of the new base drum would bear the name of the flute band and nothing more.

Big David, without realising it, had been outflanked by Eva yet again.

CHAPTER 7

STREETWISE AND HOUSE-TRAINED

Names were always a difficult issue when it came to dealing with inward investment in Ulster. Names were loaded words used as weapons in the propaganda war waged between the local politicians on each side of the sectarian divide. In Ballycarson the names of public structures comprised a veritable Who's Who of those who had encouraged others to take up arms in the centuries of civil unrest. The effect of this belated civic recognition was to give a cloak of respectability to those who had held the coats of the belligerents and inspired others to continue the struggle.

Amongst the first acts of the new Nationalist administration was a search for a Ballycarson street that was suitable for their great hero De Valera, the leader of one island, one land and one people. The aim of these newly elected Nationalist politicians was to show solidarity with their fellow Irishmen and women in the south by honouring a man who claimed to personify the entire island.

What the new Nationalist Ballycarson administration could not grasp was that their acts demonstrated exactly what they denied with their words. The Irish border had some substance after all. Their choice of hero demonstrated the great divide between the Nationalist politicians in the north and those in the south. The Northern Ireland experience had placed the Northern Nationalists into a political exile not of only a few miles but also a considerable number of decades. Perceptions of what Nationalism meant in the north and south had diverged irreconcilably. The Northern Nationalist politicians still revered a man who, according to some, had been a cracker short of a packet in or around the Jacob's biscuit factory in 1916. But in the fast-moving economies of modern Dublin and Ballyporeen it no longer mattered quite as much where your grandfather was on a particular day all those years ago. In Northern Ireland the identity and actions of your grandfather still determined your destiny. The sins of grandfathers were still visited upon grandchildren.

And so the Nationalist councillors in Ballycarson wished to express their new-found power by honouring De Valera. At the Council meeting held to implement the new policy, all the old political clichés were rolled out to honour or disparage the man whom the Unionists still regarded as the Devil from Eire. In choosing De Valera as their starting point for street reform, the Nationalists had a real problem because a Ballycarson street of a character similar to that of their hero was not easily found. As the Unionists only too eagerly read from their book of approved and well-used political critique, for De Valera there was no street narrow enough, long enough, or crooked enough. Eventually, the Nationalists gave up the search and plumped to rename Crown Street, which was the main street running through Ballycarson.

"A primary route would suit the character of such an eminent statesman," asserted the Nationalists.

Much to the astonishment of the Nationalists, the Unionists immediately agreed and offered to vote in favour of the renaming.

"It would suit De Valera down to the ground. It's a one-way street," laughed Councillor Montgomery Cherry.

Even the normally taciturn Councillor Dick Lamb did not remain silent. He read the line directly from his prompt card and scorned: "An arterial route would suit a butcher with so much blood on his hands."

This political impasse was a real roadblock to the new roads policy. Cooperation in local government had the potential to be even more obstructive than active opposition. An important step in the redirection of political life in Ballycarson, such as street-naming could not possibly occur by unanimous cross-party vote. What use would the policy be if the political opposition were not to be noticeably aggrieved? Maybe the Unionists had learned new tricks? It must be a political trap.

"If the Unionists vote for this, our new administration will look like a bunch of fools," was the conclusion of the new Councillor Chairperson Finvola O'Duffy.

The idea of renaming Crown Street was quietly dropped. The lack of acrimony irked, but what could be done? As a compromise the Nationalist majority voted to remove the name Crown Street and replace it with nothing. So what had been Crown Street became a street with no name. Of course this was a half measure, a compromise. But, in the world of local government, it was far better for the town to appear to be completely directionless than to give the impression that the Council was doing absolutely nothing. It was the logic of the drunken man: it is better to stagger about than stand still.

Of course, some semblance of political face had to be saved. Salvation was sought in Councillor Eugene O'Driscoll's assertion that by removing a street name the Nationalists were following the precedent of what had been done during the 1939–45 "Emergency". He declined to use the word "war" as no British government had any right to declare war on behalf of "his people" who had remained scrupulously neutral and solidly anti-British throughout the entire affair. During those dangerous times all the Ballycarson street names had been removed and a blackout imposed to stop foreign flyers and continental paratroopers from knowing exactly where they were. But Councillor Eugene O'Driscoll's recollection was selective. On the very first night of the Emergency blackout his own grandfather, the then leader of the local northern Nationalists, had organised a huge bonfire in the west side of Ballycarson. So much for the Celtic twilight. It was of no consequence that if they had been flying over the area at the time the servicemen of the Luftwaffe could have seen the bonfire for miles and could have flattened those dancing around the flames in the west side of town.

And, of course, the flames of defiance were accompanied by the councillor's grandfather's fireside chat with the enthusiastic assembled supporters. What was the substance of these words of comfort? It was a truly remarkable melange of half-baked analysis and overdone emotions. By this concoction the councillor achieved the remarkable feat of making a speech that was both base and baseless. What was really important, he intoned meaningfully, was that this very bonfire was a bright beacon of defiance in the face of British rule that had kept Ireland in darkness for centuries. This present difficulty in Europe, this continental war of that schismatic neighbouring island, was no more than a dispute between foreigners – indeed, a mere clash between evil empires – in which Ireland should not take sides. Indeed there should be complete moral ambivalence as to the outcome. Why should the Irish care who should win? There was safety and a moral superiority in neutrality as would soon be demonstrated by the positions of Luxembourg, Belgium, Holland, Denmark and Norway. In addition there was the shining example of the constructive and neutral fascist states of Italy, Spain and Portugal. They served as models for Irish aspirations. Ireland was not isolated after all! Indeed the neutrality of the free twenty-six counties will throw a protective blanket over the six occupied by the British. The Unionists in Ulster should be grateful! Instead of mobilisation and the building of the machines of death, it was essential that what should be promoted in Ireland was the living culture of sturdy children, athletic youths, comely maidens and cosy homesteads. This alone would lead Ireland into the prosperous future of poetry, dance and folk songs, provided, of course, these forms of art remained pure, untainted and morally acceptable to those who knew in their hearts what Ireland wanted.

There would be jobs for all in Ireland as peaceful prosperity blossomed! There would be no more emigration to support the British war machine. And after he had spoken, the crowd, clearly moved by his under-spoken oratory, broke into song and concluded the evening around the cosy bonfire with the popular melody:

"The year was 1939
The sky was full of lead
Hitler headed for Poland
And Paddy for Holyhead."

But it would be most unfair to represent the new Nationalist administration in a uniquely bad light. The Nationalists were not up to anything new. The Unionists had been into street-naming for decades. In latter years of their administration they had run out of heroes and many streets in Ballycarson were named after total unknowns found in the ranks of the Unionist councillors themselves or their relations. After all, was it really any worse to live in a street with no name than in a street named after an unknown? Even the local Loyalist population had begun to complain that they were living in streets named after yesterday's nobodies. The whole problem had been irritated by the fact that in Ballycarson many local politicians were interrelated and almost all belonged to petty family dynasties. In addition, the politicians usually employed their close family members as researchers and rented property from other family members who, in turn, had acquired that property from the fruits of political research paid for, sometimes several times, out of Council funds or so it was said. The result was that a small number of names dominated everything in local politics, leading to little choice for street names. Most aggrieved were the residents of a small housing estate built in the 1980s where every street had been named after the politically active members of the Lamb family. The family tree had been laid out in a series of streets branching off a main trunk road. Tom Lamb Street led in to Dick Lamb Street and Harry Lamb Street, which in turn branched into Samuel Lamb Street and Mildred Lamb Street, etc. etc. Given the presence of all the Lambs the whole area became known as "the Sheep Farm".

Of course there were complaints. "We don't want to live in a street named after any Tom, Dick or Harry. Let us stop looking to the past and, instead, grasp the future!" ran the anonymous letter to the then Council chairman, Tim Boyne.

The letter was copied to the *Provincial Enquirer*. With a view to piling on the political pressure, it was printed in full under the headlines "More Bleating from the Sheep Farm" and "Lamb to Get Chop?"

Whoever sent the letter had picked a most responsive addressee. Councillor Tim Boyne had always been sensitive to the issue of Christian names because his own had led to unjustified accusations that he was the product of a "mixed" marriage or, to adopt the local technical adage, a Roman Calvinist.

The Council chairman was stung into immediate action. Noone could accuse the Unionist Council of being unresponsive to their electorate.

"There will be no more Tom, Dick or Harry," confirmed the Council chairman in his weekly newspaper column. "In future, when we name streets, we will leave out all Christian names and, in addition, we will re-write the past." So all the Christian names were deleted from the various street names in the Sheep Farm leaving it with sixteen streets all with the name of "Lamb Street". As the newly built streets were all short and straight the overall impression facing the uninitiated map reader was of a crossword puzzle where every question had the same answer.

When it comes to political repentance over the mis-naming of streets and roads it pays to travel the extra mile. In a further, and perhaps a last ditch, effort to tart up the tarnished street-naming policy, the Unionists decided to rename the new dual carriageway bypassing Ballycarson after those councillors responsible for local economic development and regeneration. The chosen two, the distinguished duo, the irreplaceable pair, were Councillor James Morrow and his twin brother, Wilburt Morrow. Again Christian names were to be left out. The official Council press release was suitably effusive.

"The new dual carriageway, the road of the future, will bypass Ballycarson. It will look to the future and be known as the road of the Two Morrows."

With such a twin track approach, it was obvious that the future was bright for Ballycarson. The effect was rather spoiled when the politically unreliable columnist in the *Provincial Enquirer* suggested that the dual carriageway would lead to a double crossroads.

In the latter days of direct rule in Ulster the central government in Northern Ireland had attempted to water down the effect of street renaming by the use of the universal solvent. The effect was achieved not by giving the various Councils public money but by depriving them of it.

The rationale of the policy was summed up in a secret memo sent within the Northern Ireland Office: "If they cannot afford to build new streets, they will have nothing new to name." And so "the Roadblock Policy", as it became known, was approved.

Unfortunately, local politicians worked out ways to get round the roadblock. For even the most minor of public works the Unionist-run Council in Ballycarson had been forced to seek funding from private investors. The *quid pro quo* was usually a requirement that the new structure be named after the investor. The policy may have been politically neutral, as central government had wished, but more often than not the sponsors were after inappropriate advertising. In the latter days of the Unionist administration the Council had almost come unstuck when they had accepted funding from the Estonian manufacturers of cheap pharmaceuticals. They had wished to sponsor the laying of new roads into the Ballycarson industrial estate. Initially the Estonian investors had insisted that the roads be called after their own areas of speciality. It was product placement at its most basic. For a while there had been a real prospect of "Anti-emetic Avenue", "Botulism Boulevard", "Cirrhosis Crescent", "Diarrhoea Drive" and "Expectorant Expressway". The Council recruited a writer of signs, then got stuck on the letter "F". He could not immediately think of a type of road that would accompany a reference to Farmacology. The term "Freeway" was an Americanisation beyond his somewhat limited and localised vocabulary. The hiatus caused by limited literacy of the sign writer and the fact that he had reached the limit of his creative powers were perhaps fortunate. This held up the completion of the alphabetically inspired street-sign project for just enough time to enable the Estonian firm to go bust before the new name plates had to be put up. The unused signs joined much other material already dumped in the former Union Canal.

The legacy of street-naming obviously would be remembered for some time. It would seem that the Nationalists recalled the practice just as soon as they got into power. Immediately after the election, the main route leading to the Ballycarson Council headquarters was renamed and became known locally as "China Crescent". However, this was not as a result of the scrapping of some erstwhile Unionist-inspired street name. And if you thought the new name was aimed at pleasing some potential Oriental investor you would also be wrong. "China Crescent" was inspired by the Nationalist councillors taking out all the official Council crockery bearing the Queen's image, smashing it and dumping it beside the road. "We can build on this firm foundation," was the comment of Councillor Eugene O'Driscoll as he jumped up and down to level out the piles of white shards.

The cynical resident of Ballycarson may have sworn nothing had really changed. However, perhaps that downcast denizen was deluded. Immediately after the Crown Street/De Valera fiasco, the new Nationalist Council administration insisted that they had learned from the mistakes of the Unionist predecessors. This war of street-naming could be carried out by different means. A different angle of public transport was chosen. Thirty-two bus shelters, one for each county in Ireland, were built around Ballycarson by the Nationalist-run Council in the early days of their administration. Immediately after the change in the Council administration, new sources of public funding became available directly from Europe. The Unionist-run administration had previously eschewed approaching such institutions on the basis that the Council's political position would be compromised by taking funds from bodies that also gave vast amounts of cash to the local authorities in the Irish Republic. The Nationalists swept this policy aside and the money poured in for essential projects. They included the redecoration of the Council Offices, the building of ornamental gates for the Council chairperson's house, the extension of the existing kennel for the official Council Irish wolfhound and the construction of bus shelters. Only the very last of these vital and socially uplifting projects need detain us here.

The main, indeed the sole, condition of the European funding had been that the bus shelters would be located in a non-sectarian way and there would be no sectarian input in their design and layout.

Despite repeated Unionist objections, it was difficult to substantiate the allegation that the Nationalist administration had failed to comply with the main conditions. Indeed, to the most neutral of observers, it was manifestly obvious that they had been implemented in various ways.

First, the newly elected Nationalist Ballycarson Council required that the bus stops and shelters be deliberately built in locations where no buses ran. In particular, they should be built in locations nowhere near roads. The official reasoning? If noone at all could use the bus shelters, noone could accuse the Council of showing bias to those potential bus users with a particular religious or political persuasion in any one part of the town.

Secondly, the Council required that the bus shelters be built of a material that could not be painted a particular colour. This would avoid mini-murals of contentious battle scenes being added on the side of the bus shelters. In addition, although this was not admitted, it would put some of Camp David's painters out of a job. That would bring the Loyalist big man down to his real size. So all the bus shelters were made of glass. This would comply with the Council's targets to produce transparency in local government. Who cared if they were easily vandalised? At least the reconstruction projects would assist the hard-pressed glazing companies around the town, which had suffered so badly since the start of the terrorist cease-fires.

The third method of compliance with the main European funding condition was the avoidance of naming the bus shelters after sectarian war victories and battle sites in Ireland. So the Nationalist-led Council named them all after battles that the British had lost around the world.

"It's nothing to do with us if the British got a cuffing outside Ireland," ran the publicity blurb issued by the Council.

So the shelter at the Spion Kop bus stop was one of a set of bus shelters with foreign names comprising places as far afield as Arnhem, Crete, Dieppe, Dunkirk, Gallipoli, Isandhlwana, Kabul, Ladysmith, Magersfontein, Majuba Hill, Mons, New Orleans, Saratoga, Singapore, St. Valery en Caux and Yorktown.

With a view to further humiliating the British community the researcher employed by the Nationalist Council to complete the task wished to demonstrate that this list was not exhaustive. So, after setting out thirty-one specific names, he named the last of the bus shelters "Et Cetera". Councillor Eugene O'Driscoll, a history teacher in the local Christian Brothers' Academy, wasn't sure where this was but did not want to admit his ignorance to his pupils. So he told them it was a fortress near El Alamein. When one of his pupils complained that this was not mentioned anywhere in his history textbook, Councillor Eugene O'Driscoll's incisive, authoritative and conciliatory response was:

"All those history books written in English never tell you the truth. Let me tell you what really happened."

Clearly Councillor Eugene O'Driscoll was living up to his reputation amongst his own colleagues that he had gone to higher education and teacher-training college not to broaden his horizons but to deepen his prejudices.

As was the way of things, the territorial claims of both indigenous traditions led to the exclusive appropriation of all of the various bus stops. The new structures would now all serve the greater political purpose. In the new political economy that represented the Peace Process, the Republicans occupied twenty-six, whilst the Loyalists grabbed the remaining six. Complaints of inequality were futile and the Loyalist big man Big David simply decided to make the most of what he could get.

At this very moment his employees, the ancient arch conservative art critics in the shelter at the Spion Kop bus stop, were collectively nodding their approval as they used their binoculars to gaze down on a marvellous sight. It was William Henry at the Anne Boleyn Bridge surveying his painted accomplishments on the railway bridge to the accompaniment of a quiet cigarette. This, however, did not mean a silent smoke. He was attempting to mimic Eva Pfeiffer's notorious feat of whistling a Loyalist party song whilst smoking. Unfortunately, all William Henry could achieve was to blow out his cigarette halfway through the opening note.

In any event, this smoking habit was more complicated than it looked and demanded one's full attention. William Henry had to remind himself every time not to try to stub out the fag butt in the tin of white spirit. That was how another of Big David's painters, Billie King, had singed both hands last month. Billie King was clearly not too clever, thought William Henry. Nevertheless, it was a good job the fire hadn't been worse because Billie King was the flute band's bass drummer. It was about as easy to beat out march time with bandaged hands as it was to eat fish and chips wearing boxing gloves. Without Billie King battering the drum, the flute band would have a job getting out for parade.

As if to acknowledge the source of his good fortune, William Henry looked up the hill towards Ballycarson High Street and Big David's encampment and seat of power. And who was that coming down the hill? Speak of the devil! The sight was unmistakable. It was the band's bass drummer, Billie King.

Billie was huge. Indeed so large of stature was Billie that when the body measurements of the flute band members were sent off to the manufacturers of the new flute band uniforms, they had sent back Billie's statistics for correction with the comment: "These can't be right."

But true enough they were. Head and shoulder above most others stood Billie King, leading to the nickname "Kong King".

Billie derived her name not only from her parents' earnest desire that their child should avoid political controversy and criminal gangs but also their membership of the local squash, badminton and tennis club, which was avowedly non-sectarian, ecumenical and apolitical in its outlook. In the eyes of the local populace it demonstrated this beyond controversy by possessing both green grass courts and orange clay courts. "Racquets wreck racketeering", was the club's guiding principle. In an attempt to steer their beloved child away from sectarian politics the sporting Kings had named her after their American heroine, the golden girl of Wimbledon in the 1970s. Unfortunately, a few years later Billie's dad's love affair with racquet sports had come to an untimely end when his wife ran off with her badminton coach. After that Billie's dad confined his activity to the tennis club bar and forsook the courts for good (apart from the forensic variety where he engaged in the bitter divorce litigation). Feeling some continuing responsibility for the matrimonial disaster, the tennis club committee did at least assist in providing summer jobs for

Billie who was employed to put up the nets and paint the white lines on the courts. But the job didn't pay well, so she supplemented her income by painting scenes of selected historical events on gable end walls for the Big David organisation. Goliath had joined forces with David.

Now as a director of the Big David organisation, Billie descended the hill towards the railway bridge followed by her recently acquired assistant. Behind her she was leading her horse, "White Rum". The name reflected the colour of the animal, but this was merely coincidence because, in fact, the name had been inspired by Billie's favourite drink. William Henry lit another cigarette and waited until Billie reached the bottom of the hill where they met for a chat whilst William Henry inspected the horse.

"You can speak German to my horse, William Henry," observed Billie. "She's a genuine reproduction Lipizzaner!"

A few months previously Billie had won the horse in a lottery organised by the Ballycarson 1690 Young Defenders Flute Band to raise funds for the new band uniforms. Given that it was surplus to immediate requirements during a lull in production, the horse had been donated as a prize by a shareholder in the Ballycarson salami factory.

The King family home, a two-up two-down semi-detached in one of the Council housing estates in Ballycarson, required some alteration to keep a horse. Nevertheless, with dreams of Westerns and Clint Eastwood movies, Billie had been unwilling to give up her new prize.

"How did you convince your dad to let the horse into the house?" asked William Henry. "What did you promise him? Free transport for life and a boost to rose production in the garden?"

"Oh no, it was easier than that." Billie King grinned. "I told my dad that we could raise some extra cash by letting out our upstairs bedroom to an eighteen-year-old German blonde who was going to pose for my next painting. So, he couldn't resist. And

I told him no lies. My very next painting was a mural of King Billy crossing the Boyne on the back of his white charger."

Indeed, after the horse was moved in with a display of complete equine equanimity, Billie's dad began to see the practicality of the arrangement. This indeed was a house-trained horse.

There was only one condition laid down by Billie's dad. "Make sure that horse has no overnight visitors. I don't want the cavalry in here after dark."

CHAPTER 8

THE DIGITAL AGE

In the King household the bedroom on the first floor at the head of the stairs was duly converted into a stable.

The bedroom door was horizontally cut into two halves so Billie could admire her equine prize as it gazed out into the landing. A manger was fashioned out of a shopping trolley borrowed, on an extended loan, from the local supermarket. For convenience it could be moved around the bedroom as the circumstances required. It was truly a case of meals on wheels.

Exercise was not a problem. Each day the horse was marched up and down the stairs and in and out the front door and set to graze on one or other of the housing estate roundabouts. It was only recently that a cloud had appeared on the horizon when the immediate neighbour complained to the Council as the horse started to kick holes in the wall separating the King household from that neighbour's bedroom. One hole in the wall was now so big that the neighbour had the head of a horse gazing out over the headboard of his bed. It occasioned some disturbed sleep.

When the neighbour first threatened to complain to the Council, Big David muscled in on behalf of Billie King. Given his distinct lack of physical bulk, the term "muscled in" could be employed only metaphorically as regards Big David. It would be more accurate to say that a diminutive Big David minced in on behalf of Billie King.

"Tell the neighbour that the present arrangement is far better than waking up with a severed horse head at the foot of the bed," was Big David's observation when consulted by a worried Billie King. Given Billie's stature, Big David had to stand on a stool to address her face to face.

However, the neighbour, a local artiste, also sought the counsel of Big David as the self-imported and self-imposed community father. "I can't sing because this animal is giving me hay fever," complained the neighbour. So after this second face-to-face encounter, Big David had to be two-faced to save the day. Contrary to his otherwise trumpeted fundamental principles of dogged adherence to unchanging truth and eternal righteousness, Big David had to compromise and tell Billie to move the horse.

"I've had to move White Rum this morning…" explained Billie to William Henry. "But Big David says he will get me a room in one of the abandoned houses near the railway down beside the canal."

"How did you get away with it for so long?" enquired William Henry. "Why didn't your neighbour complain long before now?"

The explanation unfolded. "We live next door to Charlie Rae," said Billie.

"Oh, I get it – music soothes animals, doesn't it?"

"Maybe," said Billie, "but it is really a case of see no evil, hear no evil."

Because of his undoubted disability and uncertain musical ability, Charlie Rae, Billie's immediate neighbour, used to front a dance band, calling himself the "White Ray Charles". This was no sham Irish imitation of real transatlantic talent. Charlie Rae was indeed as blind as a bat. He used to be driven about by his mother from Gospel Hall to country Gospel Hall where he would lead the faithful in country and western revival evenings. To add a touch of authenticity to his act he wore real spurs, but, given his susceptibility to hay fever, he had been accompanied by a cardboard horse.

His mother, Senga Rae, had also known stardom in her day as she had at one time fronted a trio of backing musicians comprising her three daughters. With this line-up known as "Senga and the Sengettes" she had once topped the bill of a dazzling array of local artistes at the Slatequarry Masonic guest tea. Whilst the guests supped glasses of brown lemonade and tucked into plates of square-cut ham sandwiches, she belted out country and western tear jerkers such as "My Son Calls Another Woman Mummy" and "I'm So Lonely Standing Here Since My Horse Died". During this latter performance the cardboard horse was symbolically laid on its side. Such a musical high could never be repeated and, to avoid the inevitable disappointment, Senga was never invited back.

Those halcyon days of innocent fun had now passed – ruined by Ulster's troubles, during which the population had learned to avoid night-spots. Instead, they stayed at home and listened to recorded music. Suddenly, the population had discovered a different quality of life and a better quality of music. The darkest cloud does indeed contain a silver lining. But whilst the general population enjoyed the silver lining, Senga sat under the cloud. Senga had never been able to obtain a recording contract to cash in on the boom of home entertainment, so she had felt marginalised and excluded. Apart from Senga's crowd-clearing performances, it was left to her son, Charlie, to carry the torch in these more difficult times, the era of the Peace Process.

Of course Senga was now Charlie's biggest fan, but it was clearly a case of maternal rather than musical appreciation. All Charlie's musical kit was taken round the various meeting houses in a horse trailer, also containing the cardboard horse, pulled behind his mother's open-top Volkswagen Beetle. And so it continued until Charlie's career ended in a blaze of glory on the Ballycarson bypass.

One Saturday evening the miniature musical convoy was stopped and hijacked by a crowd of balaclava-wearing paramilitaries or hooded hoods. It was immediately clear the masked bandits were only after the specialist gear in the trailer and not after the car. They unhooked the trailer and allowed Charlie's mother to watch from the Volkswagen as they set the trailer and contents ablaze with a single, well-aimed petrol bomb. It was another example of four star's finest hour. Charlie's disability precluded him from enjoying any sort of a view, but the increasing heat, the smell of petrol fumes and the unmistakable sounds of a disintegrating trailer made him increasingly agitated.

He stood up in the passenger seat of the car and shouted, "What's going on? What's happening? What's the smell?"

"We'll give you a hint," replied the leader of the gang and, in unison, the hijackers started to whistle the theme tune from the film *Chariots of Fire* and to run in slow motion around the flames.

In such minor incidents the police and army were not interested. It was all within the acceptable level of violence. But the third force comprising the Ballycarson neighbourhood watch did assist. The mystery of the affair was intriguing. To assist in solving the whodunit of the hooded hoods, the neighbourhood watch put round leaflets indicating they were looking not for the usual terrorist thugs but for someone with a love of real music.

Unfortunately, someone read one of the leaflets to Charlie Rae.

This led to an ugly scene in the street immediately outside the Third Ballycarson Free Reformed Independent Non-subscribing Evangelical Congregationalist Church. Charlie, attended by his mother dressed in her best stage frock, was broadcasting his outrage to the world at large from the backseat of the open-top Volkswagen Beetle. As if this strange sight was not enough to attract attention, Charlie Rae was impressing his views on the passers-by with the help of a microphone linked to a large black music speaker tied to the bonnet. These voluble comments on the state of society were hardly valuable and were certainly not valued by the passers-by, the minister, the Reverend Grim Jordan or the church members who had been participating in a church mission evening. The members had put in considerable effort to entice in the passing pedestrian casually contemplating repentance.

They had even gone to the length of draping a huge banner over the front door with large red letters bearing the heartfelt and heartening message "Backsliders Welcome". But the path to salvation was being obstructed by a wall of sound. The bile and vitriol spewing from Charlie Rae's lips was putting off even the most determined back-slidden, potentially repenting visitor. The racket Charlie was making was clearly the din of iniquity.

Charlie's impassioned intimations of his disgust to the public may have been merely a minor case of casting false pearls in front of real swine, but, after several increasingly acrimonious exchanges between him and the church members, the constabulary intervened.

The conflict amongst Church, state and the performing arts was brief. To avoid a further breach of the peace, Charlie Rae was invited to spend a night in the newly painted cells. It was another of Big David's successes. His painting squad had very recently administered a very attractive coat of white gloss to the entire interior.

After only a few hours in the renovated and still wet cell, Charlie Rae was released early. It had nothing at all to do with the fact the jailers felt sorry at the ruin of Charlie's country gospel star-spangled black suit by the white gloss paint sticking to it every time he walked into a wall. It was solely down to the petition seeking his release on humanitarian grounds received by the officer in charge of the station. The petition, started by one inmate on a large piece of toilet roll, was signed by every police officer on duty in the cell block and all the inhabitants of the other cells together with a number of visiting solicitors who had been holding interviews with their clients. Regardless of their political persuasion, they had all been entirely persuaded that Charlie Rae's talents were best demonstrated elsewhere after he had forcibly entertained them with an endless selection of quasi-religious tunes and uplifting melodies played on his mouth organ. Charlie Rae had kept this harmonica of hope hidden like a medallion under his shirt to provide solace in emergencies just like this one. As the harmonica was connected to a chain around his neck, the police had to let Charlie Rae out to get rid of the problem.

Since then Charlie Rae had been confined to home base as the evangelical gigs dried up more quickly than the paint on the cell walls. The organisers of such non-secular soirées were quite happy to be entertained by reformed criminals provided they acknowledged that they had seen the light, but Charlie remained in darkness and was persisting in a denial that he had ever done anything wrong. He remained an unwelcome, unrepentant, hardened backslider. His career slid back into obscurity, alleviated only by the occasional performance at low-budget weddings. Some cash-strapped fathers of the bride had discovered that the best way to ensure small wedding receptions was to advertise on the invitations that the musical accompaniment at the reception would be provided by Charlie Rae.

However, Charlie continued to dream of a wider and more discerning audience. He retained what he saw as his foothold in the musical world with a series of high-level, open-air recitals. From the tiny concrete balcony leading from the first floor bedroom in his Council house, he entertained passers-by in the street with performances on a second-hand electrical Hammond organ. This had been salvaged from the bombed-out wreckage of the Hibernian Hall on the far side of town. Although a few of the notes did not work properly, this provided an ample substitute for the instruments lost in the previous terrorist outrage on the open road. Someone had even replaced his horse by providing him with a second-hand cardboard cow endowed with an enormous pink udder. Unfortunately, the complete stylistic effect was slightly spoiled by the advertising on the side of the animal betraying its origins: "Udderly Satisfying – Milk." Still, one cannot have everything.

What the Republican terrorists have taken away, the Loyalist defenders of democracy have duly provided, thought Charlie Rae. *There was justice after all.*

In fact, the truth was the reverse. It was a group of Charlie's Loyalist neighbours who had burned the trailer for the sake of peace and quiet. It was Nationalists from the far side of town who had provided the Hammond organ and cardboard cow simply to make sure Charlie continued to annoy his Loyalist neighbours.

From then on the neighbours, including the King family, were duly serenaded with the organ played at full volume and stuck on a reggae beat regardless of the musical genre aped by the organist from time to time.

There was one modest upside for Billie King. With all the din, for a long time Charlie Rae was not able to hear the equine manoeuvres going on next door, at least that was until a hoof and then a head appeared through a hole in the wall of his bedroom. Eventually, faced with two complaining constituents, Big David made his judgement of Solomon and had favoured the musical Philistine above Goliath. The horse had to go, although on a promise of sanctuary in the lush green pastures beside the abandoned railway and disused canal. As yet these Elysian Fields had only been marginally affected by the leaching of the dumped barrels Agent Orange from the canal into the soil.

"How did you convince Big David to give you a new home for the horse?" asked William Henry.

"No problem. He likes White Rum. She's now on the organisation's payroll. Wait till you see this…" responded Billie.

She stationed the horse beside the Queen Anne Boleyn Bridge and proceeded to stand on the saddle.

"There you have it!" she observed. "Mobile scaffolding for the next paint job. And all the kit is in the saddle bags. Hand me it up, will you?"

The kit comprised paint brushes and a large pot of red gloss paint.

"I thought this painting job was done for the day," said William Henry.

"No," replied Billie. "Big David said I was to go down and give you a hand."

And hand painting it was. Billie was known as the "hands-on wumman" not only because she had a large following of male admirers but also because she alone looked after the large red hand of Ulster that took up the top left side of the rampart on the railway bridge.

This was no ordinary hand. It was a six-foot-high symbol of Ulster's independence – the O'Neill's severed hand – repeatedly visited and photographed over the years by legions of Orangemen and Dutch tourists from Antwerp to Zeebrugge. In this digital age people on the modern European Grand Tour diverted to Ballycarson for this very purpose. Obviously they still hungered for real culture. There was even a visitors' book open for signature for a modest charge, in the security hut at the foot of the bridge, manned twenty-four hours a day by the ever vigilant attendant, Councillor Joe Hutt.

Normally, those people who make gestures with fingers do so because of a lack of vocabulary. But this complete hand spoke volumes for the political persuasions of the area. Further to that, local peculiarities were in evidence too. This particular painted hand had one thumb and five fingers. Yes, five – not just four fingers. It comprised five fingers and a thumb. The unintentional excess had been added by an over-enthusiastic Billie King in her first year of painting. But, once painted, the symbol's removal would have resulted in considerable loss of political face for Big David not to speak of the waste of a lot of white spirit. In the political jargon of the day, a "more constructive solution" was sought. The Council historian, employed by the then Unionist-run Council, saved the day.

In those blue-sky days of unchallenged Unionist Council hegemony, a special ceremony was arranged and duly boycotted by the elected local representatives of the then Nationalist minority. The arch of the bridge was decked out in purple and blue and an orange ribbon was cut underneath the arch. A plaque was unveiled. Speeches were made. Drinks were drunk. Champagne was eschewed. France, with its links to revolutionary ideals, was a country politically and religiously suspect for such events, even though its flag was white, red and blue. At least that was the Unionist party line. The truth was more mundane. The fact was that the local source of French wine had been shut down. The Élysée Café had been closed by the Council environmental health officers. Gaining the reputation of the "Ill Easy Café" amongst the locals on account of some slapdash food preparation, the café had attracted a dawn raid by the protectors of public cleanliness and hygiene. They had discovered a scandalous amount of long out-of-date drinks and considerable volumes of crème fraîche of an uncertain vintage. The upshot was that the supplier of local French delicacies was no more. So, instead of French-sourced liquor, to facilitate major corporate and municipal celebrations such as that going on at the railway bridge, bottles of German Sekt were opened in celebration. This was regarded as a neat political stroke as it would go down well with the large local German community who worked at the salami factory in the Ballycarson industrial estate.

Whilst all this was going on, at the far side of the railway bridge the more hard-line Unionists held their own re-naming ceremony with glasses of white and brown lemonade and orange juice. Long gone were the days of "United We Stand, Divided We Fall". They were there to abstain in person. In the heydays of the Unionist ascendancy in Ballycarson anyone running a Loyalist splinter group with more than three members was regarded with suspicion as having sold out to the establishment, whatever that was. Yes, it was a sad truth, observed by the traffickers in tried and tested truths in the shelter at the Spion Kop bus stop, that some of these people had been political Protestants for so long that they had forgotten what they were protesting about. The real fact was that it was amazing the Unionist administration in Ballycarson had lasted so long. Undoubtedly it was a case of persistence beyond the call of talent. But, for all that, it was a mere local application of the universal truth applicable to politicians: durability is longer than ability.

Yet something substantial and concrete had appeared out of this petrified political protest. What was once a mere anonymous, abandoned railway bridge on a long-closed branch line in the townland of Drummullaghfurtherland had been renamed "The Queen Anne Boleyn Bridge". The repute of such an important and solid structure was clearly enhanced by this addition of the auspicious name of the first Protestant Queen of England and mother of Queen Elizabeth I of England, the scourge of the Irish. The fact that Anne Boleyn had never been a queen of Ulster was irrelevant.

What was truly important was that the local historian had discovered that the loyal Anne Boleyn actually did have five fingers and a thumb on her left hand. A digit for each county of Northern Ireland and for each point of the star in the Northern Ireland flag. Clearly she had been destined for this role even if she didn't know it. So, in her immortal memory, the six-digit hand on the disused railway bridge was restored and repainted every year since.

Given his resounding success at justifying the error, the Council historian was quietly headhunted by the Local History Organisation and put in charge of overseas marketing.

There was one last twist to the parochial politics surrounding the bridge-renaming ceremony. Flushed by their success with the Queen Anne Boleyn Bridge, the Unionist councillors looked round for further similar publicity opportunities that might prove useful in the run-up to the impending local elections. Councillor Robinson Sydney Milliken hit on a scheme of renaming the five remaining disused railway bridges around Ballycarson after the remaining wives of Henry VIII. It was a fond coincidence that the only bridge in the west side of town, the Nationalist area, could be re-named the "Catherine of Aragon" bridge after King Henry's first, Spanish and manifestly Catholic wife. The whole town could be brought into the renaming scheme. Noone could claim the Unionists had given no thought to their Nationalist neighbours. This was a genuine cross-community policy. The bridge renaming was genuine bridge-building. Even better was the possibility that the one railway bridge in what had become the German area of town could be named the "Anne of Cleves" bridge after the fourth wife who came from the German town of Kleve. There was a real chance to pick up the ethnic, floating voter.

With a growing premonition of impending defeat in these elections, the Unionist administration feared for their place in history. They forced through the motion to carry out the bridge renaming at the final meeting of the full Council in the dying days of the last Unionist administration. Perhaps there would be an Orange sunset after all.

The first act of the Nationalists after electoral victory was to enrol a motion to rename once more the renamed bridge in the west side of town

"Queen Catherine of Aragon has nothing to do with us. We don't need these pseudo-aristocratic connections. We want an ordinary name with obvious local connections linked only to the common Irish man and woman," was the Nationalist policy asserted forcibly by Councillor Michael Lavery Fitzmaurice. So Catherine of Aragon was voted out.

"Spanish Onion to Be Removed from Irish Stew" ran the next headline in the *Provincial Enquirer*.

So the railway bridge in the west of town was renamed yet again, but this time after an individual hailed as a genuine local, working-class, Irish Republican heroine.

It was reborn as the "Countess Constance Markievicz" bridge.

CHAPTER 9

CARY GRANT

As his name suggested, Cary Grant claimed to have connections with the big time in America.

He tried to foster this impression by his choice of associates. He once had a girlfriend called Holly Wood, but his mother disapproved of her as she was a barmaid in what was regarded as a disreputable drinking establishment near the Peace Wall dividing the town. The hostelry in question was originally known as the Stagger Inn and comprised two Portacabins left over by the contractors who had built the wall. Attempts by a new German owner to move it up market and rename it as Hanover Lodge had failed. An unfortunate typing accident in the Council's liquor licencing department had resulted in a licence being granted to Hangover Lodge. The name stuck and Cary's romance was doomed.

Cary's social life and many short-term loves had been dominated by his mother. In truth she had been the determining force in his entire life. He had received his name just because his mother was a huge fan of the big screen. Cary was conceived in a burst of passion after a showing in the Ballycarson cinema of one of her idol's latest releases. There would be no such excitement in future years because, shortly afterwards, the IRA burnt the cinema to the ground after the owner was tardy in paying his protection money. It took two days for the local fire brigade to quell the blaze because the paint supply in the next-door hardware shop had also caught fire. Big David had had to source his supplies elsewhere for weeks and the annual painting of the gable walls had been threatened. The price of paint followed the flames as they, too, went through the roof.

Still the Peace Process had stopped such flagrant extortion. Now, noone paid protection money. Instead, businesses paid a similar sum of money to the same people at the same time every month, but the payment was known as a "community contribution". In addition, noone had been beaten up since the start of the Peace Process and the paramilitary cease-fires. But there had been a massive increase in the number of people falling down flights of stairs. A small step for a man could become a giant fall for late payers. Even most modern bungalows built with an EU grant had a single step outside the front door and the injuries sustained in falling from that single step could be surprisingly severe. The newspapers locally called it "Front Door Freefall Effect". Somewhat at odds with the suggested direction of travel, the sociologists at the local university explained it as the "escalator effect" of the Peace Process and several academic conferences were arranged to discuss the theoretical underpinnings of the doctrine. The participants resolved that there should be more research and pencilled in a conference in Monaco where the comparative aspects of the phenomenon could be subjected to scrutiny. The Ballycarson Council also debated the issue, but, despite the application of the best political brains available, there was no cheerful outcome. They thought it was too costly to award grants for the installation of ramps outside bungalows so that those who had been beaten up or knee-capped could get their wheelchairs into their own houses. However, a decisive step was taken when the Council voted to have an annual site visit of select councillors to comparable facilities in Australia and various parts of North America.

Despite the cinema's fiery destruction and the magnificent efforts of the fire brigade, the flame of love had obviously burned on for Cary's mum. Over the next few years she produced four more sons. Although she had only one screen idol, names were not a problem. However, she had a bad memory, so she gave them all names that rhymed. For simplicity's sake she had named her five sons Cary, Larry, Harry, Barry and Garry. Five ginger-headed sons in total, followed by five ginger-headed daughters, Cora, Dora, Flora, Nora and Lora. Obviously the Grant family were big on memorising the alphabet and practising simple rhyme but were not otherwise strong on imagination. It was just like the content of much local poetry and since there was an EU grant to produce more of that doggerel, so reasoned Cary's mum, the state might give her a grant or some sort of award for exuberance in child production. It did not really work out quite like that. The reasoning behind the list of names was lost on both relatives and neighbours. Indeed, most people, apart from their mum on a good day, could not even remember the children's individual names and resort was had to a collective nickname. With some link to their hair colour, the children were known to all and sundry as "the Red Army". In future they would make up the entire front row of drummers in the Ballycarson 1690 Young Defenders Flute Band. They made for an impressive prospect. They were all of equal stature, giving a level and balanced front row to the musical unit. The benefits did not stop there. Cary's mum reckoned that their equal heights would make it easier for them to carry coffins. If death was a great leveller, it surely was appropriate that every coffin was carried on an even keel and not at an oblique angle. The potential for money-making at Masonic funerals opened out. So, as a substantial side earner, the family hired themselves out to suitable local undertakers for a decent rate.

It had been consistently rumoured in the byways of Ballycarson that Cary Grant was in some way related to the former American soldier and president Ulysses Simpson Grant who was of Ulster descent. It could hardly be said that Cary had ever denied the possibility, but that was largely due to the fact that he scarcely knew who the man was.

Only once had Cary attempted to use his very vague knowledge of the great Ulster American hero to his advantage. That was when he applied for a job as a decorator in the renovation of a new tourist attraction sponsored by the Council – the ancestral home of a great-aunt of the former soldier and president. Upon scrutiny of the job application the councillors were immediately excited at the positive publicity possibilities. Inspired by the equally attractive prospects of a day out, Councillor Eugene Gerald Fitzmaurice hit on an even better idea. There were ancestral homes of relatives of US presidents all over Ulster. Ballycarson had the ancestral home of the great-aunt of this particular president, but the neighbouring Council had the direct line of descent – the ancestral home of his maternal grandparents. Why didn't the Council visit the neighbouring area and arrange for a photoshoot at the ancestral home of the president's grandparents? It would be a day out at taxpayers' expense. However, the councillor sought to guard himself against possible accusations of a junket. There was a precedent for borrowing these neighbouring facilities and linking the historic town of Ballycarson with the homes of illustrious deceased heroes. Councillor Eugene Gerald Fitzmaurice's oratory rose to the occasion as he saw the chance to convince his fellow councillors. To clinch the vote he referred to locally applicable precedent. In his own parish noone had died for a few years. The parishioners there had not had the benefit of a funeral or a wake and were worried about getting out of practice in relation to the usual formalities and festivities. So their parish priest saved the day. He had borrowed a corpse from the neighbouring parish so his parishioners could practise their celebrations. And what was the moral of this tale? "The benefits of a deceased were made for sharing," observed the councillor. And so it was also with dead presidents and ancestral homes. His odd logic proved convincing to an already persuaded audience longing for another day out. The Council required their rapidly expanding Department of Communication, Reports and Publicity to pass the word to all three local papers that there would be a major photographic opportunity the next afternoon outside the ruined steading. Their potential employee Cary Grant would pose with his brushes and bottle of thinners outside his and the former president's grandparents' ancestral home. In the spirit of openness required by the Peace Process, the job interview would be carried out live and in public.

Unfortunately, not one of the three local papers, the *Provincial Express*, the *Provincial Enquirer* and the *Provincial Observer*, fully lived up to their names. Whilst remaining provincial, none of them was particularly expressive, enquiring or observant. Consequently the expected scrum of local paparazzi did not turn up. Perhaps it was because all three papers had just been taken over by the new local media tycoon, Pat Buller, who had made her money in the supply of cattle for the processed meat and offal market. She was known in the trade as "Cow Pat" and her penchant for ruthless business efficiency and trimming the fat had led her to send only one sixteen-year-old photographer with an antiquated tape recorder. This solitary individual was to take a snap and provide a report for all three of the papers whilst the remainder of the newspaper staff attended the salami factory open day and annual formal dance known as the "Ballycarson Meat Ball". The highlight of the evening was to be the judging by Cow Pat's American cousin of the "Ballycarson Miss Reconstituted Steak of the Year" beauty contest.

"Get a different angle for each paper," the editor had instructed. In the eyes of the sixteen year old this meant telling Cary to turn his head left, then right and then face straight into the camera.

Those organising the interview and press shoot for Cary Grant at the president's grandparents' ancestral home should have stuck to photographs alone. Before the assembled ranks of councillors could protect Cary from the lone press inquisitor, the cat was out of the bag.

The initial enquiry seemed simple enough: "Why should you get this job?"

If Cary had stuck to a simple response of "painting is what I am good at", he would probably have got away with it. But he was inspired to see someone, even a solitary sixteen year old, ready to scribble down and record his words – yes, his very words. Noone had ever done that before except when he ordered sausage and chips at the local German fast-food restaurant "Best Wurst". So, duly encouraged, Cary told the trainee reporter that the former president, his close and admired relation, had put in a good word for him by acting as his referee.

"President Speaks from Grave" was the headline that week in all three papers.

So the councillors resolved not to offer the painting job to Cary, despite protests that he was apparently very good at whitewashing. Although a number of the councillors, of all political persuasions, suspected they might need his skills in the future, this was a time for drawing the line.

Success was grabbed from the jaws of failure. After his appearance at the Council interview, Cary was recruited for a part-time job. It involved a double role paid for by the joint committee of Big David's Volunteer Defenders and the Local History Organisation. They recognised him as someone not only with a talent for painting but also with his finger on the very pulse of dead history. He could do this in his time off from the family business of moonlighting as an undertaker's assistant.

So it was that Cary was sent as the third musketeer to the ramparts of Ballycarson's Loyalist defences. Just as the red hand on the bridge was being refreshed, Cary arrived on the scene. He was carrying three large American flags.

"What are you doing here?" asked William Henry.

The response indicated that international matters had moved on further and faster than anyone had expected.

"Big David wants these put up on the bridge. He doesn't want our end of Ballycarson left out when the Yanks turn up and the big presidential visit goes ahead."

The flags were handed up to Billie King, who inserted them into the three vacant flag holders. Since 1922, these had been symbolically left unfilled to represent the Ulster counties of Monaghan, Cavan and Donegal that had been "lost" to the Irish Free State.

Surely the filling of these long-empty flag holders compromised the traditional position of Unionist solidarity with the small remnant of their brethren just over the international border? Maybe not. Perhaps it was, as Big David expressed it, "only a temporary renunciation of a legitimate territorial claim to parts of the Irish Free State". But it was a political gamble that had to be taken in these difficult times to secure a greater and more immediate end.

With political pressure like this, the leader of the Free World was bound to cave in.

CHAPTER 10

STEAMING AHEAD

True to their collective name, the members of the Red Army were colourful characters. Their family nickname and local fame arose not only because of their ginger hair colour. Their clothing, shirts, trousers, jerseys and socks (the last being now more apparent as the trouser legs had shrunk by several inches) had all taken on the homogenous, reddish-purple colour associated with the repeated boil-washing of every item of apparel in the same load. Yet far from shrinking from involvement with washing machines, it was clear that the members of the Red Army were buying up every washing machine thrown out or dumped in Ballycarson. A keen observer would have noted that they had a particular fondness for washer-dryers of the older German variety. These were the ones with no condenser and a long plastic hose requiring the kitchen window to remain open to extract the steam.

In addition, every one of the brothers had a face that bore the obvious signs of attempting to shave too quickly, or rather too early. As teenagers only too eager to get on in life, each of them had tried to force their advance into the adult world. Even before a hair had appeared on any of their faces, all of them had tried to dry shave, leaving them all with fiery facial rashes and one or two reddish scars. With the constant irritation, the shared skin condition had never really settled down, despite repeat applications of medication. It was almost a metaphor for the political situation in Ballycarson itself. At least that was the frequently expressed view of their uncle Councillor Robinson Sydney Milliken who maintained that the family skin irritation was something about which nothing could be done. It was just a condition they all had to live with. Indeed they should make a positive merit out of the affliction. When one of the brothers looked in the mirror every morning he would know for certain that the beaming reflection could not be that of anyone else. They would all know that they belonged to each other in some deep and unexplained way. In a very real sense they were all wearing their colours. It was just like those annual colourful demonstrations of public loyalty to a particular cause. By this stage in the family's political lesson of the day, everyone, except the speaker, had given up listening. Indeed, apart from the speaker, they had already left the house. There possibly was more to be learned from the subtleties of the political philosophy of Councillor Robinson Sydney Milliken, but noone had waited around long enough to learn it.

Ignorant of the true facts and unconvinced that even the most routine acts of facial hygiene and daily cleansing could be explained in terms of politics, their worried mother had taken her five sons along to the local surgery on repeat occasions. Dr. Magda Todstein, one of the local G.P.s, had explained to Mrs. Grant that this sort of problem usually settled down as the boy in question became a man. But somehow or other it appeared that these five lads remained perpetual juveniles even after progressing into their twenties and thirties. Recently, however, their father reported that all five had improved slightly in regard to their shaving habits. They no longer shaved into a beer glass in the front seat of the transit van on their way to work. Instead, they stopped in a lay-by and used the wing mirrors to improve their aim with the blade. However, the ongoing facial skin irritation continued to puzzle the local medical specialists.

Perhaps this family skin condition is worth a letter to *The Lancet*. There might be a genetic cause just like with the local politics.

So thought Dr. Todstein out-loud as she drove to work one Friday morning.

"It might even be worth a research paper written by me. Yes, I could be someone once again. I could be invited to give talks at the university instead of lunchtime chats with those dim-witted social workers. Why do they always look so displeased when I turn up instead of my male colleagues?"

The doctor's inquisitive musings were interrupted as some white foam blew onto her windscreen. She had just stopped at the T-junction opposite the lay-by beside the pub that had once been known as the King's Hotel. She used her wipers to clear the material on the windscreen, but it only made a greater mess. Slightly irritated, she employed the wash-wipe for additional power. That was the great thing about these German cars – they were prepared for every eventuality. That was engineering with foresight. She was sure that these words of wisdom would sound better in German. Before she could move off, however, more foam landed on the windscreen. She wound down the side window to see where it was coming from only to have some more of the floating substance hit her square in the face. She wiped it off and looked at the assaulting material. If she was not mistaken, and as a former pathologist in the former D.D.R she was not usually mistaken, it contained small traces of hair and had a slight perfume redolent of a soap of some sort. As this was not the usual form of product of the weather in mid summer, even in Ireland, the doctor pulled her car onto the verge and stepped out to investigate further. It was in the lay-by that she discovered the source of the outbreak of the sweet-smelling foam.

This was the very lay-by on the Loyalist east side of town that had been the subject of repeated international controversy over a series of years. Dr. Todstein had heard of it even whilst she lived in the D.D.R. Its reputation had breached the iron curtain. First, it was because of the travelling fish. Then, there was concern about the effects of the imported liquid pollution found there. Thereafter came the notoriety because of the spectacular fall off in trade and the impact on businesses in the town. And, lastly, the repeated futile attempts on the part of the Council to twin it with similar venues elsewhere in the world as a site of special scientific interest. So much history in a small sheet of tar beside a public road! It was a wonder the Council had not put up a plaque to celebrate the locale. *Oh, it seems they have*, thought the doctor as she noticed the sign in question with a lot of small print – a clear sign of a Council sign.

By sheer good fortune and a pleasing concatenation of geographic and political phenomena, Ballycarson had been a strategically placed town and this lay-by was itself strategically placed just outside the town. The complex history of the lay-by was clearly related to this doubly strategic role. As the main town just north of the official international border crossing, Ballycarson had provided a convenient stopping-off point for lorries passing from the west-coast ports in the south to the east-coast ferry crossings in the north. Yes, all corners of Ireland met here just as if it were the centre of the St. Patrick's cross. However, it was a crossing point the long-distance lorry drivers had to bear simply due to a lack of alternatives, at least that was until the building of the Ballycarson bypass. But during the period of time in which Ballycarson had maintained its primacy as a crossing point – or a bottleneck, depending on one's perspective – there had been a paucity of hostelries to cater for the throughput of lorry drivers. Indeed the only overnight accommodation in the town had come in the form of two army camps. They were already fully occupied and outsiders unwelcome. So the lorry drivers had resorted to sleeping in their lorries parked in the two roadside lay-bys at the edge of the town. Yes, after failing to find any suitable foreign twinning candidates, the Council had simply twinned the one lay-by on this side of town with the other at the far side of town.

Fortunately, each of the lay-bys was located beside one of the two town pubs, respectively the former King's Hotel owned by the twin brothers the Unionist councillors James and Wilburt Morrow and the Irish Presidential Hotel run by the mother-in-law of Nationalist Councillor Eugene O'Driscoll. Here was an example of keen cross-community commercial competition enhanced by personal animus. The relationship between the two sets of publicans had been poisoned at an early date during the Unionist hegemony when the owner of the Irish Presidential Hotel had applied for a liquor licence. A typing error in the Council offices had led to the licence being issued in favour of the "Irish Presidential Hovel". Councillor Eugene O'Driscoll took this confusion of consonants to be a deliberate slur, indeed an attempt to defame, issued by the lackeys of British imperialism incited by his mother-in-law's commercial rivals, councillors James and Wilburt Morrow. The animosity had never grown weaker as the years passed and Councillor Eugene O'Driscoll waited for time to take revenge.

It was the first of these lay-bys on the Loyalist side of town that had come to the attention of the Russian spy satellites. After the fall of communism the operators of these unseen tools of world supervision had diversified into commercial and academic ventures just to stay in business. One of these new opportunities was the tracking of basking sharks in the Atlantic just off Galway Bay for one of the forward-looking universities in Scotland. Each shark in the grand experiment had been fitted with a brightly coloured, waterproof tracking device. The transmitting apparatus was attached to a little orange collar with a badge advertising the corporate sponsor, a chain of burger bars in Aberdeen wishing to diversify into fish cakes, and identifying the university department in question. In a three-page feature on this novel application of Scottish science to preserve Irish wildlife, the local newspaper in the Gaeltacht commended the cross-jurisdictional Celtic co-operation. The happy, uplifting story was prefaced with a headline that was picked up further north by the *Provincial Observer* and, for the benefit of English-speaking readers (i.e. everyone likely to pick up the paper), translated as follows:

"Orange Collarettes Worn by Sharks"

The inevitable row in the northern counties erupted when the headline was read to grandmasters of the local lodges. A boycott of the university in question was threatened and the entire relationship between indigenous Scots and the Ulster Scots was threatened. This unthinkable tragedy was narrowly avoided only when the professor of Scottish Gaelic at the relevant university confirmed that the original newspaper words used could also be loosely translated as:

"Orange Collarettes Worn by Big Fish"

Yes, that was a more flattering term. The grandmasters were contented in that they knew they were indeed the big fish, albeit, admittedly, the pond was quite small. So the muddied waters were cleared. Academic freedom was preserved. The university experiment continued and the west-coast sharks continued to be tracked.

Shortly afterwards the same university received a phone call at an odd time of the day when none of the academics were at work. It was half past two on a Friday afternoon and the call was taken by the university porter. The foreign-sounding caller informed the university that he had found a dead shark washed up on a Connemara beach. It was presently being eaten by seagulls but quite a lot remained untouched. When the finder of the fish had phoned the experiment-sponsoring burger bar named on the collar worn by the fish, they had informed him that they did not as yet have a demand for so big a fish, although it was still fresh enough for human consumption if suitably prepared. The seagulls were no use as it was outside the period in which they sold their special deep fried Christmas gull-flavoured nuggets. "Phone the university instead. Maybe their refectory could use the stuff." So advised, the caller contacted the natural history faculty of the university using the number conveniently stamped on the orange collar. The message was taken by the porter who said he would get the professor to call back on Monday. Days later the problem was resolved when the professor's research assistant duly called. She was interested in those sea eagles. How many were there? Only after a few minutes of pointless discussion at cross-purposes did it become clear that the sea eagles were the product of the porter's mishearing of the reference to seagulls. Eventually the main point of the call was addressed. "What does the university want me to do with this shark?" asked the west-coast Irish man once again. Yes, he could arrange for it to be transported to the university if they provided the funds and a suitable finder's fee. But he could not send the seagulls too unless they provided him with a net. Oh, that wasn't necessary; the university had plenty already. And he would phone again if he did see any sea eagles.

And so it was that the decomposing shark was loaded onto a lorry and sent north to Scotland via the bottleneck at Ballycarson. Just as the lorry passed through Ballycarson the university in Scotland received a second call, this time from Russia. To their total disbelief the practised operators of the satellite had tracked a shark leaving the Atlantic and progressing over land at a speed of fifty miles an hour to a place called Ballycarson. What sort of fish existed in Ireland? Could some of their Russian scientists come to have a look at this amazing creature? Were Irish sharks evolving into some form of high-speed amphibian or bird? What sort of fowl was this fish?

When the news of the telephone exchange became public, the *Provincial Observer* ran a supplementary special edition bearing the headline:

"As We Told You Before:
Sharks in Ballycarson."

With a trail blazed by this first pioneering shark, a trade route grew
up. The product for transport was shark liver from Connemara
to be manufactured into some sort of mysterious medicinal
panacea in Scotland. After a day's hard driving, the fish-carrying
lorry drivers would arrive at Ballycarson wishing for a stop and
refreshment. They wished to empty a bottle down their necks at
the bottleneck. The owner of the Irish Presidential Hotel soon
realised the importance of fostering this trade – but not, most
definitely not, at her establishment. What had convinced her
more readily than any words could was the attendant smell. As
each lorry remained parked in the lay-by, a dark, oily, offensively
stinking liquid seeped out of the transported shark liver, ran
down the side of the lorry and onto the tar where it collected in
large, evil-smelling pools. Difficult though it may be to speak of
such matters, it must be done. The resultant smell resembled that
of two- or three-day-old urine, only immensely more powerful
and considerably more persistent. Realising the effect of this
obnoxious stench that continued for days and could not easily
be washed away, the owner of the Irish Presidential Hotel paid
the lorry drivers to park at the far side of town at the lay-by
immediately beside the rival establishment, the King's Hotel. The
loyalty of the regulars of the King's Hotel evaporated as readily as
the pungent foul smell did not. Erstwhile unqualified loyalty to the
King was transferred forthwith and, without a second thought, to
the Irish President. The grass on the other side of town may have
been greener, but at least the beer could be drunk in comfort and
without holding one's nose.

The unfair trade advantage continued until the councillors
Morrow decided they would have to destroy their own business
forever. This was quite acceptable as long as, at the same time,
they could watch the destruction of that of their rival, Councillor

Eugene O'Driscoll, and his mother-in-law. The big idea of the Ballycarson bypass was put forward. "Release us from this stench! These decomposing bodily fluids are not our lifeblood! Not in our backyard or lay-by!" These were the convincing arguments presented to the Northern Ireland Office in a formal presentation by the then Unionist-run Ballycarson Council. Nobody bothered to think of the implications beyond the personal vendetta of the councillors Morrow. The building of the dual carriageway was duly funded as an exceptional gesture of humanitarian aid and the passing trade for Ballycarson dried up entirely. So too did the evil-smelling pools in the lay-by. So not everything was bad. One must get things into perspective after all.

As she got out of her car at the lay-by in the Loyalist side of town Dr. Todstein immediately gained the impression that international science had yet again found something of interest in this special location. The evil smell had gone and indeed had been replaced by something else vaguely resembling that encountered in a second-rate washeteria. The location was a busy place too. Five vans were parked in the lay-by and something was definitely going on. At a distance Dr. Todstein first thought that the team of five men, each with a large white hose attached to a large white machine, was somehow cleansing the area. Maybe it was a repeat of an exercise like that on the island of Gruinard off the west coast of Scotland when scientists have to come back every so often to make sure the underlying contamination of anthrax has gone. As she got closer, however, the picture became clearer. The operation on site did indeed involve cleansing but of another and unexpected type.

In the lay-by, parked in a line, Dr. Todstein could see five red transit vans. Standing beside each van was one of the five Grant brothers – the entire male contingent of the Red Army – each holding up to his face the open end of a long, white, corrugated, plastic tube. Fearing a collective suicide attempt, the doctor raced forwards to administer first aid. Her alarm, however, was misplaced. In each case the plastic tube was the extractor vent from a German washer-dryer and, as the doctor moved round the side of each van, she saw the five machines in question were plugged into the electricity supply feeding the public street lamps. All the machines were running and hot moist air was blowing out of the tubes. Small amounts of shaving foam blew across the road. This indeed was the source of her windscreen problem.

"Dr. Todstein, I presume," was the cheerful, if unoriginal, greeting of Cary Grant as he switched off the stream of hot air from his drying machine by opening the front-facing circular door. He then explained to the doctor that they all used the extractor vents of washer-dryers to produce hot steam that they could blow against their faces and have a hot, wet shave in the great outdoors. Sure, they all still got a facial rash, but it felt better and they did not get as many cuts. This indeed was a street-side barber's shop just like those seen in the temporary housing areas in the Third World, only a little more advanced. More than that, it was one that was based on a sustainable source in that all the washing machines had been reconditioned after rescue from the town dump and other low-cost outlets. Donald Oskar Gormley had supplied well over half of their business needs and had been so kind as to give them a special deal for bulk purchasing. The news caused the doctor to revisit her plans to write to *The Lancet*.

A brief consultation in the lay-by convinced the doctor that, in a community such as Ballycarson, much remained unknown to an incomer like her. Indeed incomers forever remained outsiders. As a doctor, she was supposed to take secrets to the grave, but in Ballycarson things were more serious than that. This town remained a living mystery. What she heard and saw next merely confirmed her view.

As well as facilitating early morning shaving, the steam-producing washer-dryers went, as it were, "on tour" – if only locally. The machines had become the power behind a peripatetic parlour of personal pampering. The Red Army ran a series of mobile saunas. Each involved the pumping of hot, moist, machine-produced air out of the washer-dryers and into the back of each of the red transit vans through a hole cut in the door, just like a cat flap, to facilitate the insertion of the long white hose. In every location the public electricity supply to the street lights provided the requisite power. Each red transit van was fitted out with two wooden benches in the back upon which the health-seeking populace could sit. Clearly these were the economy seats. The requisite machinery comprised nothing more than old washer-dryer machines rescued from the lost and found or the canal or acquired by equally sustainable means. Refitted, revamped and filled with the family laundry of the Red Army and their customers, the machines could blow in as much warm, damp air as necessary in two-hour cycles coinciding nicely with the time for which each health-seeking person paid. The customers could have their clothes washed whilst they waited – even the very clothes they had been wearing when they arrived. "Saunas while you wait." What other washeteria offered such service? This was better than a coffee at the barbers! Participants – or rather, paying clients – were allowed to choose their own fragrance of fabric conditioner to scent their sauna from a house-list or even to bring their own bottle, provided always a corkage charge was paid. Every opportunity for making money had been considered. "Taking Health Back to the Steam Age" was the business strap-line stencilled on the side of one of the vans. Another bore the logo "We Take the Shirt off Your Back".

There was a political dimension too. Those who enjoyed the mobile saunas came from all quarters of Ballycarson society and spoke freely as they inhaled the hot, steamy air. So economy class was really business class too, at least in the van parked at the front of the lay-by. The participants in this local ritual let vent to their secrets as their pores breathed. The whole arrangement was another great source of information for Big David to whom the Red Army forwarded all they overheard, in exchange, of course, for more washing machines at a discount. Big David knew details of the paying clients' lives that Todstein had never imagined. She was left in the dark to deal with her patients and the consequential exponential increase in acute asthma attacks and allergic skin rashes.

I wonder if there is a paper in it after all, thought Dr. Todstein as she walked back to her car. *Perhaps not* The Lancet … *Maybe* The European Anthropologist, Lost Tribes of The World *or* Washer Woman's Weekly.

CHAPTER 11

THAT SINKING FEELING

A first glance at Big David (otherwise known, though most definitely not within his hearing, as "Camp David") might lead the casual onlooker to suspect that he scarcely lived up to the image he tried to portray.

The self-proclaimed saviour of Ulster Loyalism in Ballycarson had not been born in Northern Ireland. He wasn't even a child of Ulster émigré stock reared by his parents on a version of long out-of-date politics who had returned to re-educate the populace in the pure, distilled truth and to restrain dangerous signs that the locals were about to compromise and move into a new era.

No, Big David was a four-foot-eight, ostensibly effeminate immigrant from Vietnam. He was one of the boat people who had fled poverty and oppression. As a teenager he had been placed in an overcrowded boat by his parents only to find the rusting hulk sinking below his feet a few days later far out from land. By chance the doomed crew were picked up by a passing British registered ship and, contrary to the then policy of the British government, taken to Hong Kong.

Big David's fate was decided because of a lie during his interview with the immigration officials of Her Majesty's Foreign and Commonwealth Office. To avoid repatriation David and the other refugees had lied about their origins and claimed to be from Tsingtao, China. The officials from the Foreign and Commonwealth Office knew this was an obvious lie. Big David and the other refugees knew they knew this was a lie. So there was transparency and a mutual recognition of transparency in the entire process. But it was also a convenient lie if only because lies were the currency in which the Foreign and Commonwealth officials were deft at dealing. With this manufactured world they felt more at home than with the hard facts. Better an obvious and transparent lie than an obscure, opaque and awkward truth. For British interests in the Far East, it would look good to have fewer refugees from Vietnam. So the teenage Big David and the others were noted down as arriving from mainland China. This was an embarrassment, but it was far less of an embarrassment than more incomers from Vietnam.

To rid themselves of such moderately embarrassing arrivals, the high flyers in the Foreign and Commonwealth Office hit on the neat idea of linking the fate of the refugees with the captain of the ship that had picked them up. Since he came from Northern Ireland, the refugees would be resettled there. It was indeed fortunate there were some new vacant houses in Ballycarson. Her Majesty's government could even gain some useful publicity from the event. There could hardly be a more convenient spot for the new arrivals from Tsingtao, the former official German colony in China. They could move in beside the long-established, unofficial German colony in Ulster.

The vacant houses in Ballycarson were new but lay idle and unoccupied due to a mistake in design and location. Whether they liked it or not, everyone in Ballycarson was told that they did not wish to move into this ill-thought-out housing scheme. What they really wanted, so they were told, was to boycott this new housing by remaining in their existing substandard houses. The building of the new houses was an attempt by a Hamburg-based firm of architects to impose a foreign model of society on locals. Germany may have succeeded in managing its own religious divide, but that was no reason to apply similar solutions here. So ran the prejudiced parochial political pronouncements.

The big problem was that the new houses were part of a

new model village in an urban setting, with new streets and new public facilities all designed by someone who sincerely wished to accommodate local peculiarities. Clearly the instructed architect had been only partially briefed leading to a manifest demonstration that a little knowledge is worse than none at all. The rumblings of discontent started when Councillor Eugene Gerald Fitzmaurice indicated that it was outrageous that the new model housing scheme in Ballycarson was to be named after the army of the butcher of Drogheda and Limerick. Cromwell's New Model Army, of course, had nothing whatsoever to do with the New Model Village in Ballycarson, but the accusations had touched a raw nerve and irritated an old wound.

But perhaps there was a hidden political agenda after all. Only when the New Model Village was fully built was it discovered that it comprised a new Orange Hall in Green Street and a new chapel in Orange Street. In addition, in the blurb on the back of the glossy brochure sent from the Hamburg architects, the designers had expressed the hope that they had catered for all local sensitivities and that the houses would be fit for both "staunch Catholics" and "devout Protestants". What sort of continental idiot could have made such mistakes unintentionally? No, it all must have been planned deliberately. The New Model Village was roundly condemned by all local politicians as being overtly ecumenical in its layout. It was an outrageous attempt to impose a political solution on people who had already been told what they really wanted by the local politicians.

Still, such niceties would not matter much to incomers from the Far East, thought the Foreign and Commonwealth Office. And even if they did, that was all to the good because it might encourage them to return to China or wherever it was they really came from.

"This form of internal exile within the United Kingdom of Great Britain and Northern Ireland will encourage others not to follow in their wake", ran the internal ministerial memorandum.

So the memorandum was promptly leaked to a news reporting service in Hanoi. But the earlier duplicity and lies backfired. The message did not have the desired effect. The Vietnamese news reporting service didn't report the leaked memorandum as it referred only to the resettlement in the U.K. of Chinese asylum seekers. "What's this got to do with us?" asked the editor. "It does not affect Vietnam." So the information in the memorandum was dumped.

Nevertheless, the group of refugees including Big David rejoiced on hearing of their destination and boarded the plane to Belfast International Airport. Thus began their lives in the mysterious West. State schooling and state institutions in Northern Ireland demanded that one of the established religious traditions should claim Big David and his co-refugees if only for the purpose of indicating where they eventually should be buried. So, the fact that he went to a controlled state school and not a maintained convent school determined his future forever. Whether he liked it or not, and regardless of his own religious beliefs, for all official and unofficial purposes Big David was to be perceived as a Protestant. But Big David was alive to the possibilities and manifested his newly acquired origins and loyalties by wearing orange suits and bright orange silk shirts with matching socks and underpants. This man from the Far East was determined to become more extreme, more unreasoning and more loyal than anyone else. He was going to become a real local politician.

To be educated is one thing. To have money is another. Big David intended to have both. To make him feel at home, the politically correct teacher at the state school had ordered a book of the sayings of Confucius together with several dozen Chinese cookbooks. It was all the more appropriate, the teacher indicated, that the school library should provide this material as the great Chinese philosopher taught in Tsingtao where Big David reputedly had been born. Forced to read this stuff in Ballycarson, Big David gained, for the first time, a vague and confused familiarity with the teachings. It would serve him well in later life when he recalled an uplifting, encouraging and entirely suitable definition of altruism:

"Be content with what you've got and make sure you've got a lot".

A shoestring budget was not Big David's idea of fun. From day one in Ballycarson Big David engaged in extra-curricular activities intended to raise extra funds. For him the local gang of boot boys provided a foot in the door of the local economy. Before long Big David's talents with the boot boys came to the attention of Councillor Montgomery Cherry who ran the whole operation in the east side of town.

Councillor Montgomery Cherry was indeed a man on the make who had never quite made it. However, he did have the whole market of polishing and shining boots sewn up, particularly black boots. Yes, the black polish economy in Ballycarson was booming with two army camps and a police station providing a well-trodden path to success. But it was only partially for this reason that Councillor Montgomery Cherry had earned his nickname, "Cherry Blossom". The real reason was his vanity. He did not wish to admit to his greying hair and receding hair line, so he supplemented his thinning locks with his own black boot polish applied daily to his scalp with the best of brushes made of finest bristle. The result was a deeply enhanced, shining colour and a very, very straight fringe. Both aspects were useful in his election posters to demonstrate an honest, unadulterated outlook on life coupled with his belief that all the important political issues were only black and white. There was no room for grey or for fudging at the edges. The only downside to this instant honesty came in unexpected downpours. Then his delicately painted hairline ran in streaks down his forehead and cheeks.

This boot boy business was a trade in which Big David's talents shone. A basic secondary school education had endowed him with little in the way of formal qualifications but, instead, provided him with the ideal reference from the headmaster. That reference, sent by second-class mail to the personnel department of the boot boy business, was a condemnatory one-liner:

"If David is not already in jail, he will be soon."

The condemnation proved to be Big David's recommendation.

Here is a future leader! This is the ideal man for the job in hand, thought the personnel officer at the boot boy business.

And, for once, the thoughts of the personnel officer were accurate. Within a few years of his recruitment, Big David found himself in charge of the whole boot boy organisation as the business of politics demanded more of Councillor Montgomery Cherry's time. Now Big David really was the big man. No longer was he the penniless, persecuted, political refugee. No, now the boot was on the other foot.

But Big David didn't want to change the very organisation that had given him the chance to shine. Honoured tradition had to be maintained and polished, and not brushed aside. Above the main door to the L.H.O. hall Big David had repainted in white exterior gloss the traditional slogan of the descendants of the Ulster Plantation: "One Law, One Land, One Throne." With the remains of the tin, the two long-standing tractor tyres that acted as planters for the orange lilies in the entrance hall were tastefully refreshed. And the tyres did not stand alone. Outside the main door to the L.H.O. hall stood two of Big David's bodyguards both now dressed in orange-coloured suits, silk shirts, socks and underpants to match the attire of Big David. The effect, thought Big David, had been spectacular. Consequently he extended the whole sartorial requirement to his entire workforce. They would be known thereafter as "the Orange Shirts" or maybe "the Young Orange Front". The latter variant of the name caught on but only in part. Because of their attire, Big David's workers became more widely known as "the Orange Y-Fronts".

One of the orange-shirted bodyguards at the door of the L.H.O. hall was a six-foot-ten heavyweight. The other was a four-foot-three featherweight. It was a deliberate political choice. Noone could accuse Big David of not dealing with all levels of society. But within the contrast there was uniformity. Both bodyguards had the best in black, shiny, well-polished, waterproof footwear. Big David was not going to have the same situation arise as occurred when Councillor Montgomery Cherry was boss and supplied his bodyguards with cheap, substandard ex-army boots. Back in the bad old days of slipshod shoes one of the bodyguards had kicked an intruder so hard that the sole of his boot had been ripped off. The intruder was eventually charged with damage to Councillor Montgomery Cherry's footwear. What an embarrassment! Who would employ Big David to clean or supply footwear if that were to happen again? No, things had certainly been tightened up after Big David took control. His men now all had the best of laced boots. And the vetting of the staff had also improved. He personally investigated the backgrounds of all applicants for his employ and knew all his employees by name. However, there was a complication with the two bodyguards at the front door. The first name of both these bodyguards was "Robert". So Big David had to distinguish them in some way. Consistent with their physiques, they were respectively known as "Bob the Blob" and "Bert the Squirt".

To update himself on the international situation Big David was sitting watching the large-screen television mounted on the wall of his office. The news bulletin was clearly coming to an end. A nameless female aide to a nameless government minister was making an announcement about the release of a big name Nationalist paramilitary, now with multiple PhDs in sociology, criminology and governmental studies duly earned in jail, as part of the ongoing Peace Process. The whole event was to be beautifully and sensitively choreographed as the latest of the PhDs was published in paperback at a subsidised price and launched at a Champagne reception in the centre of the city of Newry. A website was also to be produced to explain the contents and keep it constantly updated. With material this good every effort was to be made to bring it before a public who were hungry for the truth, whatever that was.

"…and finally," soothed the soft-spoken, soporific spokeswoman, "I would like to reassure the public that this man is no more dangerous than any other murderer."

Big David clicked on his remote control and the screen went blank. Things were obviously getting out of hand. This was time for the green phone – the hot line to contacts on the other side of town.

He took the green mobile phone out of a locked drawer in his desk and, after putting on a white glove, dialled the number of one of his main business and political connections on the other side of town – the second generation Italian émigré "Wee Joe". Wee Joe's central position in the esteem of the Nationalist community derived from the fact that his dad – Big Joe – had been a prisoner of the British for two years. Better still, he had been a prisoner without trial – he had simply been picked up and interned. It was not that Big Joe was an internee following upon political activism – far from it. Big Joe had been picked up asleep in an Italian army bunker as the Allied forces stormed ashore in Sicily in July 1943. Thereafter he had been interned in Ulster at the open prison camp near Ballycarson from where he was allowed out all day to assist on local farms. He couldn't wait for the war to end – he had never worked so hard in his life. But he had spotted a commercial opportunity in Ulster and decided to stay after hostilities ceased. Noone else ran a decent café. *The key to success is integration*, thought Big Joe and decided to adopt the surname of a local worthy – what could be better than a politician? What could be worse? But there seemed to be so many politicians in Ballycarson and it obviously was a successful line of business. So Big Joe copied down one of the more popular names from the various election posters appearing in the windows of various houses. The name was "Forsale". It had a certain Sicilian ring about it. It was only years later that

Big Joe found out that these were not election posters but estate agents' posters. The word he adopted as his new surname was not a politician's name but two words comprising a politician's motto. Still, after emblazoning the name in green paint on the sign above his new Iceberg Café in Irish Street, it was too late for Big Joe to climb down. So he made the best of it. When asked by all concerned how to pronounce his name he attempted to disguise the original mistake by suggesting a three-syllable single word and not a two-syllable word or, worse still, two words each with single syllables. "Forsale – as in doolally and blind alley," was his stock answer to enquiries about his name.

"Just like the local politics," was the common riposte of the enquirer.

A generation later Wee Joe Forsale had succeeded his father as the host at the Iceberg Café in Irish Street, Ballycarson. Originally the café had been set up by its owner as a place of respite from the politics of the town where locals could go to discuss what really concerned them. Over time it became clear that the local politics did really concern the locals and the café became a place to discuss nothing but politics. Even the long-standing menu on the café wall mirrored the direction and development of the local political climate. In large black letters it read:

"Today's Special – The Same as Yesterday"

With such a prominent position in the social circuit of the Ballycarson populace, Wee Joe Forsale had strong links with local Nationalist politicians, or at least those with strong stomachs. In addition, although he was a Unionist, Big David knew him well. Such contacts with the other side were best not advertised, so Big David had to keep the connection low-key. However, the cut that Big David received from the supply contract for salami for pizza toppings at the Iceberg Café provided sufficient cover. A lot could be hidden under those pizza toppings.

Being of Italian extraction, Wee Joe Forsale was known to have an extensive collection of Dean Martin CDs and was rumoured to have relatives in Pittsburgh. If these weren't enough to confirm close contacts with the Americans, anybody who was anybody or wanted to be anybody visited the café for deep fried pepperoni pizza when they came to the west side of Ballycarson. This put Wee Joe in an ideal position to provide information on any visitors to that part of the town.

This time the undercover information provided to Big David by Wee Joe was most revealing. Earlier that week two men – one white, one black; both dressed in identical smart suits – had stopped by the Iceberg Café in a hired car. As they handed out no uplifting tracts and buttonholed noone on the pavement, they clearly were not the usual well-dressed mid-west American Evangelists, although that was what they purported to be. The rumour had immediately gone round that these men represented the dark and unseen side of the Peace Process in action. The rumour mill confirmed that the black guy was probably a Nigerian diplomat accompanied by his bodyguard on an undercover visit to inspect the destruction of an IRA arms dump. But this didn't wash with Wee Joe. To his knowledge not a single bullet and not a single ounce of explosives had been handed in for years. Everyone knew the Peace Process had nothing to do with the disarmament of paramilitaries. In addition, noone was as conspicuous as an American trying to appear inconspicuous in Ireland. So too had the cover story actually provided by the two men proved unconvincing.

"And what would you gentlemen be doing in Ballycarson?" Wee Joe had asked them as they waited for their pizzas to fry in the deep fat.

"We're here to look up our ancestors and to found a new Church," said the black guy. "I'm from Baltimore. My name's O'Reilly – Martin Luther O'Reilly."

"And my name's O'Reilly too," said the white guy. "Francis

Xavier O'Reilly. But we're not brothers, just first cousins. Our grandmother originally came from round here and landed in New York after surviving the *Titanic* disaster."

"O'Reilly. Oh, really?" replied Wee Joe Forsale. He didn't believe a word. He knew that these particular pilgrims would be sending home not postcards to be read by religious superiors but briefings to be scrutinised by presidential advisers.

With murals on his café wall dedicated to the maritime disaster, Wee Joe Forsale was the local expert on the sinking of the Belfast-built liner. He knew that passenger list backwards. If these guys' grandmother had crossed most of the Atlantic in the *Titanic*, then Wee Joe Forsale had come up the River Lagan in a banana boat. In addition, he had seen all sorts of religious revivals and these guys clearly were singing from the wrong hymn sheet.

However, with a view to being helpful, Wee Joe Forsale had directed them towards Councillor Finvola O'Duffy's carpet and linoleum factory where the visitors could kill two birds with one stone. It was there that they could buy new floor coverings for the supposed new church in an establishment that claimed to have made some of the original floor coverings for the ill-fated transatlantic liner. The factory still did a very fetching and relatively inexpensive number in lifeboat-white linoleum.

For Big David, more worrying news was to follow. Wee Joe Forsale reported that the two phoney religious carpetbaggers had duly visited the carpet factory. There they had ordered a forty-yard roll of carpet. Just like the perpetrators in other American political scandals, they had been caught in this attempt to cover up. The carpet was stated to be for the aisle of the new tabernacle and for important occasions such as weddings, funerals, parades, etc. However, the two Americans had wanted a waterproof backing and the length ordered was enough to run from the front door of the Hibernian Hall to the roadside in the street with no name. In addition to that, when they were offered the colour red, they declined and requested green!

Clearly, someone was intending to make a spectacular political entrance on the west side of town, leaving Big David's east end out in the cold. Unless, that was, he could arrange an even more spectacular event on the east side of the Peace Wall. It was time to lift the blue phone and check the status of the new flute band uniforms...

CHAPTER 12

THE SALAMI FACTORY

For the design and manufacture of the new flute band uniforms Big David had given the contract to a local concern whose name was known throughout Ballycarson. As a strategic choice it was an obvious one. In a town like Ballycarson where everyone knew everyone by name, you could not win power and influence by dealing with anonymous multinational corporations. So the contract was awarded to the X and Y Partnership.

The X and Y Partnership was a marriage of science and religion. More to the point, it was a husband-and-wife team comprising the Reverend Patrick Xysomathumarsai and his beloved spouse, Ms. Williamina Wye. As a medical missionary from the former German colony Tanzania, the Reverend Xysomathumarsai had arrived in Ballycarson a few years previously with a name noone could pronounce. When asked to explain what his name meant, he indicated that in a now long-defunct version of his mother tongue it meant "preaching" as his family were marked out as preachers. Some doubted, but others believed the happy tale. So, reasoned even the believing locals in Ballycarson, if that indeed were true, Xysomathumarsai was indeed something easier done than said. Out of politeness, the man's name was immediately abbreviated to "the Reverend X". So too his spouse Ms. Wye, a local lass, had retained her maiden name not as an early symbol of Ulster feminist zealotry but simply because she had not been able to complete the marriage certificate appropriately with her husband's surname. In any event the name "Ms. Wye" seemed appropriate for a scientist who was supposed to retain a questioning outlook on life.

To say Ms. Wye was a scientist was really to put a romantic and unscientific slant on the true facts. In fact, she was an industrial chemist who had previously worked at the Ballycarson nylon factory prior to its takeover by an east European investor. The plant then stopped making nylon and started to produce odd chemicals for the local reformed paramilitaries who seemed to have moved into horticulture in a big way. Maybe they were seeking new green credentials, but they certainly ordered a lot of nitrate-based fertiliser. Not having the desired cross-transferable skills, Ms. Wye lost her job. Having been laid off, she now worked freelance. That had proved to be her big break as she turned from fabric creation to fashion design. She came to prominence with the design of the new aprons for the local Masonic lodges and the new butcher's shop. For her new commercial concern the trade name employed by Ms. Wye was "Cover Up". This was immediately noticed by Big David. Here was a skill he might be able to use.

It was at the butcher's shop that Ms. Wye first met her husband. The Reverend X had been in Ballycarson only for a few months when he was outraged at the news that Ballycarson was to witness the opening of a new shop entitled "The Joys of the Flesh". To protect the populace from the anticipated sex shop he mounted a one-man protest outside, praying that the locals would be delivered from temptation. It was only when he witnessed a delivery to temptation that he realised the truth. When a lorry-load of salami and sausages arrived for unloading he discovered "The Joys of the Flesh" was the new butcher's shop. He and some other enquiring and hungry passers-by immediately went into the establishment to buy lunch. It was the occasion of a life-changing experience. The eyes of X and Wye met over rashers of thick-sliced middle back bacon and trays of pigs' trotters. From then on things looked up. Romance blossomed for the woman of clothing and the man of the cloth. Career prospects looked up too and the X and Y Partnership was introduced to Big David via a large order to manufacture aprons for the workers in the Ballycarson salami factory.

After the Council, Ballycarson Salami Enterprises (known in the trade as "B.S.E.") was the third largest employer in the town. In the private sector it was outstripped in size and importance only by the O'Duffy carpet and linoleum factory. Big David was the real power behind B.S.E., but the organisation was still fronted by its original founder, Frankie Alphabet. Frankie, now past retiring age, had not been entirely pushed out. He had been given the honorary title of B.S.E. President and was still allowed to make his presence felt.

That magnanimity was typical of Big David. He didn't want to muscle out the man who had created the firm's original success story – the "Big Mick". Each week the factory still churned out thousands of these frozen succulent beefburgers topped with homogenised lettuce shaped in the form of a shamrock. In their attractive green polystyrene boxes these were still selling hand-over-fist in Boston, Baltimore and Brooklyn and any other such location where homesick third-generation Irish-Americans longed for granny's home cooking straight from the old country via the freezer. Just as with his racket with genealogical records, the business motto had to be "nothing knocks nostalgia". And what was nostalgia except history, processed, shaped and packaged to present advantage? It was just like the meat trade after all.

Now Frankie was in the twilight years of his power, but he still toured the salami factory every day in his battery-powered, orange and blue scooter for the disabled. He had a special basket on the front enabling him to pick up special deliveries for his staff. It clearly was a case of Frankie Alphabet remaining a butcher's boy to the end of his days.

Of course Frankie Alphabet was not the man's true name. But this was not an alias adopted purposely to draw a veil over a previous career in the paramilitaries – he had never been that sort of butcher's boy. Frankie Alphabet was simply an abbreviation.

Frankie Alphabet's full name was "Franklin Delano Roosevelt Messerschmitt" or "F.D.R.M." for short. Here was a man of letters. He had almost as many initials before his surname as most junior Council officials had qualifications after theirs. So the shortened version "Frankie Alphabet" was coined merely to save time in conversation whilst still acknowledging, with due and appropriate regard, Frankie's baptismal linguistic extravagance.

Frankie's full name betrayed the fact that he had been born during World War II in the dark, hungry days of food rationing and before the emergence and importation into Ulster of Spam fritters with extra grease. He had received the citation of honour "Franklin Delano Roosevelt" as a demonstrative list of given names symbolising eternal and unswerving loyalty to the Allied cause. But the motivation behind the endowment of these names was not just the usual one. Frankie Alphabet's father was no mere G.I. at the American camp located just outside the town. Instead, the list of names was intended to throw some cover over the tracks of his reputed true origin. It had been widely suspected that Frankie Alphabet's father was really one of the German prisoners of war who had been out on day-release from the P.O.W. camp in Ballycarson to paint Council property. So the reference to the occupant of the White House provided the whitewash and the title "Franklin Delano Roosevelt" was intended to provide his mother with a shield against any allegations of disloyalty.

However, there was no escape from the surname "Messerschmitt" as this was not only the German prisoner's name, but also his occupation in Civvy Street, or whatever was the equivalent German Strasse. In addition, it was the type of plane he had been flying when shot down over Belfast. So the perennial joke on the shop floor of the salami factory was that Frankie had got off to a flying start in life, but his career had nose-dived just like his dad's.

In any event, all that was a long time ago because the German flyer, like many of his colleagues, stayed in the province after the war as the Allied bombing had left them with nothing and noone to go home to. This was the second wave of German substantial emigration to Ballycarson. And there the mid-twentieth-century German incomers had flourished. That was the perennial paradox of life in Ulster: it was only Irish history for which the locals had a long memory. They tended to forgive and forget the mistakes of others. Further to that, Frankie's dad went on to marry his mum. Loyalty like that was appreciated in Ulster. If that were not enough to demonstrate commitment, they had a total of five other sons – all of whom still marched with the flute band, whilst Frankie, their firstborn, drove out in front on his scooter decked out with the flags of the United Kingdom and the German Bundesrepublik. Such open commitment to both nations went down well in the Ballycarson salami factory where half the workforce was local German and the remainder were locals of some other extraction.

Keeping the workforce entertained at the salami factory was a serious business. In that regard things had got off to a relatively inauspicious start. In the beginning Big David had tried to cut costs by having Charlie Rae and his mother Senga serenade the sausage producers whilst the allegedly musical pair duetted on a Wurlitzer and a Glockenspiel.

"Wurlitzer is a German name and the Germans are bound to like it," reasoned Big David.

However, the salami production figures spoke volumes or, more accurately, a lack of volume. There had been a catastrophic dip during the serenades. Charlie and Senga Rae were cut so more sausage could be sliced.

A compromise was reached with the use of taped music. But because of the ethnic make-up of the workforce strict time limits were placed on the music played over the tannoy system to comply with human rights requirements. Every hour on the hour the music altered from maudlin Irish country and western (favoured by the locals) to anonymous, pseudo-cheerful Central European pop or Oompah music (supposedly loved by the Germans). Without regard to any intellectual property rights, the Big David organisation downloaded the music by satellite from the endless supply poured into the ether by the various exponents of the respective genres. As part of a job-creation scheme sponsored by funny money from some amorphous European source, shifts of DJs changed the CDs as the hours rolled by.

And the recording industry spawned more jobs than just that. Not only did Big David provide the salami factory with recordings for entertainment, but he provided recordings for security. With his pre-recorded CDs of Pomeranian, Alsatian and Rottweiler barking, he supplied "automatic dog" recordings to businesses of all sorts. Linked to a trip switch, the sound system would click on and a suitable amount of snarling and barking would start as soon as an unwanted intruder tried to force a gate, door or window. Ballycarson Salami Enterprises favoured the absence of genuine dogs within the factory because it assisted in quelling some widespread rumours about the content of their products. There remained the potential for accident, however. When one of the DJs turned up after a heaving morning's drinking, the automatic dog CD was played over the tannoy system instead of the normal country and western entertainment. "He must have had a rough night!" a worker was heard to remark.

All this barking could have been hushed up but for the fact that there was an anonymous complaint made to the Council that the Germans were getting more than their fair share of tannoy airtime.

"The dogs were German breeds and were clearly barking in German. We could not understand a word. Yours disgusted, Ballycarson," ran the letter addressed to Councillor Fitzmaurice.

Councillor Fitzmaurice was a man known not to mince his words when it came to the salami factory. After an enquiry the Council formally requested Big David to ensure some CDs were made of the barking of Irish wolfhounds, Irish terriers, Irish spaniels or Irish setters.

"You've got plenty of choice with this array of local breeds, so there is no excuse," read the official letter of condemnation. "In the future we want to hear breed-balanced barking."

Despite the justified and completely understandable outrage at Big David's ignorance of local dog breeds, at an emergency meeting of the councillors' Canine Concern Committee, specially called to deal with the issue, it was indicated that, this time and this time only, the Council were prepared to go easy on the factory. Next time matters would be different. A strong mitigating factor for the present was the excellent supply of low-fat bacon at a special low-fat rate to the Council canteen.

"Leniency Linked to Lean Meat. Next Time Fat Will Be in the Fire" ran the headline in the *Provincial Observer*.

However, the detail of the Canine Concern Committee minutes provided a further insight into the machinations of local government. It was noted that Councillor Finvola O'Duffy had suggested that in the future unfortunate incidents of a similar nature might be avoided if the CD output could be monitored and playlists vetted in advance by a new Council-run body to be entitled the "Music and Cultural Heritage Office". This had been immediately rejected by the member representing the Republican and Unionist Feminists (known as the "RUF women") not only because it would place a politically correct dead hand on genuine artistic creativity but also because of the unhappy acronym "MACHO". Consequently the proposal had been speedily rejected as the agenda moved on to the more important dog-related issue – the privatisation of the Zapper.

CHAPTER 13

A SPARKLING FUTURE

A traditional comforting image coupled with ruthless innovation. That was how local political and business dynasties reflected an image of the past, exploited the present and secured their future. Councillor Finvola O'Duffy knew the secret only too well. Dressed all in black, with a discreet black armband on her right sleeve, she suited the part of an undertaker. Only her greying hair and pale complexion somewhat spoiled the overall sombre image. But even here there was a traditional Irish advantage. From a distance she had the appearance of a settled glass of stout. Here was a woman who did not want curves. Looking in the mirror she thought to herself, *I hope my bum does not look big in this or I will look like a bottle of Coke and not a bottle of Guinness. I had better wear a trouser suit and lose a few pounds to complete the shape. A black cheroot would help as well.* So the local gatekeeper to the afterlife studiously maintained her image. In her own eyes she was the local beauty, eternally pristine and ever eager to keep her reputation so that she might live up to the accolade first won by her, some decades previously, in open competition at the Thirteenth Annual Rural Ulster Female Undertaking and Funereal Assistant Beauty Contest. It was at that august gathering in the annexe to the Ballycarson Parochial Hall, wearing a demure black swimsuit lit by a sudden blaze of glory projected from the flash bulb of the cameraman from the local paper, that she had been crowned with the title "Miss Underworld 1982". From then on there would be no change. Here indeed was a woman who, at least as regards her outward appearance, had traded all of her tomorrows for a single yesterday.

But external impressions are not the whole picture. When it came to making money Councillor Finvola O'Duffy knew how to seize the day. Profit was right here, right now. For Councillor Finvola O'Duffy business was booming. She had recently launched a loyalty card for her customers giving them exclusive access to the benefits of "the Coffin Club". Each of them had the shiny black card in their wallet and collected tombstone points every time they attended a funeral organised by the O'Duffy business empire. Thirty Coffin Points afforded to the holder a ten percent discount on the full works at an O'Duffy funeral. A steady procession of custom was rolling in, or at least was being carried in. What was the attraction? It was not just the monetary discount, convenient though that was, to allow the savings to be spent on the wake. Membership of the Coffin Club had social benefits too. The Coffin Club ensured a large attendance of mourners at every participating funeral. The grieving family was assured of solicitation on a large scale even for the greatest scoundrel. Esteem for the deceased was acquired by flexing the black plastic card.

For Councillor Finvola O'Duffy the political future looked bright too. The real significance of the Nationalist victory in the recent local elections became apparent only in the working out of the detail of the post-election administrative agenda.

In accordance with regulations on Private Finance Initiatives and Best Value Policies the operation of the Zapper was out-sourced, causing a major shift in the commercial and political balance of power within Ballycarson. The Zapper operation contract had been awarded to Councillor Finvola O'Duffy's One Stop Store comprising pet supplies, floor coverings, jeweller's shop and funeral parlour. Because of the last of its functions, the One Stop Store was known throughout Ballycarson as the Final Stop Store. "You Won't Walk Past Our Window" were the words on the advertising poster outside the shop. Everyone knew that would be true eventually. To complete the picture of funereal and retail harmony were two granite headstones set on either side of the front door to the shop. The first bore the word "Reliability" where a family name should be and, underneath, the words of comfort "We'll be the last to let you down". On the other, the heading "Cost-effective" with the sentimental under-text "Rest In Peace: One year's free credit on all headstones". On the face of it there could be no easier way to ease oneself in to eternity.

The awarding of the contract for the Zapper shouldn't have happened as it had, at least if the double control system designed by the human rights lawyers and the electricians had worked. However, all this had been short-circuited by Councillor Finvola O'Duffy.

The terms of the Zapper privatisation contract and the design of the machine itself required that there had to be "dual control" with two separate keys to operate the machine. The concern of the electricians was that no single employee could start the machine by accident and find himself trapped inside with shocking results. So, two special keys were issued, each attached to a special key ring. The system was simple enough to understand. The key ring bearing the letter "L" was attached to the key that, when turned, connected the Live wire. The key ring bearing the letter "N" was attached to the key that operated the Neutral wire. It was known in the electrical trade as "Mutually Assured Non-destruction". The contractual clauses added by the lawyers were designed to ensure cross-community benefit. According to the principles of the Peace Process, a Council contract could be awarded only to firms engaging employees from both traditions. So in the eyes of the human rights lawyers the "L" key ring was to be held by an individual who was a Loyalist whilst the "N" key ring was to be operated by a Nationalist.

Inevitably these theories were just as detached from reality as the key rings were detachable from the keys. In the event, one employee only ended up holding both keys and operating the machine alone. Sole power rested with Councillor Finvola O'Duffy.

The job of holding the two keys was given to a particular employee who had proved herself well capable not only of being in two places at the one time but of being two persons at the one time. This extraordinarily talented individual was known locally as "Val Kerry Val Kerry". So named was she not because of some bizarre local tradition of repetitive double-barrelled names. No, the name "Val Kerry Val Kerry" had been conferred upon the originally named "Val Kerry" because she was well known to have voted twice at a considerable number of local government and national elections. However, she had never been prosecuted for personation because in the era of the Peace Process the authorities took the view that it was better to encourage the citizens to vote than leave them to resort to alternative means of being heard. In the bureaucratic jargon of the Peace Process, Val Kerry was to be regarded as being merely "over zealous in her exercise of the democratic franchise".

The strategic investment in the Zapper contract had enabled Councillor Finvola O'Duffy to achieve what she regarded as a political and commercial double whammy. At a stroke, as Councillor Finvola O'Duffy reflected happily, not only had she secured control of a potentially lucrative source of income but also the Loyalist community had suffered a major reverse. Big David was immediately deprived of a source of live guard dogs for his security business.

It was not long before the shortage of potential guard dogs began to bite into Big David's profits. But the automatic dog bounded to the rescue. Who said that man's best friend had to be a real dog? Instead of being crowded out by a pack of live hounds, the recording studio echoed to the barking of Big David's directors, William Henry, Billie King with a backing pack comprising the Red Army, and Frankie Alphabet's sons. Particularly successful was the recording known as "Howling Hell Hounds". The whole revamp of the quasi-canine recordings was a roaring success and, unaware of the background, clients complimented Big David on the amazing improvement in the quality of the product.

"You could say I've collared the market with a new supplier," responded Big David modestly.

Had it not been for the restrictions imposed by copyright and intellectual property rights, Big David joked he would have been tempted to release the CDs under the label of His Master's Voice.

Indeed the benefit to Big David was even more widespread. The on-costs of providing the human barkers were cheaper than the costs of the real dogs. Instead of having to provide cans of the locally produced dog food "Happy Mutt" he now could supply his barking directors with "Big Micks". Both were products of the salami factory – indeed they had substantially the same content – but the latter was marginally cheaper to manufacture and was subjected to less rigorous environmental health controls. The only snag was that his human pack of hounds was putting on weight at a rather alarming rate. If this continued unabated Big David would soon not be able to fit the entire pack into the recording studio for each recording session. Perhaps he would have to consider the manufacture of a diet version of the product. He would have to substitute the existing meat substitute with something even less nourishing. The broad vista of an entirely new line of production and sale opened out. Yes, there was potential for profit there too.

However, not all of Councillor Finvola O'Duffy's political machinations were dogged with failure. A worthwhile consequence of the privatisation of the Zapper was the potential for benefitting Councillor Finvola O'Duffy's own business interests. The truth of the matter was particularly shocking, but everything was perfectly compliant with all relevant Council regulations and policies. The minutes of the relevant Council meeting showed that, after a suitable disclosure of interest, the contract had been awarded to Councillor Finvola O'Duffy because she was able to promise operation of the Zapper in a manner that would comply with recycling directives and minimisation of land refill. In short, she would dispose of the canine corpses without burial. So, in future, the Council would avoid howls of protest such as those heard when the site of the last pet cemetery was redeveloped as a tourist interpretative centre and watch tower for the Ballycarson Peace Wall. Instead of fearing the ghosts of dogs past coming back to haunt them, the councillors were impressed that the remains of the electrocuted dogs were to be incinerated and compressed.

The discreet black-rimmed notice in the window of the O'Duffy Final Stop Store confirmed that it had been providing a cremation service for the grief-stricken owners of pampered pooches for a number of years. Business had been lively. The disposal of un-owned dogs collected by the Council would be an adjunct to that service, using the existing state-of-the-art facilities. All this demonstrated, thought Councillor Finvola O'Duffy, that she had a social conscience by providing a service for the most vulnerable animals in society. That would look good in the next manifesto, particularly if she could have a picture taken beside a dog with both of them wearing an appropriately coloured rosette or collar. However, outwith the periodical election campaigns, she could adopt a different approach. For a caring outward appearance with cross-community appeal it might even be better if she could find various miniature breeds of dog. She could then adorn the dogs with variously coloured collarettes and appeal to surviving families of members of various select organisations.

Of course private enterprise did play a part in the economy of the cremations. Disconsolate pet owners wishing to say fond farewells could pay extra for the "Silver", the "Gold" and even the deluxe "Diamond" service.

The "Diamond" service was exactly what it said it was. "Wear your pet with pride" were the words in the notice in the shop window, causing only a minor ripple of offence amongst those who thought it had something to do with fur farming or the new fashion of lizard-skin boots. But Councillor Finvola O'Duffy's talents were not aimed at the provision of pathetic pelts or furry footwear. No, she was interested in doggy diamonds. After cremation the ashes were condensed and returned to the owner to brighten the hand that fed. And the jewellers employed by Councillor Finvola O'Duffy would ensure the gem would be set in an appropriate ring supplied at an appropriate price. So from Councillor Finvola O'Duffy's perspective there was no incongruity of mixing loss and grief with goods and services. The pet owner's loss was her gain. All grief was good grief. The phoenix of a financial return would rise from the ashes of despair.

This market was of course principally aimed at the Pomeranian and miniature poodle market where the owners were likely to be sufficiently well heeled to afford such extravagance. The problem was that such miniature breeds produced little in the way of ashes, resulting in tiny diamonds and commensurately small profits. So the O'Duffy business mind hit on the solution of padding out the remains with the ashes from other dogs – the abandoned dogs – without, of course, unduly worrying the paying owner. Naturally, Councillor Finvola O'Duffy had some misgivings about using the remains of the abandoned dogs in this way. She had a conscience after all. However, she prevented the pangs of conscience from developing into scars by ensuring that the blend for each diamond comprised only dogs of a similar or better pedigree. Yes, there was discrimination even in death. It wasn't a case of "adulteration", "impurity" or even "homogenisation" after all. Indeed with a suitable mixture some dogs might even be upgraded to a higher canine caste. These would be augmented ashes. So much for death being a great leveller.

So proud indeed was Councillor Finvola O'Duffy of her service to society, she even coined a slogan in delicately crafted doggerel for her business card:

"The ideal blend
for man's best friend.
The perfect match
for that final dispatch."

To Councillor Finvola O'Duffy it was clear that such local artistry must have come to the attention of those rumoured to be arranging the proposed visit from the White House. A message had been received by the Ballycarson Council that the president would find a gift of a local product most acceptable. So Councillor Finvola O'Duffy instructed her jeweller's to import a miniature silver replica of an Irish wolfhound. Its eyes would then be set with locally produced diamonds. With such an animal as a paperweight on the mantelpiece in the Oval Office the Nationalist triumph would be complete and Big David and his Loyalist crew consigned to the international doghouse.

CHAPTER 14

BARKING MAD

It all seemed like Councillor Finvola O'Duffy was on a continuing roll of success. In addition, this particular roll looked like it was about to be recognised internationally. However, appearances can be deceptive. The dog warden and lost property man, Donald Oskar Gormley, knew there was much less to Councillor Finvola O'Duffy than met the eye.

How did he have this talent for clairvoyance? Perhaps it was because Donald Oskar Gormley was reputed to be one of the Ballycarson travelling people. But that was not to say he was a Romany, a Sinti, a gypsy or even a tinker. No, Donald Oskar Gormley simply had no fixed abode. He just lived and slept in whatever vehicle he possessed from time to time. He had no home to go to but went everywhere with his home. His I.D. card for his Council job indicated his address as "in transit", which was sufficiently accurate, he thought, because for a couple of years he had lived in the back of a Ford transit van.

And what of Donald's political clear-sightedness? He had no crystal ball. It may simply have had something to do with the fact that he did not let the acquisition of possessions clutter his view. But he was no aesthete or social outcast sitting in judgement on the norms of Ballycarson society in general. He did not despise faith, piety or religion. He simply preferred to see them put into practice rather than argued about. Deep down, he had a suspicion of the mixture of politics and religion encountered in the political chat rooms on both sides of Ballycarson. He saw how religion was used there to further the aims and aspirations of politicians but never to circumscribe them. Putting it another way, he had reservations about the sort of God who hated the same people the politicians hated.

Donald's lack of permanent accommodation didn't appear to worry him in the slightest. He had the respect of the local population on both sides of the political and religious divide. Not only did he possess this rare commodity but he had not struggled or schemed to obtain it. It seemed to come as an unsought by-product. How was this so? The answer: Donald knew the secret of status in Ireland. To be truly respectable in Ireland everyone had to believe you were really up to something, but nobody should know for certain what it was. And Donald made sure that as few as possible really knew what he was up to because he had only ever told his secrets to Gretel.

In addition to being somewhat secretive Donald was a sophisticate. Unlike the inhabitants of the shelter at the Spion Kop bus stop who still believed politicians were local heroes to be admired and courted because they could achieve something, Donald had a low regard for local politicians. They thought he could do nothing for them, so they did nothing for him. The contrast between him and them was stark. Whilst Donald's wreck of a vehicle staggered from one overnight destination to another, they loved to be seen being driven about at speed in a large limousine regardless of their destination. In fact, Donald suspected that for most politicians the destination didn't really matter at all. For them, what mattered was just the fact that they gave the impression of going somewhere at speed. The flag on the Council chairman's official car had changed after the recent elections. The car had even been re-sprayed a different colour and the leather upholstery refitted to match, but the limousine itself was still the same and so were the expenses claims.

"No slush funds" had been the promise in all the political manifestos at the last election.

Yet Donald knew all about the Zapper, the doggy diamonds and resultant income known as the "ash cash stash".

So much for "all's changed, changed utterly", reflected Donald as he watched yet another Council limousine sweep past.

Whilst the politicians were addicted to switching from one pressing issue to the next, as the potential for re-election demanded, Donald's life remained full of continuity as regards the things that mattered to him. Donald had been into recycling long before it ever became politically fashionable. Over the years he had driven a succession of vehicles that had been abandoned around the town and then removed by the Council for destruction. Given his obvious success as Lost Property Officer with the refurbishment of a couple of abandoned bikes, the Council had superimposed greater responsibility on him by adding the care of discarded motorised vehicles to Donald's empire. This cloud of additional responsibility had a rusty lining. By privately appropriating the vehicular debris of the town, Donald had eventually traded up from a motorbike and sidecar, through various half-wrecked, oil-burning hulks to an ice cream van recently decommissioned from Wee Joe Forsale's home delivery service at the Iceberg Café. Donald parked his transport at various accustomed night spots round the town. These night spots were not places of entertainment – they were simply the places where Donald slept for the night.

"It's Friday night, so it's the Black Lough lay-by," he said to his travelling companion Gretel, "and stop licking my face."

Gretel was a German beauty, a quarter of Donald's age, with black and brown hair. A real dog, indeed an aristocrat amongst hounds, a true German shepherd. A decade previously she had been abandoned as a young pup, picked up by the abandoned dog patrol, unclaimed and destined for the Council's Zapper. Donald had fallen in love and rescued her from Death Row by hiding her in his shed in the Council yard.

But Gretel's close encounters with the final call to the great kennel in the canine hereafter had not ended there. To keep her alive for long Donald had to get her out of the Council yard, un-noticed. He hit on the idea of disguising the dog as his granny by dressing her in a fur coat, a long blonde wig and goggles, and wrapping a headscarf over her head and muzzle. Donald was just going to drive her out of the Council yard in style. It was in the days of Donald's motorbike and sidecar and, to stop her jumping out of the sidecar and giving the game away to the security guard, Donald had attached Gretel's leash to the sidecar seat belt. Unfortunately, he could not find a proper helmet to fit. Gretel's ears were just too big.

Donald would have to wait until Half Inch O'Neill was on duty as security guard on the main gate. That man had been given his nickname not because of his propensity to theft but from the thickness of his lenses and the distance he was reputed to be able to see if he was not wearing them. Even with the benefit of his special prescription glasses, Half Inch O'Neill demonstrated his visual skills when he spent fifteen minutes at a local football match haranguing the linesman for giving a corner. Why had the linesman stood unwaveringly and taken such abuse without retaliation? Was he a model of tolerance or just deaf? No, the subject of the verbal assault turned out to be the corner flag and not the linesman.

So when Half Inch O'Neill came on duty, Donald started his motorbike and headed for the main gate with his dog in disguise. The ruse worked, although there was a difficult moment when Half Inch O'Neill gave the slouched and crumpled-looking passenger a somewhat unfocussed second glance and observed, "She doesn't look too well."

"She's just dog-tired," replied Donald nonchalantly.

The security guard continued his advice like an agony uncle. "Travelling in that wagon without a helmet? I think she's mad," he opined, pointing to the occupant of the sidecar.

"You are right. She's barking," replied Donald and sped out of the Council yard as the barrier lifted.

They accelerated out of the main gate at much more than a

safe speed. The tyres squealed as they turned right at the junction into Constitution Street. Gretel, however, was as yet unused to motorised transport and stood up, only to become unbalanced. The force of the turn shot her out sideways over the side panel of the sidecar and into mid-air. With one end of her leash attached to her neck and the other to the seat belt she was dragged along in the air two feet above the ground, a leash's length to the left of the vehicle. It was only when the still attached and airborne dog nearly hit two drunks walking along the pavement that Donald realised that he had come close to unleashing a hell hound on the local population. Fortunately, noone believed the drunks' story about a flying dog, but reports of their experience were analysed and chewed over for days by the senior sociologists in the shelter at the Spion Kop bus stop.

A few days after the great escape Donald's lay-by was visited by the Council's environmental health officers dressed in white suits and facemasks. Donald thought the bottom had fallen out of his world. Gretel would be collared. But joined-up government had not as yet reached Ballycarson and the officials in question were not there to repossess the dog. They were there to deal with consequences and not cause. There had been complaints about dog mess in the lay-by and a pile of empty "Happy Mutt" dog food cans in the sidecar. After an inspection, a written recommendation was taped to the motorbike that Donald should change his vehicle, get rid of that smelly carpet and install easy-to-wash-out flooring in the sidecar. Better still, he should upgrade to a car. Didn't he know he was probably in violation of the Council's policy regarding vehicles in multiple occupancy? Why did he not get a stable address? "I've got a dog, not a horse," Donald muttered under his breath but quietly decided it had been a shave rather too close.

So Donald acquired an old Volkswagen Golf. To comply with the Council notice previously received, he ripped out the existing carpets. However, he was not prepared to sink to the level of asking Councillor Finvola O'Duffy for a dog end of a reject washable lino for his mobile kennel. Instead, he rummaged in the lost property shed until he found an unopened bag of Portland cement. Donald then proceeded to enhance the floor of his new car with a one-inch thick layer of easy to hose down concrete.

The inspiration for this firm foundation had come from the stories Donald had heard about his great-grandfather. Prior to the Great War the vast bulk of the population of rural Ulster had lived in houses with mud floors. Exceptions were rare but one such was Donald's great-grandfather who had furnished his house with a granite stone floor. This entirely level substantial construct was not a product of that man's skill as stonemason. The truth was that he lived near a graveyard and had simply appropriated many of the headstones of his close relatives for his own use. The stones were placed face down so the floor of the house presented an entirely smooth surface free of dirt, grime and general squalour. At the turn of the century this stone floor was a real and enduring feature. Noone else had such easy to assemble, easy to clean, prefabricated flooring. In addition, if anyone broke in and stole the stones they would be easy to identify and retrieve as the family name was already chiselled into every one of them.

The inspiration from the gravestones did not stop there. Donald recalled how he had been told that most of the neighbourhood used to go to Donald's great-grandfather's house for a Friday night ceilidh. On one such night an argument arose about the age of one of the former worthies of Ballycarson who had been Donald's great-great-uncle. The argument was quickly settled with a pickaxe. It was not that the participants had come to blows. It was merely the case that Donald's great-grandfather had nipped out the back and had returned with the implement. He then proceeded to use it to lift part of the floor and read off the precise figures to supply the answer from the lifted gravestone.

So, inspired by past events, Donald smoothed and finished off his concrete car floor as Gretel looked on.

"Let us put our marks on this floor too. So if someone steals it we will know it is ours," said Donald to Gretel.

He proceeded to scrape the date and his name in the wet cement floor and encouraged Gretel to put her paw print immediately beside it.

"A bucket of water should see to the dirt every week," he said to Gretel as he smoothed out the screed round the seats and took care to trowel out small indents around the pedals. "That's a weight off my mind." Donald smiled as they stood back to admire his work. "That will last for years."

But a weight off Donald's mind was a weight on the springs of the car. Unfortunately, the new floor outlived the car. But it was only when Donald was cruising over the speed ramps laid on the road outside the police station that the weakness in his solid foundation became apparent. The back of the car floor collapsed onto the road. The police laughed so much they forgot to book Donald. It was time for another vehicular upgrade.

Donald's most recent mode of transport and place of residence, the ice cream van, had come onto the market as a result of a musical mistake – a cock-up rather than a cacophony. Big David's recording studio provided material for businesses on both sides of town, although political realities necessitated that those on the Nationalist west were supplied surreptitiously and via an intermediary. What occurred was that the package was tied on the back of a trained messenger dog that was sent off with its message to the addressee. Originally the breed of dog used had been a Saint Bernard and the package had been tied round its neck like the traditional barrel of brandy. However, a few years later, at a time of increased tension between the two communities in Ballycarson, Big David feared that a breed of dog linked, however tenuously, to a religious personality could be identified with one side of the sectarian conflict. He did not want his dogs kicked in the streets as happened to the Dachshunds in London during the Great War. The Saint Bernards were retired to security duty at the Council yard and Rottweilers and Doberman pinschers were substituted on the mail deliveries. So the black and tan warriors became the standard means of covert cross-community commerce.

For added security with really sensitive cargo, each dog had a handler disguised as a blind woman with a white stick. A woman it had to be because each handler carried a handbag with further important contents and no self-respecting Ballycarson male would take on as risky a job as to be seen with a handbag in public. No expense was spared on high-tech equipment. The handbag was armour plated. To be more accurate, each handbag was actually an old-fashioned metal kettle with the lid padlocked shut.

For Big David one would have thought when it came to recording mistakes it would have been a case of once bitten twice shy. However, in a virtual re-run of the barking disaster at the salami factory, the CDs provided to the various firms had been mixed up. Instead of a cheerful musical jingle for an ice cream van, the messenger Rottweiler delivered Wee Joe Forsale a CD of the British National anthem, which was intended to be played at the end of the performances in the Loyalist cinema in the east end of town. When this melody of loyal affirmation was played over the ice cream van tannoy in one of the large Nationalist housing estates in the west side of town it occasioned considerably more than a pointed letter of complaint to the Council. A riot ensued releasing all the community energy that had been pent up and suppressed during a long series of Senga Rae's concerts. The ice cream van had been saved from being completely torched only because the petrol bomb thrown into the vehicle had extinguished itself in the cargo of litres of melted vanilla ice cream.

With the prospect of such a heated reception no more drivers could be found to volunteer for the housing estate ice cream run. So the ice cream van was abandoned. Eventually it made its way into the hands of Donald Oskar Gormley.

Clearly the purpose of the ice cream van changed when Donald acquired it. On the side of the van the original phrase

"Ballycarson's Big Cones" had been partly obliterated with the two last letters obscured by rust, leaving the words "Ballycarson's Big Con". Whether accident or design had erased the final two letters, noone knew, but, again, this new message added to Donald's street credibility and afforded an element of mystique to the products he sold from the van. Here was a fraud in plain sight. The man in question was not only up to something, but he was advertising the fact to all and sundry. The authorities were doing nothing. Were they afraid of him?

Location is everything in the retail trade. To Donald Oskar Gormley this truth was known only too well because his particular trade required a very particular location. The trade was smuggling and the location was the border – exactly on the border.

Yet again Donald had learned his lesson from family history. During the 1940s his grandfather had run a public house in a village straddling the Irish border. So as the North went to war and enjoyed the delights of double summer time, the South remained neutral and slipped an hour behind if only for part of the year. The difference between these local time zones was particularly convenient as the front rooms of the Gormley public house were in the south and the back rooms in the same building were in the north. The international frontier was marked by a thin but distinct white line painted on the wooden floor of the hallway. When the Gardai in the south arrived to ensure that time had been called, the drinkers moved through to the back of the building and toasted their health in the next room. Of course, the reverse was the case when the Royal Ulster Constabulary arrived. Things being as they were (and still are) in Ireland, it was quite impossible for both police forces to arrive at the same time. The passing of war had done away with the general economic need for double summer time. But a pressing political need emerged to demand a local retention of the phenomenon in Ballycarson, if only for one day a year. In the dying days of the last Unionist administration the cultural office of the local authority recognised that there could be substantial cultural advantages if the clock went forwards every year at 11 o'clock in the evening on 11th July. The Glorious Twelfth would arrive an hour early. And if the clock then went back an hour at 12 o'clock in the evening on the 12th itself, the already remarkable day could be extended by an hour and become even more remarkable. The cultural advantages of an extra hour's flute-playing activity were obvious. Unfortunately, the proposal for a longer day for musicians itself became a victim of time. The Unionist administration fell after defeat by Nationalists at the elections. The proposal was never mentioned again in the new political climate.

But time stood still in other respects. In accordance with family precedent, on Saturdays Donald parked his ice cream van exactly on the border with the back door projecting into the south and the side window just within the north. At the back door the customers came to collect deliveries of cameras, CDs, computers, video- and smartphones, and other electrical goods, whilst from the side window were sold delicacies such as cigarettes, bottles of schnapps and cans of lager. Works of literature were obtainable from the cab. This was the Saturday cross-border market, an irregular, regular department store – and an international one at that. Noone had noticed that this form of trade had become wholly irrelevant in the new EU single market. The border had ceased to have any real commercial meaning. But that was part of the problem in Ballycarson. A tradition had sprung up over the years. It, above all else, gave meaning to an international border that both political traditions exploited whether they could say so in public or not. Just because the world had moved on and made the commercial activity largely meaningless was no reason to abandon the time-sanctioned business. Indeed, respect for previous years of political and commercial effort demanded that the tradition be kept up. The more obscure and meaningless it was the better for all concerned and the further removed from present reality the more difficult it was to criticise.

Home deliveries could of course be arranged, but these were more expensive and meant carting material across the border using Donald's extensive workforce of drivers. Transport for such home deliveries had to be specially arranged. Small items were smuggled inside beehives carted on the back of lorries as the army and border police were known to be afraid of bee stings and never looked inside. Larger items were wrapped in plastic and smuggled inside the refuse of farms or building sites in slurry tankers or skips.

It was by the last of these means that Wee Joe Forsale had received his regular deliveries of literature from Donald. These were the "dirty" books he was keen to hide from his wife. It was not that they were porn magazines. It was just that because of the means of transportation in slurry tankers they acquired a certain smell, which lasted for a few weeks after unwrapping and would have caused a matrimonial stir if opened in the kitchen.

Wee Joe Forsale's literary aspirations had started in a small way. Originally he was a mere technician – a collector of the technical manuals of boats, buses, cars, strimmers, water pumps and lawnmowers. His prized possessions were the instructions and warranty for the first diesel Mercedes Benz purchased in Ballycarson. However, in the last few years he had moved on to what had obviously become his real life mission. He was dedicated to collecting large sets of dictionaries and encyclopaedias.

His first venture into the field had been to collect the several published volumes of a peculiar hagiographical and overblown work entitled *The Alphabetical Encyclopaedia of Ulster Politics*. Unknown to Wee Joe, this particular collection had never been completed as every volume was already complete in itself. Each book was a complete bore. Even amongst the family members and employees of politicians (a wide enough potential constituency in itself to justify the publishing venture in the first place), the readership fell off sharply when it was realised that nothing ever changed in Ulster politics and each volume basically repeated the contents of the first one. Still, the published set of books, even if incomplete, was well bound in expensive black faux leather and had golden letters on the spine of each large volume indicating the range of coverage in each volume. On the shelf behind the coffee machine in Wee Joe's café, his customers could read and were intrigued by the wording on each consecutive volume: *Abhorrent to All*, *Born to Corruption*, *Destined to Fail*, *Fools to Govern* and *Payments to Politicians*. And there the alphabetically arranged volumes ended. Apparently, enough had been said on the topic.

Despite this disappointment, Wee Joe Forsale's taste for encyclopaedias had been whetted. He widened his search out to other topics and acquired volume after volume. He felt sorry for these extended paper tomes as new electronic media appeared likely to render them extinct. He was particularly fond of pre-war editions of these encyclopaedic works where one or two volumes were missing. His role in life, he thought, was reconciliation not of people but of books. The thrill for him came not from actually reading the contents. Wee Joe simply wanted to find the lost volumes and complete the dozens of sets that now filled his spare room, garage, his store and all other available space. Perhaps the truth was that Wee Joe had become more like the natives than he dared to admit. He retained these ancient literary works no matter how misleading their outdated wisdom had become in modern times. So too, in select parts of rural Ulster, history, no matter how incompletely or inaccurately recalled, was never truly scrapped. "The good old days" – that was a phrase to describe the present usually followed by the words "long may they continue!"

As regards the actual contents of the books Wee Joe Forsale's personal motto was "the volume of volumes speaks volumes". Wee Joe Forsale was one of those men who thought the obtaining of knowledge involved the mere acquisition of more and more material. It didn't matter that the books acquired by him were never actually read. For him literary analysis simply meant stacking the valuable volumes in the right order. Wee Joe had only the vaguest of notions that he wanted to build up a resource he could eventually leave to the town library for the edification of future generations. Just like the local politicians he could endow the future with yesterday's solutions and today's irrelevancies. Unfortunately, the present political situation made that impossible as yet. The sad truth was that Wee Joe's weakness for literature left him vulnerable to blackmail, denunciation and worse.

In the land of saints and scholars one might have anticipated a traditional respect for education and learning. Unfortunately, in the eyes of the self-appointed guardians of each of the two communities in Ballycarson this was the case only with the "approved" sort of education and learning. Wee Joe Forsale's tragedy was that he lived in the Nationalist west of the town, but the principal object of his most recent literary passion was the *Encyclopaedia Britannica*. Mere possession of a work with such a name so brazenly printed on the cover left Wee Joe dangerously exposed to investigation by the self-appointed Nationalist community guardians. Wee Joe knew only too well what had happened to the instruments of one of the local Nationalist pipe bands when they had started to learn the competition march "King George the Fifth's Army". At any time Wee Joe could be exposed and pilloried by those carrying out the community protection and continuous revolution on the west side of town. It was all the worse for Wee Joe because his wife was a local woman with well-known hard-line Republican sympathies. The potential for denunciation came from within the home itself. So Wee Joe had rows and rows of encyclopaedias backed in brown paper lining the walls of his shed and packed in boxes in his industrial freezer. Some far off, happy day, he thought, the brown paper could come off, the truth revealed and wisdom could come in from the cold.

In the meantime Wee Joe traded up-to-date information obtained from his wife for more and more books, which he acquired wherever he could. The main recipient of the information – and also the main source of the books – was Donald Oskar

Gormley. It was a pattern of trade that repeated itself many times. Donald supplied smaller quantities of similar illicit material to other individuals all around Ballycarson, again for information. The end result was that the best informed man about town was Donald Oskar Gormley.

CHAPTER 15

POLITICAL FACTS
AND FIGURES

The election of the first Nationalist administration in Ballycarson since the Ulster Plantation had been a watershed for the town. At least that was the view of the Nationalist parties. The very course of world history had been changed. It was not just in relation to those run-of-the-mill issues such as freedom, justice and equality. No, the transformation had gone much deeper than that. It had even managed to affect some of the Council's procedures. The new Nationalist administration repeatedly trumpeted the fact that they were fully determined to extirpate some of the well-entrenched practices of their Unionist predecessors.

Every new governing body needs a big idea. The big idea of the Nationalist administration was to concentrate on their appeal to the collective heart of the Irish Diaspora the world over. If Ireland were seen to be completely and demonstrably miserable, these homesick and rootless émigrés would feel sorry for the old country.

So it was time to get rid of some so-called improvements in Council functions introduced during Unionist hegemony. Those new highfaluting Council titles could go for a start. Council Chairperson Finvola O'Duffy knew where to apply the axe. In the very last crisis of the previous Unionist administration, the Council chairman, Tim Boyne, vainly tried to keep some of the less loyal Loyalist rebels in line by doling out promotions. All the councillors were endowed with the new title of "Alderman" in a special week of ceremonial activities commemorating some previously overlooked anniversary. It was an elevation to a higher status universally applied – at least within the local political elite. The snag, then, was that the currency of civic recognition had been debased. When there was a forest of aldermen, how would you see the wood for the trees? So the policy of appeasement by promotion had not pacified the Loyalist rebels and they proceeded to bring down the administration on a point of principle. The Council minutes did not identify what the principle was and, when asked, the disloyal Loyalists could not immediately remember. But it was still a point of principle, probably one so fundamental that it did not need to be articulated, and that was all that mattered.

The elections came and went. A new era was ushered in. In the new Nationalist administration, the Council Chairperson Finvola O'Duffy was determined that there would be no reversion to such trading in titular upgrading. It was degrading. It was time to stick to practicalities and to polish up pre-prepared pious and backward-looking stereotypes. She was presently arranging for the aides of the United States president to be taken on a misery tour. This would involve views of two of the overgrown graveyards and the silted-up Union Canal – that clogged-up ancient artery of commerce would have to be renamed immediately (it was fortunate that the sign at the side of the canal had rusted over and could not easily be read). Lunch, comprising a plate of steamed cabbage and a bowl of thin gruel, would be served at the site of the old poor house kitchen. Thereafter, the real highlight, the afternoon would be spent at the dentist's surgery in Irish Street where at least one hunger striker had had a tooth pulled as a child. Tradition had it that the British National Health Service, somehow recognising this particular child's future role in the armed struggle and wishing to punish him in advance (without a trial) for his as yet undiscovered contribution to rebellion, had paid for the extraction but not the anaesthetic. It was a classic tour of pain, misery and degradation. But the vehicle or means of transport appropriate to a grand misery tour had to be ready. No detail was to be left unprepared. Councillor Finvola O'Duffy had noticed that the green minibus that was to be used in the tour had a broken headlight. That would leave a bad impression. She had just ordered one of her volunteers to smash the other one so they would match. Uniformity was everything even if it meant leaving everyone in the dark ages. Yes, that was the principle put into practice. Everything and everyone should have that down-at-heel look. The minibus driver should have a broken arm, bad teeth and a poor haircut. Better still if he spoke in broken English as if he had been forced to learn it. That would make the Irish-American visitors feel good because they could then think *Just look at how far I have come since my folks left this place!* Such pleasant thoughts from closed minds would lead to opened wallets.

In the main office of Councillor Finvola O'Duffy an enormous plasma screen was showing the latest preparations for the American presidential visit to Ballycarson. The pictures were of a large, recently constructed wooden stage. It had been erected in good time by the Ballycarson Council in a location tight up against the Peace Wall. This was the perfect backdrop for the eagerly anticipated presidential address.

Not willing to lose out on such a readymade propaganda opportunity, Councillor Finvola O'Duffy already had some of her employees and supporters try out the venue. They were making uplifting speeches from the temporary but lavish podium bedecked with an Irish tricolour and several adverts for special deals at the O'Duffy carpet and linoleum factory. Councillor Finvola O'Duffy asserted it was only a test run for the presidential big day, although the test had now been going on for ten times longer than the projected main event. These test speeches were being broadcast on three of the publicly funded community channels as a form of breakfast TV. It seemed to many that it was an encouragement to get the populace out to work early. However, for Finvola O'Duffy, it was an all-day breakfast.

The original point of the community TV channels had been to enable both of the Loyalist and Nationalist communities to receive programmes dedicated to their own needs and distinctive tastes. Very much as an after-thought to secure international funding for the protection of minority interests, a third channel was dedicated to the recent German incomers. The Peace Process would be fostered in that each community would feel they had been selected for something special. Indeed that aim was the principal reason why the project had received substantial financial support from diverse European sources. This diversity remained intact until Councillor Finvola O'Duffy got her hands on the position of leader of the Ballycarson Council Broadcast Committee. What was once cast broadly was now cast as narrowly as she wanted. Two of the channels simply showed the simultaneous pictures of the same events. Those events were chosen by Councillor Finvola O'Duffy as editor in chief. There was nothing wrong with that, opined Councillor Finvola O'Duffy in the preface to her new glossy official Broadcast Committee report. One channel showed what the Nationalist community wanted to see and the other showed what the Loyalists did not want to see. It was a classic case of diversity within unity. The third channel, dedicated to the local Germans, showed the same pictures except that the programming was twenty-three hours behind. That, reasoned Councillor Finvola O'Duffy, was roughly the equivalent of an hour ahead, but it let her have plenty of time to edit out unwanted and unexpected incidents and re-write history for her Central European constituents in a manner more to her liking. The German-aimed programmes were broadcast at Central European time just as if the anticipated viewers had been in Berlin, Frankfurt, Stuttgart or Munich. Noone could complain of ethnic insensitivity. The lavish funding remained secure.

Despite her overall control of matters, things on stage were not always to the councillor's liking. With current live events or even with repeat practices for future live events, not all could be stage-managed. It looked like one of those unwanted and unexpected incidents was in the making. As she watched the screen, Finvola O'Duffy was on the phone to one of her aides at the podium site.

"Move that tricolour a bit to the right," she growled. "It is blocking part of the advert for our new floor covering range. Better still, get a slightly smaller flag and a bigger advert. No, make it two more adverts and put them on the Peace Wall itself."

One of the adverts for the O'Duffy floor covering business clearly bore a large picture of the *Titanic* underneath the words "The Lino that Launched a Liner". It was the classic product of the factory.

Councillor Finvola O'Duffy continued her instructions. "Make sure that poster is right beside the president when he speaks and can be seen by everyone. The president will want his image associated with a ship and a floor covering of such quality and endurance. Maybe we need a new strap-line. What about 'the Lino that Outlasted a Liner' or 'Waterproof Floor Coverings Are Our Speciality'?" The questions did not anticipate any answer except "Yes, ma'am, immediately, ma'am."

As the televised backdrop was being reorganised to suit the councillor's retail requirements, she could clearly hear that the series of practice speeches was continuing. The nameless employee presently behind the microphone was explaining how he, as a political prisoner, had been let out of jail early. He had not renewed his active military involvement with the volunteers against the British war machine, but, instead, he was assisting the Nationalist effort and Peace Process by working at the O'Duffy carpet and linoleum factory. It was the same struggle, he explained, carried out by different means. Because she employed volunteers, the councillor was able to undercut all the Loyalist-owned businesses for miles around and it was all paid for by the European Union by grants under the work programme known as "Head-starts for New-starts". It was an utter disgrace that the

Unionist press had simply derided this valuable programme as "Kick-starts for Up-starts".

Here again was another unexpected and unwanted incident, albeit one of potentially greater political and commercial magnitude.

"Get that guy off the stage immediately," shouted Councillor Finvola O'Duffy. "He will let the cat out of the bag."

The tactless employee's potted public politico-economic analysis was brought to a sharp end. He was swiftly replaced by a similar man expressing similar political sentiments but with considerably more acceptable subtlety and less factual revelation. Yes, Councillor Finvola O'Duffy had made a lot of money out of ex-paramilitaries working for her on early release schemes so they could be rehabilitated into a peace-loving society. She had even been nominated for a Peace Process award for her boundless enthusiasm in accepting the old volunteers into a workplace environment. She liked the mixture of the spirit of volunteering and the professional ethic. She was the professional businesswoman and the government could pay for her volunteers. But the financial secrets of the success of her floor covering business had to be kept under the carpet.

That's more like it, reflected Councillor Finvola O'Duffy as she heard the new speaker, another released volunteer, indicate that the local population should all be glad because the new Nationalist-led Council had made a number of things in Ballycarson better than they had been for him in the jail. Even as a political prisoner, who had gained a PhD in Sociology, Internationalisation and Republican studies, it had been tough for him on the inside. Content with the substance and phrasing of the renewed message, Councillor Finvola O'Duffy let the broadcast words slip from her immediate attention. She had more important and pressing things to attend. But the plasma screen remained switched on and the incessant and un-altering political message continued to form the background noise of her day's activity. She would have been lost without it. It formed the wallpaper music to her life.

Another phone rang in the office. The ringtone was the opening bars of John Philip Sousa's "The Stars and Stripes Forever". The call itself brought important news. The news had finally broken that the president of the United States would be arriving in Ballycarson in two days' time. It was time for the full weight of the O'Duffy political and commercial machine to swing into action.

The combined application of political and commercial weight often involves waiting. However, that did not matter. "It will not take us long waiting two days," was the inspirational message of Councillor Finvola O'Duffy as she broadcast the information over the tannoy system to her workers at the O'Duffy carpet and linoleum factory. "Get the presidential green carpet ready by 6 p.m. tonight." And, just as she clicked off the switch to the tannoy system, a further thought crossed her mind. After the American president had gone home the carpet might even suit to cover the aisle of the chapel at her own wedding. It wouldn't be a second-hand carpet, after all, just a pre-enjoyed one. That was no mere play on her own much-used, sales-orientated words. For the carpet in question would never have had a previous owner. She would have owned it all the time. It didn't matter at all that the carpet in question was really a large section of Astroturf that her workers were cutting into slices. She had recently re-acquired it when the local Gaelic Athletic Association Club went into liquidation and could not afford the payments on their new artificial playing surface. It was a good job Finvola had supplied this surface on Hire Purchase as it had always remained her property and she just had her repossession men roll up in lorries to roll up and roll away the surface. Yes, those legal and commercial technicalities were truly vital especially for an event such as a dynastic marriage that had such potentially important legal and political consequences in rural Ulster. And the further benefit? She could confirm she truly had a "Green" wedding in every sense of the word. Her guests would benefit from that genuine reproduction outdoor feel as they walked up and down the grassed chapel aisle on her big day. And the final bonus? On the day after the big event the carpet could be cut up even further into smaller sections, sold and fitted as extremely hard-wearing carpets for council house floors in the west side of town. And, as for the final cut-offs, she might even be able to sell them to the Americans cut up even smaller into one-inch square pieces of genuine reproduction Irish greener than green grass. There would be no waste at all. It was all win-win for Councillor Finvola O'Duffy.

It was true that Councillor Finvola O'Duffy was engaged to be married. She had been so engaged for thirty years. The real oddity was that, despite his long standing, her fiancé appeared to have little to do with the matter. You might have thought that after the expiry of such time in such a close-knit community the information as to the existence of the engagement would have filtered down to him. But outward appearances indicated that the date of the long-delayed wedding was hardly a pressing engagement. Indeed, among the more sceptical in the Ballycarson chattering classes, particularly those in O'Leary's bar, there were some who believed the fiancé in question was wholly unaware of the whole arrangement of betrothal. These persistent rumours had occasionally troubled Councillor Finvola O'Duffy, but only occasionally. One such occasion was now. On the basis that actions speak louder than words, she resolved that a dramatic act was needed to put the rumourmongers to silence. She had decided to stage a public event demonstrating the climax of three decades of espousal. That would settle the rumourmongers.

The fact of the matter was that the engagement had started out as an attempt to harness two potentially great political forces within the Ballycarson Nationalist community. The man in question was Councillor Eugene Gerald Fitzmaurice. He had come to the notice of Councillor Finvola O'Duffy all those years ago at the very beginning of his long-running Street Traffic and Signs Initiative. In those terrible days of Unionist and Loyalist hegemony Councillor Eugene Gerald Fitzmaurice had hit the headlines with a brilliantly designed publicity campaign. It was he who had initiated the now celebrated "Cones' Hotline", the very first project in Ballycarson to be sponsored by the European Union, or the E.E.C. as it was then known. A call centre had been set up in the vacant ice cream and chip shop beside the Hibernian Hall to receive the calls of anxious Nationalist travellers in Ballycarson and the surrounding district. The drivers could use a free-phone service to report the location of traffic cones that troubled their consciences and political sensitivities. The core of the constitutional issue at stake was the fact that, apart from the reflective white strip in the middle, the plastic devices were all coloured orange. It was no wonder that motor insurance was not available in Ulster at a reasonable rate. The relentless rising tide of traffic accidents was caused, no doubt, by Nationalist drivers who could not keep their minds on the operation of driving after becoming enraged by these ubiquitous symbols of Unionist rule. Now, instead of aiming to demolish the cones by driving at them or even stopping to throw them over the hedge, the drivers could use their mobile phones to call for assistance as they drove along. Upon receipt of phone messages from troubled callers, action squads of painters were sent out to paint the top of the cone bright green. Given that the middle of the cone comprised a reflective white strip, the overall effect, after green painting of the top, was that traffic was directed by a device resplendent in the colours of the Irish tricolour. In Nationalist and Republican circles there was great satisfaction all round. In the attendant blaze of glory Councillor Eugene Gerald Fitzmaurice was identified as the most eligible man in west Ballycarson. Here was a man who appeared to have an endless supply of green paint.

But it pays not to rush into things, particularly when they involve matrimony. Why repent subsequently even if at leisure when you could repent in advance at a stately pace? Indeed, Councillor Finvola O'Duffy realised that engagement gave her many of the benefits of matrimony and none of the drawbacks. In particular, she did not have to apply her own political policies to herself. Unfortunately for Finvola, her brand of traditional Nationalist values meant that the policies of her party had been determined by the cousin of her great uncle who had assisted at the founding of the particular splinter group of the political party and the writing of its constitution. These fundamentals could not be altered now, but it was all too inconvenient that the corporatist values espoused by the cousin of her great-uncle should mean that if Finvola married, her influence would be subsumed by that of her husband's family. In particular, if she adhered to her own inherited views, her vote should pass to her husband as head of the traditional household. The obvious compromise was to remain single, albeit semi-detached, for the sake of outward appearance and decency in public life. That way both she and her fiancé could have a vote each. To cap it all, Councillor Finvola O'Duffy was never really sure that his branch of Nationalism was completely sound, so it would be useful to retain the ability to vote against him in committee should the need arise.

In her speeches at the annual splinter group political conferences held, as one might expect, in camera in the committee room at the Ballycarson cheese factory social club, Councillor Finvola O'Duffy had repeatedly expounded upon the necessity of an annual review of policy. This review was most certainly not to suggest or enable change but to ensure that basic, unalterable principles were still being adhered to. The review was an auditing exercise. The message she had delivered at the most recent political event still resonated, at least within her own mind, and would be worth re-using next year and the year after that. Indeed, there might be a chance to slip some of the same well-worn phrases into her speech of welcome to the United States president. The only snag was that the message would then be public. No, upon reflection, that would never do. Perhaps it was best to repeat the comforting words to herself like a morning prayer just to make sure she was not going off course in both her public and private affairs.

And so Finvola silently dictated the dogma to herself to ensure she had retained a true and fair view of the political and historic situation in Ballycarson. Life was like a profit and loss sheet. All true Nationalists in Ballycarson had to carry the torch passed on to them by previous generations. Noone should forget that previous generations had suffered and sacrificed so much. The present Nationalist generation should claim that ancestral suffering as its own. The suffering of ancestors hallowed all present efforts. Oh how those well-practised words just rolled off her tongue. What Finvola was not prepared to admit was that she personally had suffered and sacrificed not at all. In the great balance sheet of life she could roll over these never to be forgotten ancestral losses indefinitely and make as much gain as she liked without having to account for any profit. But it did not do to upset her supporters by overly ostentatious wealth. In fact, the present-day adoption of the poor mouth avoided any recognition that she had accumulated wealth, power and influence beyond the wildest dreams not only of her ancestors but also of most of her contemporary constituents. But that was the sort of off balance sheet financing that was best kept secret. In addition, Councillor Finvola O'Duffy felt obliged to put into practice the mirror image of the prejudice that she regarded as having so penalised her forebears. And she not only felt good about it, but had also convinced herself that it was the right thing – indeed, the only thing – to do. The responsibility for moral choice was not hers – the decision on that matter had been taken generations ago. Yes, in politics, the long view, grounded in unarguable pre-history, was the true mark of the stateswoman.

And the long view was the way in which Finvola regarded her engagement to Councillor Eugene Gerald Fitzmaurice. The thirtieth anniversary of the original proposal was the same day as the imminent presidential visit. But despite the speed of the passing of those thirty years, the ravages of time had begun to show in the relationship and in the ring itself. Events were conspiring, if not to undermine, at least to challenge her long-held strategy of matrimonial delay. It was becoming clear to her that she could no longer keep the issue of her engagement ring on the long finger.

It was apparent that the political wing of a dissident sub-set of the Real Continuity Provisionally Acting Official Thirty-two Counties IRA were mounting a challenge to her long-held financial and political superiority in Nationalist circles in west Ballycarson. Inevitably, the challenge had come by proxy. In this regard it was her fiancé who was the weak link. When the Ballycarson bypass project was first unveiled, it appeared to be a potential boom time for the family of her fiancé, Councillor Eugene Gerald Fitzmaurice, who owned all the stone quarries and had been contracted to supply the foundations and underlay for the entire project. He was going to make a killing. Unfortunately for him, the persuasive representatives of whatever version of the IRA was then dominant arrived at the quarry head office one morning. They announced they were also going to make a killing unless the business was handed over to them forthwith. Clearly they were dissident Republicans as they did not turn up in chauffeur-driven government cars. One could be dominant as well as dissident, it seems. So the continued struggle of the volunteers and their splinter groups metamorphosed into the going concern of shattered stone supply and the British government paid by direct debit as the road was constructed. Only several years after the new road was opened was part of the truth revealed when the road started to sink in several places. Only a fraction of the required shattered stone had actually been delivered, but the stated price had already been paid in full directly into the accounts of the IRA. So much for secret funding of terrorism! For those in the know this was a public fact. State-sponsored terrorism had come to Northern Ireland.

However, there was one, albeit comparatively modest, upside. Noone apart from the quarry office staff had been allowed to know the details of the hostile takeover of the stone quarries.

These people were actively persuaded (and reminded several times that they should remain persuaded) not to tell anyone. So the true extent of family humiliation of Councillor Eugene Gerald Fitzmaurice remained hidden and only odd, somewhat garbled, versions of aspects of the story leaked out. Some reports were turned to the councillor's advantage. In particular, Councillor Finvola O'Duffy's fiancé took public credit as the man who, by sheer political skill, had negotiated the free transfer of the ownership of his family's quarries to a splinter company of volunteer workers – it was initially suggested that the new owners were a form of community co-operative or society. He was also the man who had somehow diddled the British government out of millions. What a statesman! What generosity! He himself, so the managed version of the story confirmed, had not made a penny directly out of the transaction or from the official government payouts. What self-sacrifice! What restraint! However, as a result of a fortunate but unforeseen side effect, Councillor Eugene Gerald Fitzmaurice knew that he was now able to recoup some money for the sacrifice involved in his attributed altruistic efforts. He had branched out into motor repairs and crane hire. He was making a fortune in axle repairs and removal of immobilised cars thanks to all the potholes on the new bypass. Chunk by large chunk, the hole in his family finances left by the loss of the quarry was being filled in.

So even if the full truth were to emerge eventually, Councillor Finvola O'Duffy's fiancé had clearly not lost all attraction and influence after all. Maybe he was worth marrying, if only for his persistently positive public image and improving private finances. But perhaps she would leave it a few more years yet just to see how he turned out.

CHAPTER 16

OUTFLANKED AND OUTDATED

Given the available cross-community communication channels it wasn't long before there was a major leak of the details of Councillor Finvola O'Duffy's proposed presentation of a miniature jewelled dog to the United States president.

One of Councillor Finvola O'Duffy's diamond and carpet cutters let the secret slip when he tucked into his regular portion of deep fried pizza and chips at the Iceberg Café. The news was immediately relayed to Donald Oskar Gormley in exchange for a skip-load of discarded volumes of out-of-date knowledge. For both Donald and Wee Joe it was a good deal. For Donald, a whisper of present-day gossip was worth a lorry-load of stale hard facts. For Wee Joe Forsale, in contrast, true knowledge never had a sell-by date.

Gossip can be the gift that keeps on giving. There was a second recipient of the first-hand rumour. The same message was next passed on by Wee Joe via the green mobile phone to Big David in exchange for a substantial discount on the next delivery of sliced boloney. For Big David, it was a high price to pay, but, with the local political stakes as high as they were, up-to-date intelligence was never too expensive. The tiniest piece of new information could provide insight, relief, delight and political salvation. It was indeed a crumb of comfort. But it had to be new. As regards political gossip and influence, if you were out of date, you could be out on your ear. So Big David kept his ear to the ground to avoid having to land on it.

Things had not being going well for Big David that morning on other fronts. In fact, it had been a consistent diet of bad news. Big David was presently on the black mobile phone receiving the report that Council environmental health officials had just raided the salami factory on a tip-off. They had ordered the suspension of the manufacture of traditional square sausage. Apparently there had been some inconsistency with the sell-by dates shown on the product. That summed up the basic problem with Northern Ireland, thought Big David. There was no consistency in anything here. In food manufacture the sell-by dates continually moved on and changed every day. In politics time stood still and policies were set in stone. This part of Western civilisation comprised a world of meaningless contradictions.

The environmental health official on the phone would not let matters drop. It seemed that someone had complained that the sell-by date on the side of a particular batch of square sausage was long past. Normally, if it had been a few days out, noone would have bothered. But in this case it was well over 100 years out of date. It was all very well for food to be made according to a recipe handed down from great-great-granny's third cousin, but it was unacceptable for this to have occurred with the ingredients of the actual product or even the very product itself.

When it came to the sausage meat the environmental health official knew he was on a roll. He didn't mince his words. He was so excited that the black mobile phone sounded like it was spitting consonants into Big David's ear. Clearly, the official was delighted he had caught Big David at last.

"I want you to sort this out fast. It's a matter of grave concern," were his final words as the phone went dead.

Little does he know how true that is, thought Big David.

Big David had long hidden the truth about the manufacture of square sausage. He had consistently played up its rumoured, but otherwise completely baseless, association with arcane Masonic ritual to divert public attention from the real facts (and to gain extra sales from hungry Lodge members). The truth was that the square sausages were given their regular shape by the use of granite tombstones irregularly borrowed from the churchyard and incorporated into a convenient homemade square sausage press. This was not a case of cutting corners but simply the use of corners already cut by a most skilful Victorian funereal stonemason. You could not get craftsmanship like that today. Furthermore, not any old tombstone would do the job. The original tombstones had been chosen most carefully because the family name of the deceased parties had to be "MacLean". This name, and the associated details of date and place of death, was then carefully partially grouted in by Big David's modern-day craftsmen to leave visible only the word "Lean". This single remaining word, Big David thought, would make a suitable raised projection on the processed meat in the granite sandwich although the true culinary effect was obscured somewhat by the word appearing back to front in mirror image on the surface of the meat product. Unfortunately for Big David, the truth forced its way out like the meat substitute in some overfilled hamburger. The grout obscuring the year of death "1881" cut into one particular grave stone had fallen out. This left the white fatty deposits in the meat product to make an unfortunate undesired and unexpected impression within the tiny stone indents. Against the nondescript brownish-grey background of the cooked meat slurry, the white date "1881" stuck out in a manner that was incapable of being missed even by the most casual inspector. It was this very date on the meat that had been discovered by the environmental health official. He condemned the entire batch of product.

The demise of traditional square sausage-making was staring Big David in the face. If he didn't get down to the salami factory fast the real truth would get out and the Council official would close the place down for good. However, it did not pay to act too fast. A little thought could buy him the time needed to cover up the facts.

The best way to keep the regulatory dogs off his tracks, thought Big David, was to throw them a bone. In other words, he would employ diversionary tactics by spreading a false story of more immediate interest to the authorities. However, the false story he was now wishing to leak to the Council would have to be substantially inflated before the Council officials would bite. That was no problem, as Big David was a master of generating hot air. William Henry was immediately summoned on the orange mobile phone and instructed to contact Donald Oskar Gormley. William Henry was to negotiate for the purchase of one of the contents of the box of long-discarded bicycle pumps held in the lost property shed in the Council yard. That black bicycle pump would then be planted in the Schwarzwald Konditorei. What was the leaked story to be? The German baker was cutting costs and icing his doughnuts with the use of a bicycle pump. As the environmental health officer's wife was one of the cake-consuming social workers, he would be spurred into rescuing her from substandard and potentially dangerous icing practices. A mountain would be made out of a molehill; an iceberg out of the icing. And the square sausage production would be saved.

That problem was solved at least for the moment. But it clearly was not a good day. No sooner had Big David put down the orange mobile phone than yet another phone started to ring. This time it was the special green mobile phone. The call came from Big David's secret source in the Republican community, known by the code name "Deep Throat". This name was no mere allusion to the top source in the Watergate scandal (although the Ballycarson "Deep Throat" also was close to the Republican leadership). The truth was more mundane. The Ballycarson "Deep Throat" was Wee Joe Forsale's wife. She simply swallowed all the whiskey and sausage meat Big David could send her way and, in exchange, proved particularly loquacious. So Big David had two independent sources within the same family on the other side of town. In fact, totally unknown to each other, the two members

157

of the Forsale household constituted a double-cross-community fount of information. Double the flow of facts: marvellous. Corroboration of the substance of rumours: even better.

Deep Throat's revelations confirmed her husband's earlier reports of the likelihood of a presidential visit to the west side of town. For the Loyalists and Unionists in the east the news was particularly dispiriting. It was rumoured that the American officials were hoping to hold a ceremony at the pig sty beside Sevriano O'Donnell's farm in the townland of Ballydrumbairn. The Council-employed historian and archivist was almost ready to declare that this was the site of the ancestral home of the present American president. It was just a matter of the relevant birth and death certificates coming to hand. The whole thing was Councillor Finvola O'Duffy's trump card. This sty would be one in the eye for the Loyalists and Unionists.

Big David rang off and considered this new west-side story. In fact, like most news in Ireland this genealogical information was not at all new, but it was depressing to hear it repeated from two such well-connected sources. It confirmed the rumour that had been going round ever since the election of the American president the previous year. The enterprising farmer in question (and, in the tradition of true genealogists, one must award him his full name – Joseph Mary Brendan Mulcachy Xavier Sevriano O'Donnell) had even opened up a visitors' book for his pig sty. With an undisputed, but as yet unproved, claim that he was the president's long-lost, closest living Irish relative, Joseph Mary Brendan Mulcachy Xavier Sevriano O'Donnell was already conducting guided tours for any visiting Americans (on a paid basis of course). He was cleaning up and, as long as he kept that sty looking filthy and ancient, he would continue to clean up.

Faced with this potentially disastrous news, what would Big David do? Resorting to type was a possibility. The public hurling of abuse and the insidious propagation of outrageous half truths were reputed to be endemic in Ulster politics at a local level. If Big

David was going to rescue the Loyalist position in Ballycarson, his first thought was that he would have to discredit this pigsty. For that purpose, mud, mud and more mud would have to be slung. In fact, shovel-loads of mud would have to be shovelled. And for Big David, a true worshipper in the temple of unadulterated mud, what could be better?

But, for once, a strange and more sophisticated thought crossed Big David's mind. Perhaps digging up the historical truth would be even more effective than the slinging and shovelling of mud. But in Ireland, the historical truth, for all its oft-stated unchanging nature, was sometimes more liquid than solid. It was a truly fluid substance distilled over centuries. In America, the president's visit would be heralded by the political pundits as a showpiece of ethnic solidarity aimed at the Irish-American vote. It would be portrayed as the reunion of the victims of natural disaster and political oppression separated by the cold waters of the North Atlantic and over a century and a half of struggle. The sons and daughters of destitute Irish men and women who had been forced to leave during the potato famine could once more embrace their countrymen whose ancestors had suffered equally from the same tragedy but who had faithfully remained in their native isle. But was it not also the truth that many of those Irishmen who had remained in Ireland after the famine were the very middlemen who had exploited their destitute compatriots before they emigrated? Was the present meeting of long-lost cousins not really a case of reconciliation rather than reunion? And were indeed the vast bulk of Americans now claiming to be Irish not really the descendants of a much earlier wave of emigration when Ulster Scots had fled political and religious persecution and ended up founding the United States? And perhaps most of these Scotch Irish had nothing at all to do with the Irish famine? And maybe most of the modern Irish-Americans were more closely related to Ulster Loyalists than to Irish Nationalists?

These deep thoughts were interrupted by yet another phone

159

call from Deep Throat. For another crate of spirits and a case of salami she would show Big David how to derail the Republican roadshow. The deal was done instantly and Deep Throat spilled the beans.

"All you have to do is find a closer relative of the president – a Loyalist. If you do that, the president will visit your side of town instead."

Big David leaned out of the front office window. "Get my official limousine! We're off to the L.H.O. hall," he yelled down to the dedicated duo comprising Bob the Blob and Bert the Squirt, who were standing at the front door to the L.H.O. hall and Big David's office.

To any outsider this instruction might have appeared strange. Big David's office was in the same building as the L.H.O. hall, so he simply could have gone down the stairs. Indeed it would have been quicker to do so even though the official car was parked beside the front door. However, in a land where immediate and shallow political impression was everything, Big David had to be seen leaving and arriving by limousine even if it meant coming back to the very point from which he started two minutes ago. It was a fundamental principle that he extended to his political negotiations because it was always safest to move in circles and end up where you were already. That way one never trod on uncertain ground, one never went off at tangents and one could never be accused of selling out to new ideas. These well-tested political traditions had to be maintained even if they constituted a road to nowhere.

The diligent doublet standing guard at Big David's door were a double act in function as well as appearance. Bob the Blob and Bert the Squirt were not only bouncers but also official drivers of Big David's official limousine. That conveyance was an ancient orange Volkswagen Golf. Driving the car was a joint effort because the car had a primitive and unique form of joint controls and could be driven only if at least two people were in it. This was nothing to do with Big David running a driving school on the side and everything to do with a defect in the car itself. Simply stated, the accelerator pedal no longer worked. But the car could still be driven as long as the front passenger pulled hard on a fan belt attached on a wire running under the dash to the remains of the original accelerator cable inside the bonnet. Clearly good timing and synchronisation were needed when a gear change was required. But Bob the Blob and Bert the Squirt worked as a team and were used to this. They clearly knew each other's minds. That was perhaps less an achievement than at first it might seem. Cynics stated they even shared their only single thought.

Big David jumped into the back of the car, the mutually complementary drivers took up their posts and they all headed off for a two-minute circular jaunt inevitably leading back to the very spot from which they came: the front door of the L.H.O. hall.

Big David made a quick phone call from the back of the car. The voice at the other end assured him that the genealogists in the L.H.O. hall had already prepared the historical papers on the local celebrity known as Mason Auchrim Carson (or "Mac" for short). This local celebrity was a man with tattoos of King Billy on his arms, legs and torso. Here was a man with an orange bath, an orange tea set and an orange fake suntan. More importantly, here was someone who could be proved by documentary evidence to be a relative of the American president and, in that regard, Mason Auchrim Carson was closer than anyone known to be living in Ballycarson.

This will stymie the latest Republican plot, thought Big David.

He was right. For the American president there were no votes to be gained from the Irish-American community if he were to be photographed shaking hands with an Ulster Loyalist, particularly if his shirt sleeves were rolled up so the tattoos of the seventeenth-century Dutch prince were in full display. For the leaders of the Irish-American community all Irish relatives were worth finding except those not made in their own image. Far from being made in their own image Mason Auchrim Carson, even if abbreviated to "Mac", was a product of the Irish-American community leaders' worst imagination.

For one single moment it felt like victory for Big David and then it didn't. Suddenly, Big David realised that if Mason Auchrim Carson were to be revealed to the world, the American president would not come at all. Ballycarson would be bypassed by the presidential cavalcade. That would destroy Big David's own aspirations to stand in the spotlight on the world stage. Yes, the playing of this particular Orange card would lead to mutual simultaneous destruction of the Republican and Loyalist causes. Loyalism would not live to see the demise of Republicanism. It was an earth-shattering moment. Whilst not exactly having found a common cause shared by both Republicans and Loyalists, Big David had realised he had found a common effect.

"Get moving! Stop the car!" yelled Big David. "And get back to the L.H.O. hall immediately!"

The car started up, moved forwards several yards and then made the ordained stop. Then, after some muffled swearing from the back seat, the car began to reverse at low speed requiring more fancy operation of the accelerator cable. Had progress of the Loyalist and Unionist political cause also gone into reverse? The answer to that question remained in the balance and depended on the outcome of some further genealogical investigation. True to form, the future of Ballycarson would be determined by what was thrown up by the past.

CHAPTER 17

PETRIFIED
POLITICAL VIEWS

Councillor Eugene O'Driscoll, the history teacher in the Ballycarson Christian Brothers' Academy, usually wore the agonised grimace of a man who suffered continuously from untreated irritable bowel syndrome. Rumour had it that his outward appearance had to do with the potato purification programme that he personally had initiated several years past. The councillor had been outraged when the local branch of the Irish Potato Producers Association had advertised a "tasty tuber" festival to highlight the nutritional benefits of potatoes in all their varieties, be they red, white or blue. Since then Councillor Eugene O'Driscoll had staged a one-man protest against such obvious political bias in the tuber cultivation business and had gone on a well-advertised nutrition strike. This involved him in a lunchtime diet of boiled green potatoes or, if he was feeling particularly adventurous, fried green potato skins. "It's what's on the outside that matters" was the campaign slogan indicating the relevant colour of the skin of the potato in question but wholly ignoring the problems caused for the councillor's insides. In addition to this dietary oddity, Councillor Eugene O'Driscoll's entire personality appeared to be projected through his short, narrow moustache. He was short in understanding and temper and narrow in his mindset. He groomed himself daily to retain the *status quo* in all respects.

Today his pupils were especially worried. His facial expression bore the vaguest resemblance of a thin smile. Clearly, this unaccustomed feature indicated that something was up. The slightest hint of pleasure – no, that was putting it too high; the word was probably "satisfaction" – had come about from a double success.

The first victory was evidenced by what Councillor Eugene O'Driscoll was carrying under his left arm. It was a miniature silver rubbish bin. To be more precise it was an empty miniature silver rubbish bin. The colour of the object and its inscription betrayed the fact that the thing was actually a trophy won by Ballycarson for the "Best in Class – Tidy Town Award". The presentation of the award had occurred the night before at a glittering ceremony in a top Belfast city centre hotel. Councillor Eugene O'Driscoll had been sent, with three assistants and several official guests, to uplift the spoils of success as it was his very idea that had led to the outstanding municipal triumph. The award had been for impressive improvement in the provision of tidy picnic sites. This had been a big turnaround from the litter-strewn picnic sites that had existed under the prior Unionist administration. Political change, it seems, does lead to the greater good. Immediately after the Nationalist victory in the local government elections the newly elected Council had sought to bring to the attention of tourists who might stray into their area the revered names of deceased Republican hunger strikers. The Council had been able to do this, on Councillor Eugene O'Driscoll's strong recommendation, by naming each of the existing municipal picnic sites after one of the calorie-controlled candidates. In further honour of the super-starved soldiers of destiny, the Council had passed a bye-law that the behaviour of those enjoying the facilities now or in the future should be modelled on that of the deceased diehards. So there was a general ban on eating or drinking within the picnic sites. The prohibition was advertised in large print on the roadside signs: "Picnic Site: No Eating or Drinking Allowed". The result was spectacular. No food. No rubbish. No litter. No overflowing bins. The overall upshot: tidy picnic sites for all to behold. A civic award was guaranteed. No wonder Councillor Eugene O'Driscoll was impressed with himself. If the troublesome tourists wanted to tuck in, they could drive on to the next county and take their rubbish home. "We want tourists to continue to tour and not to stop here."

The second triumph of the councillor's day had come about because of the pupils he had sent on the school science trip. This single adventure had proved the correctness of Councillor Eugene O'Driscoll's life-long-held political principles. The two top sixth year pupils had been sent on a hot air balloon trip. It had gone badly astray when the balloon pilot had become unconscious shortly after the balloon rose into the air. Prior to the take-off the pupils' parents had been rather anxious when this man appeared to speak with a variant of English that was gargled through whiskey. The nervous mums and dads were only slightly reassured by Councillor Eugene O'Driscoll who had attempted to allay their fears by indicating that this was a lesser-known dialect of Irish that obviously had avoided contamination by English. "A mellifluous language such as that should be allowed to flourish," were the history teacher's final words of comfort as the balloon rose into the air.

The hot air balloon had set off from the school hurling pitch half a mile to the west of Ballycarson. It was then driven south for several hours in the face of a brisk north wind. Very shortly after take-off it was clear to the pupil passengers that the balloon pilot had not just nodded off but was actually unconscious. From having watched far too many repeats of poor comedy films during their homework hour, they recalled that sleepers usually wake up when they have water poured on them, but, as he lay on the floor of the basket, this individual remained oblivious to the fact that he and the pupils were being completely soaked in a storm. Fortunately, one of the pupils had brought her mobile phone and sent pictures and an urgent distraught message back to her parents. Whilst the mobile phone battery lasted, a hastily organised air traffic control centre was assembled in the Iceberg Café. The frantic parents were able to find someone who could relay flying instructions to the pupils over the airwaves. The man in question was Frankie Alphabet, who was hastily awarded the role on the sole basis that he might have inherited some of his father's wartime flying skills. Frankie Alphabet was assisted by Wee Joe Forsale who read out mathematical detail from a series of technical manuals and an ancient and outdated volume of the *Encyclopaedia Britannica*. The ancient and illicit repositories of information had proved their worth at last in this marvellous example of cross-community crisis co-operation. Incomers to Ireland, or at least the immediate descendants of incomers, had proved their worth yet again. Between the two of them, Franklin and Wee Joe were able to talk the pupils down over the phone by passing on simple ditching instructions. After the balloon had drifted across several county borders it finally landed in a boggy field in County Leitrim in the Irish Republic.

The pupils, who had been sent up in the air without additional warm clothing, were freezing and soaked but safe. The *Provincial Observer* ran a headline that particularly enraged Councillor Eugene O'Driscoll:

"Pupils Blue with Cold"

"This is a disgraceful misrepresentation of the political affiliations of the academy pupils. My scholars are all dyed in the wool Nationalists. Each is green to his spleen," was the quoted response of Councillor Eugene O'Driscoll as he spilled his accustomed bile into the reporter's sound recorder.

But there was a very silver lining to this particular storm cloud. After he had fumed at the local press, it became clear that Councillor Eugene O'Driscoll was ecstatic or, at least as mildly self-satisfied as a man in his condition could be. The series of fuzzy and rain-obscured photographs taken by the frightened phone-bearing pupil as she passed over the county border between counties Tyrone and Cavan showed no red line on the ground where the Unionists alleged there was an international border. There could hardly be clearer demonstration that the Irish authorities had always been correct not to show such a false and fictitious dividing line on their officially produced maps. There could scarcely be a greater encouragement for Councillor Eugene O'Driscoll to continue to pull down any purported indication of a pretended international border. The councillor made a note to recommend these pupils for a school award for political science and geographic studies. Their parents would be pleased. He himself might even get an award for services to advanced methods of education. To be certain, however, he had best recommend himself.

Such uplifting thoughts encouraged Councillor Eugene O'Driscoll to believe that it had indeed been the culmination of a great, indeed historic, few days for education and civic society in the Northern Counties. He was more than content with his week's work. As well as securing his future in the Irish educational hall of fame, he had just exposed an attempt to set up a false religion in Ballycarson. It wasn't just the usual persistent Protestant heresy. His pupils had been well warned against such contagion. Instead it was far more dangerous. It was the seductive new-age message that had already led astray many Irishmen and women even in the Gaelic heart-lands of County Cork, County Westmeath and New York. Just as he had long predicted, the pestilence had arrived in Ballycarson.

A stall advertising "Psychic Readings" and "Clairvoyance" had been set up in the Sunday afternoon market at the bottom of the street that used to be known as Grafton Street in west Ballycarson. The middle-aged woman providing the services was of native Irish extraction and appeared friendly. Councillor Eugene O'Driscoll even knew two of her grandparents. He had taught her uncle. Upon the councillor's approach, the woman had enquired "How are you doing?" She even knew how to say the words in Irish. This transparent attempt at false affability did not fool the councillor and led to the woman's immediate public exposure as a fraud. "You would not need to ask that question if you really were a psychic," was the devastating response of the dedicated protector of local morals. The stall was shut down within an hour. The crisis had passed. *I bet she did not foresee that*, thought the councillor smugly as he headed off to detect and pursue other renegades.

Encouraged by his success, the councillor was on the trail of a prostitution racket run from the crane hire business at the top of Irish Street. The poster on the badly painted office door advertised "Wench for Hire". Disgusting, wasn't it. "No sex please, we're Irish," was the immediate and forceful demand of Councillor Eugene O'Driscoll as he hammered his fist on the front desk in the office of the crane hire business. The unfortunate receptionist was confused and made a quick phone call to her boss who was out on a building site supervising the lifting of iron girders. Five minutes later Councillor Eugene O'Driscoll discovered the illusory call girl ring was the product of a spelling mistake in the homemade poster painted by the receptionist. "Wench" should have been "Winch". Nevertheless, one cannot be too careful and the exercise in moral cleansing had been useful after all. Everyone, even receptionists in a crane hire business, needed to know what not to do even if they had no idea what they were presently not doing. And what was the outlook of the unfortunate receptionist who had suffered the moralistic harangue? "That comedian did not even recognise me as one of his former pupils!" was her complaint. "If he had spent less time on these idiotic political crusades and more time at the school, I might have learned to spell."

It would, however, be a gross underestimate of the consistent care and sustained solicitude of Councillor Eugene O'Driscoll to suggest for one moment that he had been neglecting academic matters. He was fully aware of the reading abilities of his students because he had been training them for months on how to read classic works of literature such as the electoral register and ballot papers. "These documents are the key to success in Ballycarson," he had repeated as he wrote the words up on the blackboard.

"Make sure your name is on this list for several different addresses. Practise making the letter 'X'. You will also need to know 1, 2, 3 in case they bring in proportional representation."

Again, it would be wrong to suggest that the level of education was low in Councillor Eugene O'Driscoll's class. Rather it was the case that the councillor had unilaterally re-focussed the application of traditional educational skills so that his pupils could make the best of the world for their local political leaders. The sixth form school project for the last few months had been tailored and crafted to assist Councillor Eugene O'Driscoll in a novel and far-reaching blend of politics, history, art, religion and theology. True to the traditional toilet humour of the sixth form, the bored students had condensed these subject names to their initial letters. To describe the endless reading of lists that consumed their day, they had coined the term "the PHART Project".

Councillor Eugene O'Driscoll's PHART Project was aimed at adapting the existing voting system in local government elections. The whole idea was to render it suitable to the many voters who were struggling to read and who never would be able to read because the completion of important educational projects meant that there was too little time in the school day to open a book. The notion was that the ballot papers would carry a well-recognisable symbol to identify politicians of the two traditions. Words would not be needed. Reading would become redundant for the sophisticated electorate in the local government wards of Ballycarson. Such an imaginative and forward-looking innovation in political education for voters of the next generation had not gone un-noticed in Brussels. Extensive European funding was made available to the councillor on condition that the ballot paper symbols chosen did not have Irish or Ulster origins. One might suppose the idea was that such foreign symbols would not thereby be seen to cause local offence or occasion any form of domestic bias. Driven by his legalistic outlook on life, Councillor Eugene O'Driscoll was meticulous in his compliance with the condition. True to requirements, the symbols chosen were both animals not found anywhere in Ireland (excepting always the Belfast and Dublin zoos). For the Nationalists and Republicans the animal selected was the mole. This velvet gentleman had been responsible for the death of King Billy in 1702 when his horse stumbled on a mole hill. For the Unionists and Loyalists, Councillor Eugene O'Driscoll chose the creature that St. Patrick had driven out of Ireland: the snake.

Now Councillor Eugene O'Driscoll was off to complain to Councillor Finvola O'Duffy about bias in broadcasting on the fourth of the local community channels. The problem was quite simple. There was not enough bias. The channel in question, the weather and history channel, had been set up to be completely uncontroversial and for that purpose had received even more European investment than usual. Hour after hour of broadcasting was filled with historic weather forecasts. Repeats of rain clouds, sunny intervals, snow storms, scattered showers, high pressure areas, cold fronts and depressions filled the airwaves and provided material for stimulating conversation amongst the Ballycarson apolitical elite. But this was not good enough for Councillor Eugene O'Driscoll. He wanted the broadcasts edited so that every time the twelfth of July was featured it would show rain falling on the parade. Sunshine had to be edited out when that date was featured. It may well have been the case that the sun shone on the righteous and the unrighteous, but it was important not to encourage the latter by giving the impression that they got equal treatment.

But when he arrived at her office Councillor Eugene O'Driscoll did not receive his usual friendly welcome from

Councillor Finvola O'Duffy. She was preoccupied by troubles of her own and received him with little more than a perfunctory exchange of pleasantries. Hardly had he begun to outline the latest list of dangers threatening good morals and civilisation itself in Ballycarson when she dismissed him with the line "Get out and go back to Ballygobackwards!" Accustomed as he was to reverential silence from his pupils, who drank deep on his words of wisdom, Councillor Eugene O'Driscoll was so surprised that words failed him as he sought without success for a devastating response. Dumbfounded, he turned on his heels and headed off back to the academy. What on earth had caused such unwarranted rudeness? Clearly, it was more than his philosophy could comprehend. It must have been something to do with the real world.

There was trouble at the O'Duffy carpet and linoleum factory. The members of the workforce were resisting the attempt to extend their shifts without extra pay. For some reason the usual incentives and managerial exhortations had not yet succeeded. Only yesterday, by means of carefully worded tannoy announcement, it had clearly been explained to the workers that the new twelve-hour shifts would be imposed in eternal memory of the twelve dead hunger strikers. With such a significant number forming the proposed new structure of their working day, the workforce should feel more than honoured to be selected to renew their patriotic zeal in a commercial context. However, far from fostering fanatical fervour in fabrication, the announcement had precipitated unambiguous demonstrations of discontent. The workers had even demanded a lunch break in defiance of the exhortation to honour the hungry heroes by emulation of their efforts. If that was not bad enough, someone had gone so far as to sabotage the entire supplies of green dye necessary for the presidential carpet of honour. No substitute was available. This was serious given the imminence of the American presidential visit. The carpet, carefully woven from the hairs of German shepherd and Alsatian dogs, presently lay in an un-dyed and natural state. It

171

could not have been worse. The colour of the dog hair was black and tan. For Councillor Finvola O'Duffy the political implications were obvious and stark. Domestic and international humiliation stared her in the face.

To keep the workforce producing carpets for extended hours, Councillor Finvola O'Duffy had to play her trump card. She would impose a new time for the work shifts to finish in the evening: 1916 hours. No self-respecting Irish Nationalist or Republican could refuse to comply given the obvious allusion to the revered, if unsuccessful, revolt against the British. Additional time would have to be worked to honour the martyrs of that sacred Easter rising. Yes, it was a very clever strategy, especially since she had taken steps to ensure all her employees held suitable political sentiments or, at the very least, lived under her protection in west Ballycarson. It was certain to work. Her appointed shop stewards would ensure sufficient revolutionary fervour. Noone would be silly enough to prove un-enthusiastic in public. As an employer, Councillor Finvola O'Duffy would immediately gain an extra free sixteen minutes' work per day from every worker. A similar device could be used again. It was fortunate there were so many important Irish dates in the twentieth century. Over time, she could extend the work shift incrementally to 1922 (the founding of the Free State), onward to 1948 (the leaving of the Commonwealth) and even all the way to 1957 (the Fethard-on-Sea boycott). One could only hope there would be further auspicious dates in the early twenty-first century so she could ratchet up the working time commensurately. And, into the bargain, it was an approach her rival Big David could not use to his advantage at the Ballycarson salami factory in the east of the town. The key date in the Loyalist calendar could not be similarly employed. There was no such time on the clock as 1690.

With the immediate crisis passed, Councillor Finvola O'Duffy could now turn her attention to the organisation of the public event to celebrate the thirtieth anniversary of her engagement.

Something traditional would be best – a traditional procession along a traditional route with traditional music and traditional dress. She plumped for an evening street march by her supporters up Irish Street, through the town and out to the graveyard. In all of this she would be accompanied by flaming torches and a strutting bodyguard. This particular tradition had been handed down to her from her childhood hero – actually her distant cousin – Eoin O'Duffy. She could remember the days when her grandfather told her fireside tales of their much admired relative and his pre-Emergency street rallies with the legendary blue-shirted warriors and the uplifting speeches accompanied by the mesmerising chants of "Hail O'Duffy! Hail O'Duffy! Hail O'Duffy!" The torch had now been handed on to her. Those fond and flame-lit days and nights would come once again to west Ballycarson. But first of all, Councillor Finvola O'Duffy had to ensure that there was indeed something to celebrate. She had to look her best as she was the focus of the celebration. When she lifted her right hand to salute the crowd she wanted them to see the light of the flames reflected from the new engagement ring.

Inspired by the hindsight of reviewing her ancestor's political achievements, Councillor Finvola O'Duffy was never short of foresight. Indeed only last week she had been preparing for this very moment. She had ordered a new engagement ring because the original thirty-year-old ring had worn out. Diamonds were not forever; true love, it seems, does take its toll. The replacement ring was now being crafted at public expense by the released and cost-effective volunteers manning the jewellery side of her business. Tradition had to be maintained. Just as with the treasured original, she herself had chosen the replacement ring. She had chosen it alone. What had it got to do with anyone else? Just as with the acquiring of the original ring there had been no need to involve her fiancé except to invoice his sand and gravel business for the price. The second diamond was certainly the most expensive rock her fortunate fiancé had ever purchased. That said, Councillor Finvola

O'Duffy consoled herself on the basis that he would be able to recover the amount spent as a tax-deductable expense provided he hid it under his quarry accounts under the term "supply of stone". An eagle-eyed tax inspector might consider it odd that stone was being supplied to a quarry instead of by it, but that was a small risk that probably would not materialise. In any event, to have her fiancé attend the jeweller's for the choosing of a new ring would only have taken his mind off those essential, continuous political campaigns. And, as Councillor Finvola O'Duffy recalled to her great satisfaction, she owned the jeweller's anyway. Business and political priorities had to be maintained. It was just a paper exercise after all.

A diamond suitable for the renewal of such a dynastic engagement does not come along every day. This acquisition of renewed sparkle had required considerable preparation. Councillor Finvola O'Duffy had had to bide her time until she had assembled a suitable quantity of canine ash to make an especially large doggy diamond. The final product had come from a mixture of the ashes of Great Danes and Scottie terriers. The employees who attended to the manufacture proudly called the resultant mixture a "Grottie".

"It is a pity these mutts don't have gold fillings. We could have extracted that to made the ring shank also," Finvola thought as she watched one of her employees set the new diamond in the new ring.

"But I suppose that if the dogs had metal like that in their teeth that would short circuit the Zapper," responded the employee much to Finvola's surprise.

It was only then Councillor Finvola O'Duffy realised she had been talking aloud. How many more of her secrets had she been revealing to the world? Perhaps, without even realising it, she herself was the long-suspected leak of inside information to Big David. "When it comes to political security you can trust noone – not even yourself," she concluded thoughtfully. The employee nodded in agreement, flattered that Councillor Finvola O'Duffy had once more taken him into her confidence.

Councillor Finvola O'Duffy's engagement plans had indeed leaked out some weeks before. For all of that time reliable sources had spread the story of Finvola's plans to renew her sparkle by having former political prisoners create a new diamond. But the reaction from the Loyalists in general and Big David in particular was not what one might have expected. Unknown to Councillor Finvola O'Duffy but to almost everyone else's knowledge and surprise, the whole crew, including Big David, were being most gallant. To celebrate the symbol of Finvola's renewal of marital promise, Big David had secretly instructed Eva Brunette to teach the Ballycarson Young Defenders Flute Band a new tune as a musical appreciation of his long-standing political adversary and her new ring. In addition, new band uniforms of a particularly surprising design had been covertly designed by Eva Brunette in an attempt to update the image of the band. Big David had first exploded with rage when he discovered the unsanctioned proposal, but, on re-consideration of the potential to hijack preparations for Councillor Finvola O'Duffy's intended celebration, he realised an opportunity had arisen to turn the new design to his own advantage. He readily ate his previous words of wrath to Eva Brunette and sanctioned a famous rock and roll outfit as a way forwards for traditional Loyalism.

When all was ready, in their new white sparkling Elvis Presley "Las Vegas" outfits, the band assembled outside the jeweller's shop where, at that very moment, Finvola was examining the large stone fabricated by the ex-prisoners. And what was the tune they played to celebrate the ex-prisoners' renewal of the diamond for the engagement ring? It was none other than "Jailhouse Rock".

CHAPTER 18

WORKFORCE WORRIES

Despite being the butt of a very public Loyalist musical joke, Councillor Finvola O'Duffy had not lost any of her long-standing confidence in her own special abilities. Nor was she deflected from the course of self-appointed leadership, wisdom and truth that she knew was hers by virtue of birth-right, bank balance and natural ability. She knew that all she needed to do was to look into her heart if she wanted to know what her Nationalist constituents wanted. That was an easy thing to do as she had such a big heart.

"So much for Détente!" yelled Councillor Finvola O'Duffy as she stomped down the shop floor of the O'Duffy carpet and linoleum factory. Her closest security aides scurried behind her in an attempt to keep up with this woman of boundless energy. The Loyalist musical appreciation of her renewed engagement had rankled, at least after the joke had been explained to her by reference to a book listing Elvis Presley's back catalogue of hits and a dictionary of English slang.

"Clearly Big David is getting information because things around here have become too lax. How did he know I would be at the jeweller's shop at exactly that time? How did he find out about the new diamond? Did I inadvertently tell him myself?"

It was clearly a major worry. If the Americans heard about the nature of the workforce or the source of the carbon, it was just possible that the president would refuse to accept the miniature silver replica of the Irish wolfhound with its eyes set with locally produced diamonds. How was this information leaking out? Surely she herself could not be the source of the leak? But even if she was, someone else had to be passing the information on as she herself had not spoken directly to Big David since she had made the decision about making the new ring. With no answers immediately forthcoming, Councillor Finvola O'Duffy resorted to type and ordered an immediate crackdown on leaks.

Have you ever tried to stop a leak by cracking a whip? Not even in rural Ireland, where one can still find the traditional skills of plumbing and good horsemanship, can such a phenomenon be achieved. Was Councillor Finvola O'Duffy cracking up rather than cracking down? Nothing so dramatic than that. The reaction was really nothing new. The long-term outcome of the increased level of security was preordained, but the O'Duffy security aides knew they had to go through the motions if they were to keep their jobs and their perks. Well, upon reflection, there were not that many perks really, but the jobs were worth retaining given that there was nothing else readily available in the immediate locality. The wheels of the O'Duffy security machine were set in motion. The seasoned carpet factory employees looked on with a degree of resignation. They knew from experience that the big flap would last only a few days, maybe even a few hours, and then all would be back to normal.

It did not take long for the new security arrangements to have noticeable public effects. That same morning at the Ballycarson salami factory Big David observed that many of his German workers had arrived very late for the early shift. When Germans don't arrive on time, even in Ireland, clearly something is seriously wrong. Why had he not got word of this possibility in advance? Immediate investigation was required and a note was dispatched to the all-seeing overseers at the Spion Kop bus stop.

From their position of prominence at the Spion Kop bus stop the community supervisors could see extra activity at Checkpoint

Charlie. But for several hours they had not been alive to what was really going on. Councillor Finvola O'Duffy had managed to divert their attention by a double, tactical master-stroke. It was a case of diversion accompanied by disguise.

The diversion came in the form of very obvious on-goings in the tiny and overcrowded chapel graveyard. The activity comprised an out-of-doors practice performance of a new musical written, so everyone assumed, in honour of the soon-to-arrive American president. As they gazed at the sentimental story being played out by a troupe of actors, the art critics in the Spion Kop bus stop were drawn in to the tear-jerking theatre amid the tombstones. A vaguely familiar tune could be heard above the normal noise of the town as it drifted up and over to the Spion Kop bus stop. Recorded music was being relayed to all and sundry by two enormous stacks of black speakers, each the size of a tombstone, and it was obvious the ill-prepared actors were largely just mouthing their parts. The performance was so bad it was impossible to ignore. This was just what the impresario Councillor Finvola O'Duffy had intended all along. The play's storyline itself was not up to much and followed the traditional mould. There was a series of sentimental, tear-jerking songs performed by a singing nun with a very poor south German or Bavarian accent. Then a family of Austrian extraction, called "Von Klapp Trapp", were forced to flee a housing estate in Ballycarson after suffering discrimination at the hands of a repressive right-wing Unionist administration. The action became a little confusing after that, but it appeared the entire family was trying to scale a part of the boundary wall that had been disguised as a series of Irish hills.

"This looks like the same old political soft soap," quipped one of the critics in the Spion Kop bus stop.

"You'd think they would come up with something new. They used that same nun last week when they put on the first of the series of *Father O'Hagan Re-Investigates Cold Cases*," responded the other.

"Yes, this is the same graveyard where the nun found the corpse last week," said the third critic. "This is just a repeat. It's no better than the television." That was the damning conclusion of the written report penned by the leading critic and sent for filing at the L.H.O. hall via a sealed kettle and a doggy delivery.

Whilst the performing arts obviously failed to flourish in the graveyard, the tactic of disguise was applied to the activity slowly building up at Checkpoint Charlie. In contrast to the usual quota, there appeared to be a larger number of official attendants at the crossing point all acting as border guards. In addition, the seasoned Spion Kop bus stop observers eventually could not fail to see that the augmented number of crossing point attendants were all sporting a new uniform. Some semi-official ceremony was going on. It was clear that Councillor Finvola O'Duffy's cousin, councillor and vice-chairperson, Councillor Seoras O'Duffy, was pursuing his familiar theme yet again. There he was at the checkpoint announcing from a megaphone that the old crossing point uniforms had been discarded on the basis that they were a remnant of the Royal Ulster Constabulary. Even though the old uniforms had long since been shorn of any royal insignia, the very cloth itself had now to be discarded as the threads themselves were steeped in a history of partiality. Instead of these ruined rags of ill-repute, the Nationalist-led Council had now acquired, at a modest discount, the uniforms, helmets, belts and boots of the former East German border guards. The professionalism of that sadly disbanded but efficient force would rub off on the new Irish wearers. The newly attired crossing point attendants lined up for admiration by the tiny assembled crowd of bemused onlookers. A number of Council photographers had arrived and, at the invitation of Councillor Seoras O'Duffy, took plenty of official snaps, presumably to record the event for posterity and to fill the walls of another corridor in the newly expanded Council offices. To the experienced onlookers in the Spion Kop bus stop it appeared a tedious repetition of innumerable similar ceremonies that had taken place since the fall of the Unionist-led administration in Ballycarson. The traffic wardens had received similar uniforms and an identical oration just last week. The month before it had been the attendants at the public toilets. In contrast to the tiresome tirade of Councillor Seoras O'Duffy, the graveyard theatrics retained a certain charm, if only marginally. It was little wonder that the attention of the spies at the Spion Kop bus stop drifted back to the tombstone thespians. It was all as Councillor Finvola O'Duffy had planned.

The information-collecting crones at the Spion Kop bus stop failed to see the queues of traffic that had built up at Checkpoint Charlie as the photographers continued to ensure the place in history of the newly attired border guards. The Spion Kop spies did not notice the vehicles and pedestrians backed up on the west side of the wall as the crossing gate remained shut and the lights controlling the flow of traffic remained on red. Until it was too late, they failed to observe how the photographers moved seamlessly into unison with the border guards and proceeded to establish a regime of additional body searches, photographing and form-filling as the gate was finally opened. The backlog of German workers wishing to cross to the east built up steadily. Those who possessed special skills for working in the salami factory were informed that they did not possess the newly printed green card required to permit their crossing. They would have to come back tomorrow with copies of all of their German grandparents' birth certificates. It was no excuse that these had been lost in 1943 during the destruction of Hamburg. Some official from the Russian embassy in Dublin would have to confirm officially that Königsberg in East Prussia was now Kaliningrad in Russia. In addition, each and every one of the Germans wishing to cross at the checkpoint would need to provide written assurances, with suitable translations, that none of their family were intending to overthrow the newly elected Nationalist Ballycarson Council and that none of them had worked at the German embassy in Dublin during the 1939–45 Emergency. No, it did not help that their great-uncle had worked there as the ambassador and knew Mr. de Valera personally.

For all that it was traditional, even reactionary in outlook, the O'Duffy security machine had been innovative as regards these border checks. For a single, well-chosen morning, the new border guards had caught Big David off-guard. With a log-jam of his German workers at the Peace Wall, the salami factory was immediately under-staffed. By lunchtime, the amateur agricultural inspectors in the Spion Kop bus stop could see that lorry-loads of live pigs were being turned away from the abattoir and forced to park up at the L.H.O. hall. Both the pigs and the factory managers were beginning to squeal. A dark, strong-smelling liquid was beginning to seep down the side of the pig lorries and on to the tar. It was potentially the basking shark debacle in re-run, but this time it was at Big David's front door. And Big David was nowhere to be seen. The old crones in the Spion Kop bus stop had not received any instructions for hours. However, they took modest reassurance from the fact they were not being picked out for special treatment.

Despite the increasing urgency of their telephone calls to the L.H.O. hall, the alarmed management at the salami factory could find out nothing. There was no answer except for the usual tape-recorded message:

"The office is closed. Staff are being given their marching orders during the marching season."

Worried that this meant imminent redundancy on a massive scale, the salami factory bosses resorted to sending Frankie Alphabet on his disability scooter up to the L.H.O. hall. Surely a man of such stature and mobility could resolve the informational impasse and find out something. But all he discovered was that the front door security guards, Bob the Blob and Bert the Squirt, were guarding a hall that was locked up. That was unusual. The place was normally open twenty-four hours a day. In addition, the two guards looked slightly different. Their orange shirts, ties and sundry equipment had been augmented by orange handkerchiefs placed, cowboy-style, across their faces in an attempt by the wearers to cut down the smell emanating from the liquid-leaking lorries. This semi-successful stench-stifling sartorial signal was the only initiative they had shown for years. But despite the assault on their sense of smell, these guardians of democracy had shown true grit and had stuck to their posts to complete what they had been told was an important task. To any enquirers they were to hand out a single side of photocopied words of propaganda dictated by Big David earlier in the day and printed in small type on orange notepaper. The pompous prose of political prediction pontificated prodigiously. Digestion of too much of this sort of stuff would make anyone feel they had eaten too much chocolate, probably of the chocolate orange variety, but a small snippet is bearable and is sufficient to indicate the flavour, historical mis-reference and general lack of logic:

"This Nationalist disruption is no more than an irritant at the fringe of Loyalist Ballycarson. It may be a minor and temporary tactical gain for Councillor Finvola O'Duffy, but it will soon end up in a major strategic loss for pan-Nationalism. It will just be like the Suez crisis. In due course of the day, the Councillor Finvola O'Duffy will receive a phone call from the American embassy. She will be apprised of the Americans' displeasure at this potential disruption to the president's visit. She will be informed that the great Republican transatlantic alliance will be broken off if she does not cease this interference with a strategic transport route. Then Councillor Finvola O'Duffy will be forced to climb down publicly. Loyalists will emerge triumphant from these present difficulties."

And on it went for several more repetitive and largely uninspiring paragraphs. *This is not the material to encourage troops to storm a beach on D-Day*, thought Frankie Alphabet. He was no fool. Even though at that very moment he was fortunately up-wind of the numerous pig lorries parked at the side of the road, he could still smell that something was not quite right. He knew only too well that this sort of verbal smoke screen was published simply to make sure the newspapers had something to print. Better still, if they printed it all, there would be no room to publish anything else. Further to that, the readers would struggle with the first paragraph and then give up. This form of media manipulation turned the logic of sound-bite politics on its head. What you had here was an entire meal of re-heated indigestible verbiage with seconds to follow. Franklin Delano Roosevelt Messerschmitt strongly suspected that Big David was elsewhere engaged on sensitive business that he did not want made public. He was right.

Big David had known all along that he would receive no assistance in the form of American intervention. Indeed, his sources had privately confirmed exactly the opposite of what he had publicly predicted in print. A message from the Spion Kop bus stop spoke of two well-dressed strangers at Checkpoint Charlie not long after the queues had formed. The two individuals were clearly American as they walked right up to the front of the queue and immediately engaged in some sort of exchange of views with the border guards. Other secret sources confirmed that these officials were part of the presidential advance party. But, much to Big David's disappointment, the transatlantic dialogue at Checkpoint Charlie had been friendly. The Americans had indicated satisfaction that additional security was being put in place for the imminent presidential visit. "Keep up the good work," were their last words as they were driven away. Clearly, there would be no breach in the transatlantic Republican alliance contrary to the predictions in Big David's published statement.

Big David realised he had to trade something to unblock the

flow of his supply of workers. He had to deliver to Councillor Finvola O'Duffy something she badly needed. Fortunately, he had the very thing. But, in Unionist and Loyalist eyes, it was an item so potentially disgraceful that he could not ever be seen to have possession of such an article. To avoid being cast out of Loyalist society forever, Big David had to complete the trade in the utmost secrecy and preferably through a third party. Better still, if the deal was completed by a third party who was already dead. And, when the trade was done, and when the tension at Checkpoint Charlie had then subsided, Big David could then claim his published statement about Suez revisited was right all along. Those words might have been turgid, but they were going to be proved true all along. They would be regarded as a prophesy. The great political profiteer, Councillor Finvola O'Duffy, would never wish to reveal the true facts either and she would allow him that small semblance of a public victory. However, for the future to play out appropriately, the whole thing had to be properly stage-managed.

So, alone in his office, Big David had spent part of the morning on the phone to Councillor Finvola O'Duffy. There was not the slightest hint of animosity or anger. There were no outbursts of rage. It was purely business. Both greeted each other cheerfully as old friends and then proceeded to choreograph the entire delicate event.

CHAPTER 19

A LAND WITH NO VISION

Eager to impress the security experts in the presidential advance team, the Nationalist-run Ballycarson Council for some time had been engaged in completing a variety of important precautions. In the few weeks prior to the anticipated visit the pace of precautionary activity had been frenetic. Chief amongst the new works was the extension of the Peace Wall into the new Ballycarson municipal cemetery. But it wasn't all highfaluting considerations of foreign policy and grand strategy that had caused movement on this front. With her ear pinned firmly to the ground, Councillor Finvola O'Duffy had long realised that her moderate political thinking and traditionally rigid views could always be outflanked by sentiments even more extreme than those holding the valleys and swamps of the moral low ground of Ulster politics. Months before the president's visit had even been suggested, she had heard the beginnings of the whispers to the effect that she had lost territory here. When it came to political bigotry, the excitement always appeared in the fast lane. And where was the fast lane in Ballycarson? It was in the public graveyard that she was most vulnerable to such a flanking move. What was better to protect your flank than the building of a graveyard wall?

So, as convenor of the Construction, Deconstruction and Reconstruction Committee of Ballycarson Council she ordered the extension of the wall into the graveyard. The route would split the fifteen-acre site roughly into two halves: east and west. But even those most unfamiliar with construction operations would have realised that this new segment of the security structure bore little resemblance to the part of the wall already built. Consistency lay in the fact that it was, from a vertical point of view, fifteen foot in extent just like the remainder of the wall elsewhere in town. But, in the graveyard, all of the new structure was dug into and sited below the ground. To be absolutely accurate, it was fifteen foot deep and not fifteen foot high. On the surface of the ground the visitors to the graveyard could walk on the six-foot-wide top of the Peace Wall extension as if it were a ridge of sub-sea mountains that just breached the surface of the water. It would be, thought Councillor Finvola O'Duffy, a suitable testament to her stature and political achievements: "a Political Giant's Causeway."

A striking consonance of political pressures and commercial concerns had demanded such architectural novelty. On the stage of world politics, Councillor Finvola O'Duffy could assure the Americans that Ballycarson Council was protecting the commander in chief from underground attack. Not even the CIA had thought of that. There was a local spin off too. As convenor of the Income Generation and Franchise Committee, Councillor Finvola O'Duffy had realised the potential flow of revenue from the graveyard would be accomplished only if she could get the public to sign up to burial in that area. God's acre could then become the golden acre or the gold mine. This was all the more important now that the O'Duffy carpet and linoleum factory had secured the exclusive funeral and interment franchise for the west side of the graveyard. Timeous and convenient political justification for the underground wall-building policy came from Bishop Eugene Miguel O'Hagan in his weekly broadcast to the faithful. He confirmed the western side of the graveyard would be suitable for Nationalist burials provided (and it was a major proviso that bore frequent repetition) it was permanently sealed off from the eastern part where the unfaithful others could be interred. In a densely reasoned explanation of traditional ecumenical policy he confirmed that the lesson for the day was "Balanced Burial to

Comfort One's Loss": there would be a balance brought to the graveyard by permanent division. There could be no integrated interment. The separation wall had to be underground to prevent potential post-mortem complications. Heathens and heretics had to be sealed out and limited to the east otherwise there was a risk of cross-contamination. Perhaps Bishop Eugene Miguel O'Hagan wished to hide a secret personal departure from the official religious dogma of his Church and perhaps he did believe in transmigration of the soul after all. Maybe he thought the dead were itinerants that would wander in the afterlife and visit the other side. But here was the rub. Councillor Finvola O'Duffy knew the whole official religious justification was watered-down nonsense. Given the height of the water table, everyone was going to be buried above ground level anyway, so the mortal remains would forever lie above the level of the wall. Nevertheless, whatever unease she might feel at the unhindered sideways movement of those laid to rest, she consoled herself with the thought that the flow of income would begin. "Balanced Burial to Comfort One's Loss"! What baloney! She could find greater comfort from healthy profits and balanced accounts. There was no loss in that.

How did this unusual opportunity for gain originally come about? Yet again, Councillor Finvola O'Duffy felt that her actions were justified in that she had not manufactured the situation. It had been laid on for her by centuries of history and the topography itself. So, why should one have a conscience when accepting what nature itself presents? Why feel bad about exploiting nature's bounty and history's inheritance? Ballycarson was a strategically placed market town. In the mediaeval era it was protected from attack from the south by swampy ground. No army could march across the mire and bog meadow. But, as centuries passed, technology changed and the swamp, in the eyes of the construction cognoscenti, became important as a potential development opportunity. Advised as they were by the holders of such secret commercial insights, it was into this Ballycarson swamp that the Northern Ireland Office plunged. In the stagnant political days of the last Unionist-run Council administration, fifteen acres of the swampy ground was compulsorily purchased by the central government. Their intent? To facilitate the construction of a state-of-the-art production plant for lightweight, fast speed, gull-winged amphibious tractors.

They say that the characters of nations and towns are shaped by their landscape. This sentiment certainly seemed to hold good for this ambitious business venture. The firm went into liquidation just as, in the view of the shadow supervisors of the design team in Spion Kop bus stop, the lightweight, fast-speed, amphibious tractors would have done if any of the doors had been opened during their operation. In fact, not a single lightweight, fast-speed, gull-winged, amphibious tractor was built. Nor had a single wing of the factory been constructed. It was so lightweight it had never appeared. The construction materials were so fast and speedy that they had disappeared off to other sites within minutes of their delivery to the proposed tractor fabrication site. Indeed, by the time the gates came to be finally shut on the tractor factory compound, no such gates had ever been erected. No single member of the workforce had ever been recruited. All there was to be seen on the ground was a series of small internal roads built up on ramparts to keep the road surface clear of the adjacent and subjacent watery mire. But the plans for future development were magnificent and a few signs had been put up describing parts of the future production plant and announcing that the venture was generously sponsored by the Northern Ireland Office. Because of the absence of sure foundation, all of these signs had been gradually swallowed by the underlying marsh except for the enormous location sign for the "Body Shop".

Progress on site is not everything. Off-site there had been some activity – the initial government grant of several millions of pounds had been paid over and over spent. Only after the completion of such strenuous spending efforts did the firm receiving it became insolvent and the project abandoned. All that was left was the embarrassing undeveloped fifteen-acre site and the single remaining "Body Shop" sign. The Northern Ireland Office could not get the site of this financial debacle off their hands quickly enough. To mark the election of the new Nationalist-run administration, it was donated to the Ballycarson Council as the site of the new municipal cemetery. Perhaps the "Body Shop" sign would take on new life.

Apart from the layout of the internal roads, the swampy site was not well suited for a graveyard. The sale of plots was slower than slow to say the least. Noone wanted to be buried in waterlogged ground. In Ballycarson, one undertaker explained, coffins are not built with keels. In fact, after two years of hard sell by the Council's department of recreation and interment, only one person had bought a plot to the memory of himself and his wife. As with everything else he had acquired in life, this particular individual believed he had spotted a bargain. But in this instance it was a case of buy cheap, buy dear. The buyer of the grave plot found he had to divert lorry-loads of Council-purchased stone to build up the ground and erect a mausoleum in the style of old New Orleans to provide his wife and himself with a place of peaceful last repose. There, immediately beside the site of the "Body Shop" sign, stood the modest mausoleum. It was a solitary modern folly, in effect the show house for the new cemetery, built by a dead man to himself and his wife.

The dead man in question was Donald Oskar Gormley. He had consistently cocked a snook at the sophisticated and highfaluting forms of sectarian division in his community by keeping his feet on the ground. When it came to footwear, it was rumoured that he deliberately wore a green sock on his right foot and an orange sock on his left on the basis that if he got knocked down by a Ballycarson bus the local authorities would not know where he was to be buried or who was to carry out the formalities of interment. In truth, he simply wished to be regarded as an individual free to make his own choices even in death. He did not know, however, that this trick had been tried before by a few brave souls. Such individuals were regarded as colour blind and their religion determined by the paramedics tossing a coin in the ambulance and replacing the footwear on the patient by one of the green and orange spare sets of socks kept in the ambulance especially for the purpose of designation of the potentially deceased.

Ever since he had built the mausoleum to himself and his wife, Donald Oskar Gormley was known locally as a "dead man walking". It was not just because of the threats he might have received because of his reputed ill-matched hosiery. Furthermore, he did not fit the usual category of such condemned individuals. He was not one of those who had been sentenced to death by some paramilitary organisation because of a foolhardy attempt to muscle in on their lucrative rackets of protection, drugs, prostitution or smuggling in or around Ballycarson. Consonant with his relatively sensible attitude to continued life, Donald Oskar Gormley had always been meticulous in engaging in low-key rackets without lethal competition. But quite apart from his life's choices, he had simply been lucky. Who else could see a profit in second-hand washing machines or bicycle pumps? They were hardly the currency favoured by the high-rollers of the paramilitary establishment. So if the paramilitaries and local hoods had not caused his untimely demise, who had done it? For Donald Oskar Gormley, it was much more straightforward and closer to home. It was his wife who had prepaid the ferryman and condemned him to a premature pre-planned crossing of the River Styx.

Rarely, if ever, had this particular matrimonial relationship been harmonious, despite Donald's best endeavours. Ever since the day he had found out that he was married, he had been meticulous, so he thought, in attempting to foresee his wife's every concern and was sensitive to her needs. Indeed, every time he had gone off to the town dump for a rummage, he had asked her if she wanted anything brought back. Women, he thought, love that sort of tender solicitation. In exchange for such enquiries all he received was a constant ear bashing. What sort of woman was she anyway? Over time he found himself moved out of the matrimonial home and into the garden shed. His wife was heard to joke to her friends that she had shedded her husband. The ambiguity was not lost on Donald Oskar Gormley. The shed became a tiny cell, albeit a cell located in an open-door jail as the lock on the outside had never been fixed after someone wrecked it when trying to steal the mower. As regards matrimonial visits to the incarcerated, there were none. Contact was kept at a minimum. Donald's wife knew he was still alive because the daily helpings of food she left at the door continued to disappear and she collected the empty plates. But, even with such a distance between the parties, the rows continued, although at a slight remove, as they scribbled the occasional angry note to each other. The broken-down relationship broke down a little more. The preparation of meals to be left at the shed door became intermittent and what arrived was merely dumped, by means of a shovel, in a small trough left at the door. Donald eventually perceived he was not wanted and sought solace in drink. As he found he could speak his mind, indeed open his very soul, to the bottle of whiskey and it never answered back, the binges very soon got longer. As he continued his monologue with an audience consisting only of alcohol, he disappeared for days, weeks and months at a time. His wife, however, was not completely thoughtless. On the very last day Donald had been seen at the matrimonial home, his wife sent him on his way with a flexible hip flask. "Take this with you and don't come back," she shouted as she threw him a purple rubber hot water bottle filled with a liqueur of uncertain provenance. Unscrewing the cork, Donald noticed the liquid had already taken on the purple hue of its container. "Just like a good whiskey and the famous sherry barrels," mused Donald. But there was a haunting afterthought.

"Maybe this liquid has not been in this container for ten years. Maybe it is just methylated spirits." Who cares? It was drinkable and no worse than much he had swallowed of late. Donald tucked the bottle into his belt and headed off down the road. It was the last time his wife saw him alive. That was indeed what she had always planned.

After one visit to the land of reassuring oblivion, which had lasted an uncertain but clearly very extensive period of time, Donald came to beside the silted-up Union Canal and felt hungry. The feeling in his stomach told him he had not eaten for several days, perhaps the best part of a week. When he searched for food in the nearest public rubbish bin, he found it to be a source of information and enlightenment as well as nourishment. All the facilities of modern life were laid on at this waterfront site. Following long-standing tradition, the *Provincial Enquirer* was still used to wrap-up fish suppers acquired at the Iceberg Café. The Council had issued a dispensation from public health requirements provided the newspaper was lined with a special inner liner of paper impregnated with antibacterial vinegar and provided also that the inner liner carried free adverts for the O'Duffy carpet and linoleum factory. As he ate his way down the remains of the discarded fish supper, Donald Oskar Gormley found that the newspaper wrapped round his meal for that day bore tidings of a terrible double local calamity. Not only did Donald read the obituary of his wife but also, right beside it on the very same page, was a similar, albeit rather shorter, eulogy relating to himself.

Intrigued, rather than distressed at news of this common calamity, Donald read on. He was comforted to know that all the correct policies and procedures had been complied with. Even if he were not actually and physically dead, the announcement of his death was procedurally correct. The paperwork was in order. There was a suitable audit trail. The appropriate boxes had been ticked. With that procedural propriety, it seems, Donald had been finally ticked off. It transpired that after a long period of absence on a drinking binge Donald's wife had reported him missing to the police. She had also presented them with suitable evidence of her loss. She sent the police an orange sock and a green sock together with an assortment of underwear and items of outer clothing and claimed they had been found immediately beside the swamp forming the proposed municipal cemetery. The clear inference was that Donald Oskar Gormley had deliberately thrown himself into the mire and had been swallowed for good. Well, it was good for her, his wife thought. In response the police had sent out a letter addressed to Donald care of the garden shed. The style of official enquiry letter had been meticulously crafted to seek out the relevant facts. It ran something like the following:

"Dear Sir/Madam,

We wish to check the veracity of the report that you are dead. Please return the attached *pro forma* to us so that our files are complete. Please tick Box A if you are alive. If you are dead, tick Box B.

Yours faithfully…"

A lack of response had indeed held up the official process for several months as a senior officer of the constabulary expressed reservations that there was no Box C dealing with a response from absent parties. Without clear-cut evidence from a completed box-ticking exercise, the police remained unconvinced for a considerable while. However, after continual badgering of the authorities, Donald's wife managed to have him declared dead following a lengthy absence. Both forensics and common sense had confirmed that no man in Donald Oskar Gormley's position would have left his socks and clothing behind if he had intended to come back. In any event, the same senior officer who had previously expressed doubts noted that the ancient manual of standard policing practice indicated "When he dieth, he shall carry nothing away; … naked he came into the world, and naked he must return". So, that was the matter put beyond all doubt regardless of what might be cast up by any further spurious scientific enquiry. Thereafter developments were fast but perhaps unfortunate. The very day of the judicial declaration of death, Donald Oskar Gormley's wife was found dead at the foot of the steps leading from the Register of Births, Deaths and Marriages. She had just recorded Donald's deemed death and had started to walk away in jubilation clutching an official certificate of the declaration of death. She was a free woman again. It was as if, having achieved her life's ambition of ridding herself of her hapless spouse, she had nothing more to do. Her purpose in life had been fulfilled. She had a massive fatal heart attack with the stress of the less than quiet celebration.

The reading of this tragic tale assisted Donald Oskar Gormley to sober up. He had been dead to the world for what must have been years and now it was official. Released from this earthly life's constraints and armed with knowledge of the contents of his own death certificate, Donald Oskar Gormley set about arranging the erection of a suitable memorial to himself and his wife. From the ashes of his matrimonial disaster arose the architectural marvel of the mausoleum in the swamp. Like the local poet William Butler Yeats, Donald Oskar Gormley had obtained the signal distinction of writing his own obituary. But he had surpassed the beloved bard in several respects. Donald had written the obituary not only for himself but also for his wife and their relationship. Moreover, Donald had achieved all this after his own death. For all his flirtation with theosophy W. B. Yeats had not managed that! The touching words of tenderness above the front door to the modest "Gormley" mausoleum – the very first in the Ballycarson cemetery – read as follows:

"Death appeared in lovely form
to bring the peace and still the storm."

For the tiny mausoleum there was a back door too. "You always need an escape route in a crisis. You never know when you might need it," were Donald's instructions to the bemused funereal architect employed by the undertaker. "Make sure the back door has a notice saying 'no parking in front of exit: passage required on a 24-hour basis'." As if to symbolise calmer waters at the end of the booze cruise of a troubled life, Donald quit the drink and went back to looking for gainful employment. The citizens of Ballycarson, long reverential of old traditions, adhered strongly to the principle that one should not speak ill of the dead. Consequently, doors opened widely to Donald Oskar Gormley as no-one could give him a bad reference. That was how he got the job of his choice – lost property officer at the Council. Indeed he was the ideal man for lost property collection as it was recognised that Donald was already in some way lost to the world.

On the day immediately before the anticipated American presidential visit, Councillor Finvola O'Duffy was down at the municipal graveyard on the small manmade isthmus of land forming the site and surroundings of Donald Oskar Gormley's mausoleum. Councillor Finvola O'Duffy was personally supervising the completion of the construction work for the extension of the Peace Wall into the Ballycarson municipal cemetery. The top of the new wall stretched out like a six-foot-wide highway into the site of the future Necropolis. All that was needed now as a final touch was an opening official parade.

As she signalled her satisfaction with the finished work, Finvola noticed the door to the Gormley mausoleum was secured only by a knot of rough bailer twine. Even in rural Ireland, that was an odd way to keep the living and dead apart. Surely the thread of life should be stronger than that? Respect for the departed kept her out; curiosity led her inside. There was no coffin to be seen. The small structure was so full of washing machines, builders' supplies and materials that it was clear Donald's wife had been buried elsewhere. "So this is why he bought the place." The councillor smiled. The mausoleum was a front for one of Donald Oskar Gormley's many commercial operations. Finvola smiled to herself again. She was not going to close this place down. What was the point in that? She could use this place to her advantage. It would be the site of her proposed deal with Big David.

The scene was now set for the trade-off between the rival political and commercial forces facing each other in Ballycarson. But the actors themselves had roles to play. The last phone call between Big David and Councillor Finvola O'Duffy confirmed the details. Secrecy was the watch-word, so the whole matter would be carried out in public and in plain sight. Who would then suspect that anything underhand was going on?

Evening came and Councillor Finvola O'Duffy's parade was forming up in the centre of the town. Four or five hundred of a bodyguard had assembled. The air was buzzing from excitement and the smell of diesel and paraffin from the torches that had been prepared to light the way. At sundown they would set off to the municipal graveyard for the climax of the evening. Councillor Finvola O'Duffy had good reason to feel satisfied. One would have struggled to imagine a more romantic setting for the public event to celebrate the thirtieth anniversary of her engagement. As guest of honour, she would head the parade of her relations, supporters and well-wishers. Her fiancé, if he turned up, could take the rear. That way there would be a ubiquitous presence of the principal parties, but she would keep the limelight. In addition, since she would not have to speak to the man, there would be no chance of an embarrassing public argument about the price of the new ring or policy differences on matters as diverse as the location of the proposed Councillor Eugene Gerald Fitzmaurice Memorial sewage treatment plant and the burning of the undesirable books that had been removed from the public library. More to the point, Councillor Finvola O'Duffy wanted to make sure that her fiancé did not see the vanguard of her supporters make the vital pick-up of materials at Donald Oskar Gormley's mausoleum. Even these most trusted heroes of the Republican revolution, the Truest of the True, did not know – and would never know – the contents of the unmarked cans and she did not want that inquisitive fiancé asking any awkward questions.

Whilst the romantic parade was assembling in the twilight in the centre of town, Big David was at the municipal cemetery depositing the unmarked cans just inside the front door of Donald Oskar Gormley's mausoleum. "I'm just going in to pay my respects," was Big David's explanation to his team of drivers as he took the cans out of the boot of the official car. He undid the string securing the front door of the mausoleum and slipped inside for a few moments. "I didn't know he was that religious," said Bert the Squirt to Bob the Blob. "I suppose those cans contain some sort of oriental spices to placate the spirit of the departed." Little did both of them know that the cans and their contents were actually being deposited there to placate the person who would next arrive at the mausoleum – Councillor Finvola O'Duffy.

As the day came to an end Big David was back at the L.H.O. hall and the night watch at the Spion Kop bus stop had just started their vigil. Darkness was no hindrance to them as they turned to the new weapon in their armoury for urban oversight. The three old hags strapped on their night vision glasses and gazed down at the Nationalist assembly in the centre of town. They could see every detail as Councillor Finvola O'Duffy harangued the crowd with a familiar tirade of anti-Unionist abuse. Although they could not hear the words, they were confident that Big David's sources in the crowd would ensure that by next morning the transcript would be on Big David's desk. "Isn't this great?" said one of them. "Councillor Finvola O'Duffy does not know how many of her own supporters are actually working for the other side!"

Then the lights went on in the former town square and the old hags could see nothing. More precisely, Councillor Finvola O'Duffy had ordered the torches to be lit by those in the parade.

In addition, piles of confiscated volumes of old encyclopaedias soaked in diesel were set alight at each corner of the square. The sudden concentration of bright light meant that the Spion Kop bus stop spies were blinded. Their ultra-sensitive lenses were overwhelmed. Did Councillor Finvola O'Duffy know of this weakness for visual overload? Was there a leak in the Loyalist camp? Who could tell? But in any arms-race there will always be an incentive to take countermeasures and in this case the tools of the stone-age had beaten the most advanced technology. Was it not a metaphor for the politics of Ballycarson itself? Age-old and mindless animosities continually overwhelmed new and supposedly more reasonable initiatives.

So, as the parade headed out to the cemetery, the overseers at the Spion Kop bus stop had to resort to their own unaided sight. They could see virtually nothing except a long, narrow orange glow as the parade headed to the graveyard. "Well, at least we can report there wasn't a green flame!" was the optimistic observation of one of the Spion Kop hags. The front of the parade reached the Gormley mausoleum. The unmarked cans were uplifted by the vanguard who remained none the wiser as to their contents. They thought perhaps they were extra supplies of diesel or paraffin so their torches would burn brightly the whole evening long. The parade headed up and down the new causeway provided by the top of the wall. There was a short speech indicating that this new route would be the means of breaking Evil Albion's death grip on the Ballycarson economy. Without complication the marchers returned to the west of town and the unmarked cans were delivered to the O'Duffy carpet and linoleum factory just in time for the early shift.

What was the special and secret content of these unmarked cans? Why was it so sensitive? And why did Councillor Finvola O'Duffy so desperately need it?

It was a substance that Big David had acquired years before knowing that a crisis such as that now facing him might arise. The contents of the cans was yellow dye. For some time Big David had been able to conceal the acquisition on the basis that he might need it to print the flags of the German Republic. It was a case of plausible deniability. But, in doing this, he was taking a major risk as some of the more alert of his German employees would be able to tell him that the central colour of their national flag was not yellow but gold! Even the most stupid of his employees would have known from birth that yellow dye was an unacceptable product for a leader of the Loyalist cause to have in his possession. It was capable of being mixed with blue to make green. If his workers had found out about his possession of the substance, the ensuing riot would not have been quelled by any assurance that it was to be mixed with red to make orange. In fact, such an assurance would even have made the rioters more energetic in their destruction of Big David's empire. It would have been taken as tantamount to the voicing of the taboo that Orange and Green had something in common.

So why did Councillor Finvola O'Duffy so desperately need this stuff? She had found her supplies of green dye had been sabotaged during the recent shop floor agitation about the lengthening of work hours. She was left with a carpet made from Alsatian and German shepherd hair coloured black and tan. The allusions to the previous participants in the British military machine were obvious. The present-day political and historic implications were alarming. This carpet could not be presented to the United States president as a symbol of Nationalist Republican prestige! Yet all she had in store was the blue dye for the shirts of her loyal bodyguard. The lack of green dye allowed her, indeed forced her, to seek common cause with Big David.

The yellow substance in the unmarked cans arrived just in time for Finvola's grand designs. At the O'Duffy carpet and linoleum factory it was suitably mixed with the blue dye to make green and applied to the dog carpet. The resplendent final product for underfoot presidential support was left to dry overnight.

CHAPTER 20

THE PRESIDENTIAL
ENTRANCE

One thing, or to be more accurate one person, was needed to ensure that the presidential visit went ahead on terms suitable to Big David. He still had to find someone living in Ballycarson who was not a Nationalist and who was the closest living relative of the American commander in chief. That necessity had always existed, but there was now a new urgency. The American pre-event negotiators who now arrived every day at the L.H.O. hall to establish the final details were absolutely insistent on a final conclusion to the ongoing frenetic research. By means of a soundbite they explained the logic of wooing the Irish-American vote by finding historic Irish connections to the present American president: "Nothing Knocks Nostalgia". The phrase falling from the lips of the American representatives was music to Big David's ears; indeed, it was his very own motto for his multifarious business ventures. Clearly the English-speaking nations on either side of the Atlantic were not divided by a single language.

But as the presidential representatives left to report back to their associates further up the greasy political pole, it occurred once again to Big David that the pedigree of the lost relative had to be politically acceptable to all concerned. It was clear that the Americans were seeking a Nationalist at best. A dyed in the wool Loyalist – or at least one with tattooed skin – was completely unacceptable. However, it occurred to Big David that he might still win the day if the relative found was a non-Nationalist without any of the more enthusiastic Loyalist characteristics. That was a very "big ask" indeed given the pervasive pigeonholing of personalities. In Ballycarson, as Big David knew only too well, it was almost impossible for anyone to be his own man given that he was invariably claimed by one tradition or another and deemed to have loyalties of one sort or another if only for the purpose of recording his birth or burial.

But the hunt for this remarkable, potentially unique, individual had to start somewhere if the presidential visit was to be rescued from cancellation due to potential political embarrassment. So, via Big David's dog delivery system, word went out from the L.H.O. hall to all the local Protestant Churches and religious assemblies requesting another urgent examination of their genealogical records.

In the meantime, as if nothing else were amiss, all the other preparations continued for the presidential visit.

The essential details to be established right at the start were the exact date and point of entry of the presidential cavalcade. In due obeisance to local sensitivities, and to avoid claims that one side of the political divide was being preferred over the other, the presidential aides had to engage in double talk. Fortunately, it was a skill not unknown to them in other contexts. But in Ballycarson it had a special dimension. To keep the local politicians happy the American aides even considered sending the real president and a double who could make simultaneous visits to the two parts of town. Noone would know which was the real president and political face would be saved all round. However, the aides eventually settled on a single genuine president and they determined that an announcement of the details of the visit would be conveyed simultaneously to the local political leaders on both sides of the community. At midday a single phone message would be relayed at top volume from a tannoy placed on the highest watch tower on the Peace Wall like a message sung from a minaret. This announcement had all the benefits of not being mistaken for a message from a Christian Church of any denomination. Noone in the local religious establishments could feel excluded. So this was how it was announced. After the two separate crowds of the faithful gathered on either side of the Peace Wall the broadcast phone call confirmed that the United States president would be arriving the next day.

The big drawback of such an address system was that it benefitted only the chosen few. Only a relatively small number selected by the local politicians could crowd into the public roads tight up against the Peace Wall. The whole process appeared to treat the self-appointed local political elites as legitimate privileged social classes. This rankled with those who regarded themselves as the ambassadors of the great transatlantic democracy. So, to widen the class of recipients of the glad tidings, the presidential aides hit on the further idea of a leaflet drop. It had all the merits of going over the heads of the local political leaders and speaking directly to the people. It was a symbol of democracy at its best. Freedom would flow – or at least fall – down from on high. The small fleet of Huey helicopters, acquired by the previous Council administration from the CIA to deal with the supergrass plague, were wheeled out from storage, fuelled up and made ready for service. These machines were loaded up with paper and then showered east and west Ballycarson with all the necessary written details. To warn the locals of the arrival of the flying messengers, music was played at top volume from big loudspeakers strapped to the side rails of the helicopters. Clearly local sensitivities had to be addressed in the choice of music played. There was to be no occasion for hiring ersatz dog-barking CDs and the volunteered services of Charlie and Senga Rae were hastily declined. "Let us go for something neutral – something stirring, something German!" decided the well-meaning presidential aide in command of the venture. So the helicopters flew low over Ballycarson accompanied by the deafening strains of Wagner's "Ride of the Valkyries". The Council street cleaners worked overtime to clean up the mess. In the meantime Big David quietly recalled distant memories of his original home in what had once been Indo-China.

The leaflets announced that the big day in question was the very next day: 26th June. This had been deliberately timed to coincide most happily with the exact anniversary of the famous speech of President Kennedy in Berlin. In Ballycarson the incumbent president would make a similarly historic speech from a hastily erected podium at the Peace Wall. The exact location of the structure was vital. Again to account for local sensitivities, it would be done within the site of the former and now largely abandoned Loyalist enclave in the west. Filled as it now was with Germans, it was as if this relatively small but troubled area had always been destined for this very purpose. There was a community benefit in ethnic cleansing after all. To provide the necessary room for the presidential platform and the space for the expected audience to stand, the Council ordered the summary eviction of the two argumentative Germans who had taken up residence there and the immediate demolition of any structures on the ground. Perhaps the paramilitaries could be persuaded to sell or hand over some of their explosives to speed up the task. Maybe they would give a discount if there was a bulk purchase. The Council could also claim it had persuaded them to decommission some of their weapons. The publicity possibilities beckoned.

The presidential entrance to Ballycarson would itself be effected by helicopter. Of course the machine in question would be of a much more modern vintage than the pensioned-off paper-dumping heralds used in the leaflet drop. Local political niceties had also been considered. The centre of the abandoned American baseball park just outside the town would provide a suitable landing spot for the entrance. William Henry, that ardent disciple of Big David, could be employed to paint a large letter "H" at the landing site. It was fortuitous indeed that such a letter could not be painted upside down. It was lucky too that there was such a pseudo-American facility near Ballycarson since it could act as neutral territory even though it was actually situated on the edge of the eastern side of town. The history of the imported sporting facility was bizarre indeed. The place had been constructed in the latter years of the Troubles by enthusiastic American investors. They had noticed that outside America the largest sale of baseball bats per head of population anywhere in the world occurred in Northern Ireland. Regular ship-loads of this sporting equipment docked at Belfast harbour. The potential for transatlantic profit invited the export of the game itself and not just its equipment. Unfortunately, the investors had not noticed that in Northern Ireland there was a complete absence of a corresponding sale in baseballs. They discovered only at a much later date that the baseball bats were used not for recreation but destruction by the various gangs of hoods, some of which were later to provide protection for the baseball park itself.

However, by the time the stadium was built it was too late to withdraw. The "Ballycarson Yankees" were recruited, assembled and trained at great cost. Team banners shouting the message "Go, Yankees, Go" were printed in huge numbers and fast food prepared on a massive scale, causing an enormous growth in Big Mick production at the Ballycarson salami factory. A large New Yorker of German extraction by the name of Jimmy Scheidt was headhunted and appointed as the team coach. His enthusiasm was boundless and matched only by his excitable temperament. Unfortunately, there was nothing he could do to avoid a dismal first and only baseball season in which minuscule crowds attended to watch uninspiring displays of an unknown activity vaguely resembling sport. The very last game was marred by the team coach assaulting a crowd member who had expressed his disgust at the low level of entertainment within the hearing of the, by then, disheartened Jimmy. The swearing had echoed around the virtually empty stadium. The chief photographer of the *Provincial Observer* caught the attack in a crisply taken snap just as Jimmy Scheidt's fist made contact with the fan's jaw. The very next day this image was plastered over the front page of the *Provincial Observer* with the narrative:

The coach of the baseball team was promptly sacked and the baseball park closed down. The team banners were abandoned at the side of the pitch and the fast food fed to the local pigs. The sporting facility had lain idle ever since as a testament to a hopeful but fruitless American intervention in a foreign land.

After landing at the baseball park the president would be conveyed by means of a motorised cortege sweeping into Ballycarson accompanied by American secret service out-runners. The president would be ferried in style right to the Peace Wall beside Checkpoint Charlie. Then his speech would be delivered from the new podium inside the recently cleared, abandoned Loyalist enclave. To please the displaced local German community, part of the message would be delivered in German – it was fortunate the president had vague German ancestry too! However, this venture into the central European tongue would occur only after exhortations in Irish and Ulster Scots, of course. You couldn't get much more even-handed than that.

Well, the helicopter entrance will be nothing new, thought Big David. Rumour had it that the president had to be seen to outdo the dramatic entrance of the last head of state to visit the province, the Queen. She had also come by helicopter for fear of landmines. But the "wimp factor" in United States politics meant that the president had to be seen to be unafraid, to stare danger in the face and face it down. So his presidential cavalcade would drive slowly as if to throw down the gauntlet to the local thugs to do their worst. Yet any threat had already been neutralised by deft political negotiation. After secret negotiations with the local paramilitaries, the American aides finally reached a compromise. There would be no attack on the president. Instead, it was agreed that the ambiguous sporting banners "Go, Yankees, Go" would remain to adorn the edges of the helicopter landing spot. These banners still littered the stadium and their continued presence would be accepted by the local thugs as a symbolic message to the president and his team.

To ensure the complete success of the presidential visit, further compromises had to be made and largesse distributed by the American aides. As the route from the baseball park to the Peace Wall ran through the east of the town and lay wholly within the domain of Big David, he was in a position to extract the concessions. Big David's list of demands was relayed by phone and, apart from the last, instantly accepted. The demands included:

a)   The Ballycarson 1690 Young Defenders Flute Band was to lead the presidential parade. The suggestion seemed to fly in the face of the desire of the Americans to seek out a Nationalist slant on the event. "But Loyalism can be dressed up in different ways," suggested Big David as he recalled an earlier sartorial surprise not originally of his own making or design. The Americans accepted the suggestion of the band's leadership of the parade only because the band uniforms were not traditional flute band uniforms but, instead, were sequinned white Elvis Presley Las Vegas-style outfits. It would be the second outing for the outfits. The uniforms had already proved their worth when poking fun at Councillor Finvola O'Duffy's engagement ring. Now Big David saw the chance of a double dividend. However, no matter how the band was dressed up, Big David still wanted to keep control of such a potentially revolutionary entity. The ranks of the band would be greatly expanded by placed men from Big David's security organisation.

b)   Big David was to receive the catering contract to supply food for the entire event. For all official participants there would be special packed lunches of Big Micks and sliced salami. Desert would come in the form of presidential-size doughnuts drizzled with the words "*Ich bin ein Berliner*" to celebrate the anniversary of the earlier presidential speech on 26th June 1963.

c)   The president was to visit Big David in the east before meeting any Nationalist leaders in the west. The parade would pass right underneath the newly decorated Queen Anne Boleyn Bridge and move all the way up the hill to the L.H.O. hall. The president would then officiate at the dedication of the new band uniforms and flutes and cut the ribbon on the newly renovated band practice room at the L.H.O. hall. The geriatric cameramen and women in the Spion Kop bus stop would be able to film it all for posterity.

d)   The president would inspect the Red Army. Of course this one was turned down as it might have generated awkward headlines for the president. But Big David knew how to negotiate. He had to allow the American aides to report to their superiors that they had been able to knock back Big David on something. The pleasure of reviewing the Red Army was something both he and the American president could forego.

It all looked good for Big David. He considered his negotiated achievement. There may soon be a Nationalist diamond-studded replica dog on a presidential desk back in Washington, but that would remain a minor detail obscured forever from public view. What the world would see was global television coverage of the parade, the catering arrangements and the visit of the American president to his headquarters. Who said that only Irish Republicans and Nationalists were adept at using propaganda?

But in any negotiated settlement there are always loopholes and compromises. It did not all go Big David's way. Big David wanted to stuff the flute band with his own men. Eva Brunette proved equal to the threat to band autonomy. She avoided the inevitable disruption to the musical outcome by insisting that the tone-deaf incomers would be inserted at the centre of the band so they could not be easily seen. In addition, they would be armed not with black flutes but with silent substitutes – the black bicycle pumps taken from the box at the back of the Council lost property shed. With his lack of musical knowledge, Big David believed her when she explained that these pumps could be used as "trombone flutes" and that they could be extended to reach the really high notes. Donald Oskar Gormley's treasure trove of collectables had saved the day again. Furthermore, the Americans managed to manipulate the news of the visit to Big David to deflate any problem with the Irish-Americans back home. Not only did they employ Big David's other, less favoured nickname but they also presented the whole story as some banal domestic presidential travel. The *Provincial Observer* picked up the headline fed by the American publicity machine:

> PRESIDENT
> TO VISIT CAMP
> DAVID BEFORE
> GOING WEST

During all this frenzy of last-minute announcements and back-room deals about the practicalities of the presidential visit, the search for the lost presidential relative continued with even more desperation than before. It was now the last few business hours of the day before the anticipated presidential visit and the results from the continuous clerical and congregational consultation were still discouraging. There was still no trace of any non-Nationalist close relative of the president other than the man with the enormous Loyalist tattoos. "Do the search again," ordered Big David for the third time that day. "Start at the beginning and do it again," he yelled down the phone. "I know it's a last ditch," said Big David, "but see if you can come up with anything in the German community and don't forget that church that nobody knows." It was to turn out to be an instruction of genius fortuitously found by Big David as he fumbled about in the dark.

Last on the alphabetical list of Ballycarson churches was a church that appeared to have broken the mould. It had been left to the end because it wasn't even in the alphabet, the phone book or any list at all. This was the Church of the Reverend X located in the street with no name. Consonant with this low-key approach to evangelism, the church had no noticeboard at the gate and was known as "the church with no name". Preaching from a church with no name in a street with no name, the whole idea of the Reverend X was to avoid the name-calling that blighted religious discussion in Ulster. He remembered only too well the confusion and moral outrage that had erupted when a previous Protestant church had tried to tie down its particular brand of doctrine by an overly detailed title. The Free Evangelical Non-Integrated And Non-Subscribing Church had suffered irreparable damage in the esteem of potential adherents when some local wag had abbreviated their name by use of the acronym the "FENIANS". Unfortunately, the total avoidance of any name brought difficulties too. The attempt at anonymity had hit an immediate snag as it was generally the case throughout Ireland that the only church never to have a noticeboard at the gate was the Roman Catholic Church. Within that particular church it was presumed by the incumbent clerics that, of course, everyone should know their institution. In their view, the one true Church did not need to advertise. So, when the Reverend X failed to put up a noticeboard, the local parish priest in Ballycarson was perturbed and put out by the Reverend X's presumption. Again some cross-community negotiation was needed. It was indeed pleasing to see that an outcome was achieved without anyone compromising on their strongly held principles. To avoid confusion, a notice was projected from the spire of the Roman Catholic chapel across the street onto the gable wall of the Reverend X's church. On this dark surface the projected letters of light enlightened the casual reader: "This building used to be a German church". It was a solution of genius. No noticeboard was erected within the boundaries of the Reverend X's building. No words confirmed the present use of the building. The information was useless to any visitor to the town or any bypasser who might otherwise be tempted to enter. Despite that, the terms of the projected sign were absolutely and completely accurate. It was a diplomatic achievement comprising both total historic accuracy and a present lack of utility. Even the British Foreign and Commonwealth Office would have been proud of it.

The church with no name was indeed a building formerly used by a long-dissolved congregation of a tiny German Protestant sect. All that remained of their gatherings was a large box of mouldering records. It had lain undisturbed under the church stairs for years. These were the archives that were to prove to be the salvation of Big David and the Unionist cause. It was there that the searchers discovered the familial link between the president and a present-day resident of Ballycarson.

The presidential relative in question turned out to be none other than Donald Oskar Gormley. He was German on his mother's side. As a direct descendant of the seventeenth-century German incomers to Ulster, he could be linked directly to the American president's ancestral village in the Sudetenland and was easily the president's closest direct living relative in Ballycarson. The ace in the pack was the fact that Donald had been declared dead and already held his own death certificate. If the whole "meet the Irish relative event" went badly, the president could truthfully deny he had met such a living soul in Ballycarson. It was a classic example of the principle of plausible deniability in action.

More last-minute deals had to be done to persuade Donald Oskar Gormley to appear on the presidential podium and have his photograph taken. Of course, Donald's dog could appear on stage to meet the president. But this time it was the Council and not the Americans who had to provide the majority of the incentives. Donald was promised an exclusive franchise for his activities at the border. The activities weren't rendered legal, of course, because that would spoil the fun and ruin Donald's image. Parking places for his vehicles, whatever they might be, were to be constructed at suitable locations around the town. He was to be provided with an unlimited supply of second-hand chip vans and a first call on any washing machines fished out of the canal that once was called the Union Canal. And there was to be some continuity in all of this benevolence. Donald was to have a job for life at the Council. Well, you can't change everything. But perhaps there was indeed something new. He would have a job for his afterlife since, at least in the eyes of the law, Donald was already dead.

The final touch for the presidential visit comprised the significant additions to the painting on the Queen Anne Boleyn Bridge. A huge German flag was to fly over the bridge to accompany the nine flags already there. Even in Loyalist and Unionist Ballycarson, a Republican tricolour of black, red and gold was perfectly acceptable. The symbolism extended to words reflecting the complete alignment of the theme of the presidential visit and Big David's commercial motto. Painted on the bridge to complete the spaces left beside the three NOs was the following inspiring message:

"**NO**THING
K**NO**CKS
NOSTALGIA"

Never before had two such seemingly irreconcilable interests been so speedily realigned to arrive at a more satisfactory conclusion. Never had the transatlantic alliance appeared more solid and vibrant. All that was necessary now was for the president to arrive.

INTRODUCTION

The politics of Northern Ireland are a mystery to many. The writer hopes that they will remain so even after reading this book. However, for those who wish to venture into the morass, the following is the briefest of introductions to some of the personalities who, in small or large measure, continue to affect the issues – at least, that is, within the storyline of this book. Many are dead, but that does not seem to matter.

Following the traditions of Ulster politics, no attempt has been made either to be fair or reasonable to those named. A few historic events and descriptive terms have been thrown in for good measure. The reader should remember, however, that the collective community recollection of an historic event may be more akin to fiction than fact, but it frequently becomes a phenomenon in its own right.

Some who hold strongly to certain views will be disappointed to find their heroes or political views selected for the list set out below. Such readers usually expect the whole world to be already familiar with the intricacies of local Ulster politics and their heroes to need no introduction. Fortunately, this is not the case. Most people have not a clue what these intricacies are and remain ignorant of local political celebrities. The very fact that these brief explanations are required should suggest that the world at large is usually concerned with something else. There are fourteen defined terms. Some will immediately perceive a bias in that it may be that only five can be consigned to one of the traditions to which this book applies.

The Black and Tans – the nickname of the Royal Irish Constabulary Reserve Force raised in Ireland in 1920 and 1921. It contained many ex-soldiers who had spent 1914–18 fighting the Germans.

The Easter Rising – the tactically unsuccessful revolt of Republicans in 1916. The action took place mainly in Dublin and involved locations such as the Jacob's biscuit factory. It involved the use of imported German guns. The revolt was suppressed by the British, but the immediate aftermath involved punishment of the rebels (involving execution in some cases) carried out with such insensitivity that it made martyrs out of those who participated. It was a calamitous strategic blunder by the British.

Edward Carson (Sir) (1854–1935) – successful barrister and leader of the Ulster Unionist Party. He was much involved in the setting up of Northern Ireland in 1922. Prior to the First World War he had been active in persuading the British government not to include Ulster in the Home Rule project by raising the Ulster Volunteer Force. German guns were imported to assist in the persuasion. The Ulster Volunteer Force in large measure became the 36th Ulster Division of the British Army that fought and died for king and country at the Somme in July 1916.

Éamonn de Valera (1882–1975) – born in New Jersey, USA, the son of a Spanish-Cuban settler and Irish mother, first Taoiseach and later president of Eire. Originally a militant Republican later noted for his conservatism. His visit to the German legation in Dublin to express condolences on the death of Herr Hitler, the erstwhile German head of state, on 2nd May 1945 has aroused controversy. There was no similar visit to the embassy of the United States of America on the death of Franklin Delano Roosevelt just a few weeks previously.

King Billy – William III (1650–1702) – a Dutchman alsoknown as "William of Orange" who married Mary Stuart to become joint monarch of Great Britain and, later, of Ireland. His armies, comprising German mercenaries, defeated Mary's father, James II and VII, at the River Boyne, north of Dublin, in 1690 thus securing the Glorious Revolution and the Protestant Ascendancy. The anniversary of the battle is celebrated on 12th July.

The Lagan – the river running through Belfast. The river, now clean, was once heavily polluted by local industry. Some believe that that Unionist industrialists deliberately poured chemicals into the water to make it orange in colour.

Loyalists – the more enthusiastic form of Unionists associated by some with blood and thunder flute bands.

Constance Markievicz (Countess) (1868–1927) – born in London as Constance Gore-Booth. In 1901 she married a Ukrainian aristocrat of Polish ethnicity who moved back to the Ukraine in 1913 without her. She was involved in the 1916 Easter Rising and with the Republicans in the Irish Civil War.

Nationalists – those who wish Ireland as a whole to be a nation once again.

Eoin O'Duffy (1892–1944) – born Owen O'Duffy, chief of staff of the IRA, second commissioner of the Garda Síochána, leader of the Blueshirts and the Irish Brigade who fought for Franco in the Spanish Civil War. In 1943 he approached the German legation in Dublin with a view to organising an Irish Legion to fight Bolshevism on the Russian front. His offer was not taken seriously.

O'Neills – the family from Tyrone that ruled large parts of Ulster until the flight of Hugh O'Neill into exile on the European continent in 1607.

Republicans – a term that literally denotes those who desire a republic in Ireland but which, within Northern Ireland, is more commonly applied to Nationalists of the more extreme variety.

Sinn Fein – A Republican party closely associated with the IRA. From time to time they have remodelled their policies to act, at least in public, within the existing constitution whatever it might be.

Unionists – those who wish to retain the Union of Great Britain and Northern Ireland.